The Cumberland Bride

The
Daughters
of the
Mayflower

SHANNON MCNEAR

BARBOUR BOOKS
An Imprint of Barbour Publishing, Inc.

Print ISBN 978-1-68322-691-8

eBook Editions:
Adobe Digital Edition (.epub) 978-1-68322-693-2
Kindle and MobiPocket Edition (.prc) 978-1-68322-692-5

All scripture quotations are taken from the King James Version of the Bible.

This book is a work of fiction. Names, characters, places, and incidents are either products of the author's imagination or used fictitiously. Any similarity to actual people, organizations, and/or events is purely coincidental.

Model Photograph: Lee Avison/Trevillion Images

Published by Barbour Books, an imprint of Barbour Publishing, Inc., 1810 Barbour Drive, Uhrichsville, Ohio 44683, www.barbourbooks.com

Our mission is to inspire the world with the life-changing message of the Bible.

ecpa Member of the
Evangelical Christian
Publishers Association

Printed in the United States of America.

PRAISE FOR *THE CUMBERLAND BRIDE*

"Gut-wrenching emotion with all the action of *The Last of the Mohicans*. *The Cumberland Bride* will grab you by the throat and not let go until you've closed the book. A hearty round of applause for Shannon McNear's debut novel. This is one up-and-coming author that you're going to want to keep your eye on!"

–Michelle Griep, award-winning author of *The Captured Bride*

"Take an exciting journey through the Cumberland Gap in the late 18th century with the talented Shannon McNear's well-developed characters. You won't be disappointed!"

–Carrie Fancett Pagels, award-winning, ECPA-bestselling author of *My Heart Belongs on Mackinac Island*

"Filled with unforgettable characters and a dash of romance, Shannon McNear's *The Cumberland Bride* is an adventure from the first page to the last. Just when I thought I knew what would happen next, McNear surprised me. I fell in love with this book, and I know you will too."

–Kathleen Y'Barbo, bestselling author of *My Heart Belongs in Galveston, Texas* and *The Pirate Bride*

"Breathtaking and captivating! *The Cumberland Bride* has everything I look for in a good book—great characters, a swoon-worthy hero, edge-of-your-seat adventure, and a romance that truly touched my heart. The author's in-depth research and historical descriptions swept me back to the early American frontier with all its romance and dangerous beauty. Rarely does a book keep me up at night, and rarely do I think about the story long after I turned the last page. Don't miss this one!"

–MaryLu Tyndall, author of the bestselling and award-winning Legacy of the King's Pirates series

"Shannon McNear writes vivid, richly-detailed historical novels with plenty of heart and adventure. Highly recommended!"

—Elizabeth Camden, RITA and Christy award-winning author

"Shannon McNear's *The Cumberland Bride* is a beautifully written novel with a compelling plot of brave travelers on the Wilderness Road. In wonderful lyrical prose, McNear deftly handles the building romantic tension between Kate and Thomas while weaving a fascinating tale chronicling the historical hardships between the Native American people and the waves of European settlers flowing into their land in the late 1700s. This can't-miss tale will capture your mind and thrill your heart!"

—Jennifer Uhlarik, Selah award-winning author of *The Outcast's Redemption*, a part of *The Secret Admirer Romance Collection*

"A fabulous read! *The Cumberland Bride* is gorgeously-written and rich in historical detail, with a romance that hooked me from the start. This one is definitely for the keeper shelf."

—Susanne Dietze, award-winning author of *My Heart Belongs in Ruby City, Idaho*

"Rooted firmly in time and place with rich historical details and a vivid storyworld, *The Cumberland Bride* is a beautiful tale of hope, redemption, and true love. A must-read debut novel for those who love Laura Frantz and Lori Benton."

—Gabrielle Meyer, author of *Love's Undoing* in *The Backcountry Brides Romance Collection*

"Compelling and lovely, *The Cumberland Bride* will take you on a journey of the heart as you travel with the characters into the wilderness."

—Roseanna M. White, bestselling author of *The Lost Heiress* and the Shadows Over England Series

DEDICATION

For my mothers and fathers who walked this road
before me, and for my children, who will walk it after.

Thomas saith unto him, Lord, we know not whither thou goest;
and how can we know the way?
—John 14:5

Wishikatowi!
("be strong" in the Shawnee tongue)

Daughters of the Mayflower

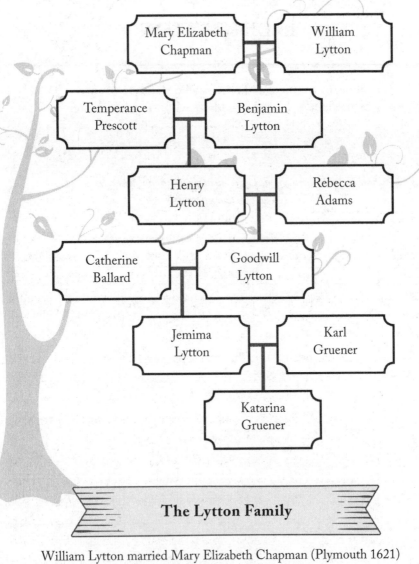

Mary Elizabeth Chapman — William Lytton

Temperance Prescott — Benjamin Lytton

Henry Lytton — Rebecca Adams

Catherine Ballard — Goodwill Lytton

Jemima Lytton — Karl Gruener

Katarina Gruener

The Lytton Family

William Lytton married Mary Elizabeth Chapman (Plymouth 1621)
Parents of 13 children, including Benjamin
Benjamin Lytton married Temperance Prescott (Massachusetts 1668)
Born to Benjamin and Temperance
Henry Lytton married Rebecca Adams (New York 1712)
Children were Goodwill and Amity
Goodwill married Catherine Ballard (New York 1737)
Born to Goodwill and Catherine
Jemima Lytton who married Karl Gruener (New Jersey 1777)
Children included Katarina

CHAPTER I

Tennessee, Spring 1794
Bean's Station

My father used to tell the story," Kate murmured as she wrote, quill scratching against the page, "of how he and his fellow Hessians sailed down the Hudson with the British, preparing to attack Washington and his forces. When they came under fire, he and the other men of good, devout German stock, broke out singing hymns, believing God would preserve them. Colonel Rawdon commenced to mocking them for such simple faith. And that was the beginning of the end of my father's faith in the British."

Kate sat back from the page with its drying ink and gazed out the open window of her narrow attic room. Noonday sun spilled across the busy settlement and rolling forest beyond, still waiting for the green of spring. A tendril of breeze touched her cheek, and she reached to catch the sheet of paper just before it lifted from the bedside table.

She loved this story. It deserved to be told, how the wicked Colonel Rawdon cut his own hamstrings, so to speak, with his disdain of the Hessians' faith in such a time. But her father had forbidden sharing it outside the immediate family, even with those considered dear friends. Things were difficult enough in this new country, he insisted, without folk knowing he'd once fought on behalf of the enemy. And so, out of love for her dear papa, she'd held her silence.

She probably ought not commit such words even to paper. But the story burned within her, begged to be told.

And 'twas but one of many.

Ink and paper ought to be reserved for practical things, Papa maintained—keeping records, writing letters. Nothing as frivolous as storytelling, and personal journals were up for debate—but this, she told herself, was a form of record keeping. If a people lost their history, what was left them? Even the holy scripture devoted as much of its pages to histories as to psalmody and exhortation.

"Katarina Grace Gruener! Where are you?"

Oh bother! She thought she'd done enough of the morning's chores to allow for stealing a half hour to write, but apparently not. "Coming, Mama!"

Kate hastily recapped the ink and wiped her quill, then slid the written sheet carefully beneath the blotter, pressed the top layer down, and tucked both in the side of her clothes chest. It should be safe there from discovery, at least for the present.

Skirts fisted in one hand, she ran down the narrow stairs of the cabin they rented while Papa surveyed for the Wilderness Road to the north. Mama stayed busy taking in washing and sewing—as if three of Kate's younger siblings were not occupation enough. But Papa and Mama had agreed that Papa would save all of his wages that he could, and Mama would endeavor to keep the rest of them fed and clothed by her industry in this little town where the Wilderness Road dipped south from the Holston and Watauga Valleys before angling back north toward Cumberland Gap.

"Katarina!"

Kate burst into the morning room on the heels of her mother's call. Jemima Lytton Gruener was a formidable woman, briskly efficient even when loving, and Kate dreaded her ire. "I'm here, Mama."

Her mother's features flattened into disapproval, her lips thinning. "How many times have I told you we haven't the luxury of you sneaking away to read in the middle of the day?"

"I wasn't—I'm sorry, Mama." Kate held herself still and tried not to feel like a chastened infant still in leading strings—as Stefan currently was, playing with a pair of wooden spoons while tied securely to a table leg. He looked up with an adorably toothy grin and waved a spoon at her.

Mama nodded once and, reaching into the side of her skirts, pulled out a folded and sealed paper. "Very well then. I need you to carry this message to the tavern to be sent out with the next post rider, and see if anything has come from your papa. Wait if you must," she added, pressing the packet and needed coins into her hand. Kate swallowed her glee as she accepted the missive, but Mama's brown eyes were sharp. "Do *not* think this is reward for being slothful this past hour. Stay no longer than necessary."

She stepped outside to the blindingly bright day. The smell of lye stung her nostrils—Dulsey, their Negro freedwoman, and Betsy, Kate's younger sister, were hard at work washing linens in the small yard behind the cabin. Waving to them, and returning the smile she got from both, she hurried on, into the muddy path running behind their cabin and half a dozen others like it, down the hill to the tavern that served as the social center of Bean's Station.

Away from the house, she slowed her steps. The spring day was too beautiful not to savor. Clear blue skies, balmy breeze smelling of the land awakening from its long winter slumber. The hilltops beckoning, and the not-too-distant mountain—except that everyone was warned not to stray from the station itself. Not without an escort. A well-armed one.

Even so, a thread of longing whispered through her. Fear followed hard on its footsteps. What was she thinking? She'd likely not last an hour out there in the wild, forested hills.

The tavern loomed just ahead, a two-story structure of hewn timber that, like their cabin, hadn't had time yet to weather. Did any of the horses tied out front belong to the post rider?

She stepped lightly onto the porch and inside. Barely a hesitation in the rumble of conversation registered her presence as she paused, letting her eyes adjust to the dimness. The aromas of baking bread and tobacco smoke permeated the air.

Seeing no one she recognized besides the settlement folk, she made her way past the tables to the woman behind the counter. "Good day, Mistress Johnson. Has the post rider come yet? I've a packet for him."

A twinkle and a dimpled smile answered her, with the tilt of a head.

"Just in and over there, speaking with Nat Carrington."

Kate swiveled to stare before she could stop herself. The Indian Affairs agent, here? Both men at the table looked rangy and trail worn—nothing terribly remarkable there, but appearances could be deceiving. She turned back to Mistress Johnson. "Is there trouble expected?"

The older woman's dimples flashed again. "Always, sweetheart. But nothing more than usual." She slid Kate a dripping mug. "Here, have some cider while you wait for them to finish talking."

Thomas Bledsoe took a better grip on his ale and leaned an elbow on the table. "Sounds easy enough."

Carrington's eyes measured him for a long moment before he gave an approving nod. "Heard a lot of good things about you, Bledsoe. And your family's a solid one. I've no doubt you'll be an asset to our government's efforts to make the frontier safe for our settlers."

Feigning a long swallow, Thomas rolled the words around in his head. "You'll pardon me, sir, but I hope I'm an asset to both the settlers and the Indians."

The other man's gaze flickered. "Of course."

"If you don't mind me asking," Thomas went on, "just whose side are you on?"

Carrington lifted his mug, but not before Thomas saw the slight hardening of his face. "The right one."

"Which is?"

Carrington didn't answer. His gaze strayed past Thomas and he nodded again, slightly. "There's a comely miss waiting to speak with you, looks like."

Thomas's shoulders were already prickling from having to sit with his back to most of the room. He twitched a glance behind him. The young woman who he'd seen come in a few minutes ago still stood by the counter, trying to look casual, but the frequent glance toward him and Carrington betrayed her unease.

"Dan'l Boone says the three things a man needs to make it on the frontier are a good horse, a good gun, and a good wife."

Thomas cupped both hands around his tankard, ignoring the sly smile that curved Carrington's mouth. "Doing well enough with the first two, thank you."

Carrington laughed softly. "Of course, no wife at all is better than a bad one. But 'tis something to think upon, for sure." His eyes slid past Thomas and took on a gleam again.

To forestall further comment from Carrington, if nothing else—surely not out of his own interest—Thomas shoved back his chair and stood, then deliberately turned and walked toward the girl.

At his approach, the girl's eyes widened and her face went a shade paler than she already was, but she drew herself up and clasped her hands primly before her. Thomas didn't fail to notice the whitened knuckles. "Did you need aught, miss?"

She threw a panicked glance behind the counter, but Mistress Johnson had disappeared into the rear of the tavern. "I—I'm waiting for the post rider, sir. I'm told you are he?"

He gave a slight bow. "I am."

One hand groped toward her pocket slit. "I have a message. May I give it to you now, or . . . ?"

"I reckon now is fine, miss."

A blush stained her cheeks as she fumbled for the packet, and between the familiar annoyance at the girl's nervousness and his habit of noting detail in every situation, Thomas found himself absently assessing her. Blue flowered gown over a red-striped petticoat, some signs of wear but not yet threadbare. Average height, perhaps a little more slender than some wished—but he was used to that, with his own sisters—rosy cheeks and fair hair peeking from her very proper cap. A cleft in her pert chin that someone would doubtlessly find charming.

But not him. And certainly not today.

Sandy lashes lifted to reveal coffee-brown eyes. Now there was a combination he'd not often seen.

She held out her hand, and after the sliver of a breath, he remembered to accept the packet and accompanying coins. He peered at the addressee, then up at her again. "You're relation to Karl Gruener?"

Startled from her missishness, she snapped to attention, instantly wary. "Yes. He's my father."

"I have something from him then. Just came from the survey camp." He dug in the satchel still slung across his shoulders.

Blast her fluttering, anyway. This girl's family was the one he'd just agreed to guide northward on the Wilderness Road.

CHAPTER 2

The wilderness was where Thomas felt most alive. He liked it best when alone, taking the road as fast as the terrain—and his mount— would allow, ears open to birdsong and the riffle of wind through the trees, head bare to the sun and sky when the day allowed. And thanks to the post-rider position, he knew well the road into Kentucky where he'd be guiding that party of settlers in a couple of weeks.

Besides the impending suspension of the post, he still wasn't sure what compelled him to offer when asked whether he knew of anyone able or willing to do so, but something about the man's earnest manner and his slightly lisping, accented speech tugged at him. Now all he could think of was how he'd miss the freedom of solitude.

After handing off the latest post delivery though, he was away south to the Watauga Valley to see family. It had been too long already, and who knew how long it might be before he returned.

The path from Bean's Station across the Holston was well worn enough, but winding due east toward the Watauga, it grew narrow and steep in spots. Thomas didn't care. Ladyslipper was as surefooted as she was fleet, and made light work of whatever trail he put her to.

Come to think, he wasn't sure just how long it had been since he'd seen his sisters. All at once? It had been years. And nothing against the others, but the eldest, Truth, remained his favorite.

Likely 'twas because she'd served as mother to them all since Thomas was nine or so. His other sisters were fine enough in their own way—he had to give them that, now that they were all grown—but none had the knack of ordering the household, of holding them together the long autumn their father had been killed after that terrible battle with Tories over in South Carolina. And then she'd had the audacity to go and marry one of those same Tories. Thomas smiled. His brother-in-law Micah Elliot had proved his worth as an over-the-mountain man many times over, after running to warn the settlement of impending attack by the Cherokee just a few days before Christmas.

And it was still their favorite story to tell, how Truth had fed Micah at gunpoint the first time she'd met him, on foot and starving from days of wandering the mountains.

Thomas wasn't sure who'd gotten the better end of that deal.

Micah had made a very decent older brother too, all things considered. Thomas could not deny his affection for Truth, and hers for him.

Crossing the southern spur of Holston Mountain, he slowed, breathing deeply of the laurel barely beginning to bloom. The sunlight fell in patches through the new leaves, oak and walnut and elm arching overhead. He hadn't thought he'd missed this bit of country—but he realized now he had.

Down into the valley and up over the next ridge he went, Ladyslipper scrambling over the rocks and finding her way as she always did. Once he descended the ridge, it was just another couple of miles over a road that once had been but a footpath—and then there, with the slope of a mountainside rising beyond, lay nestled the cabin and barn his papa had raised when they'd first come in '73. The sunlight pooled, jewellike, in the greening of the trees and the new fields spreading to either side of the cabin.

An unaccustomed tightness seized his throat. For a moment, he could not speak, then he swallowed and called out, "Halloo the house!"

A knot of children—two in skirts and two in britches—emerged from the edge of the woods, watching. So much taller than when he'd seen them last—for that matter, the youngest of those was still in leading strings then. No one on the porch though, until he was well within sight as well. Truth herself stepped out, shading her eyes, then gave a whoop and ran to meet him.

He dismounted, laughing, and caught her in a hug that lifted her off her feet. "Hie, big sister."

"Oh you!" She squeezed him so hard, it nearly hurt, laughing as well. When he set her down, mist-grey eyes met his own and crinkled. Both hands came up to frame his face. "Look at you! It's been an age. Are you well? What brings you back?"

And then the children were upon them. "Uncle Thomas! Uncle Thomas!"

He embraced them all, overcome by the laughter and their welcome. "Here, stand back and let me have a look!"

At last they disentangled themselves, still bouncing and fidgeting. Thomas, the oldest at twelve, named after him as he was named after a grandfather. Magdalene, not quite ten, and then Abraham and Rebecca, five and eight respectively.

"Jacob and the baby are in the house, napping," Truth said when the older ones were finished filling him in on their ages and latest adventures. "And Micah should be home—"

"Long about now," came a male voice, calling across the field.

Beneath the brim of his plain felt hat, Micah's teeth gleamed white against his dark beard, and though Thomas topped him by half a head, his embrace was every bit as hearty as Truth's.

"Can you stay long?" he added to the questions already asked.

"A few days," Thomas said. "Been carrying the post from Bean's Station up the Wilderness Road, through Cumberland Gap and sometimes as far as Danville and Harrodsburg, but I've agreed to guide a party of settlers up that way. Will be meeting up with them in a week at Bean's."

"Well, come on to the cabin," Truth said. "We'll be having supper before long."

The inside of the cabin looked so nearly the same, he wondered whether he'd stepped back to his own childhood. Finger to her lips, Truth beckoned him to the lean-to bedroom, and he peered in at the small boy, still in skirts, asleep on the bed. A bundle in a nearby cradle squeaked and waved a wee fist. "Ah, now," Truth murmured, and scooped the baby into her arms. "It isn't time for you to wake, but perhaps your uncle wouldn't mind toting you a bit while I finish supper. Once I change your swaddling," she added, slanting Thomas a smile.

She accomplished that swiftly enough, both of them staying silent so as not to wake Jacob, and then tucked the tiny bundle into the crook of Thomas's arm. "Here," she murmured. "She'll need to nurse before long, but meet your youngest niece, Constant."

Such a little thing. A smile pulled at Thomas's mouth. "After Mama."

Truth nodded soberly. "It took me this long to work up the nerve for it."

Thomas shifted her more closely to his chest. "She's a sweet bit."

"That she is." Truth smiled again, brushing the baby's brow with her fingertips, then turned away. "Now. Supper."

A half-made mound of biscuit dough lay on the table. As she sank her hands into the mess, gathering in the flour, Thomas was struck by the strands of silver amongst the dark peeking from her cap, the fine lines at the corners of her eyes.

When had she begun looking like such a mama herself?

He cleared his throat. "So what of the girls these days?"

She slid him another smile, as if just remembering he was there. "Well. Patience and Daniel settled somewhere about Nashborough and seem to be doing just fine. Thankful and Joe are still up on the Clinch River—I believe, anyway, haven't heard from her in long about a year—and one of the Clark boys is sparkin' Mercy. Another wedding won't be far off, I'm thinking." Her pale gaze probed his. "And what about yourself? Any promise of a family of your own soon?"

What was it about married women that they needed to have everyone else matched off as well? He shook his head. "Nope. Not looking for it either."

She smiled a little, her eyes falling to the babe who'd dropped off to sleep again, cradled against him. "You'd be a good papa. Always had the right touch with my young'uns."

"And I'm happy enough to keep it to your young'uns."

Her smile went sly. "You just haven't found the right girl. One of these days, you're going to meet one, get so attached that you won't want to be without her."

Thomas snorted. "Like that would happen." Gently bobbing the baby, he took a few steps across the floor and back. "To be honest, Truth, I've no interest in staying put. And I'd rather not leave a woman crying over me."

She stilled and regarded him gravely for a long minute. Thomas paced away again. The words sounded foolish now that he'd said them aloud.

"We can't avoid all the heartache," she said softly.

He could think of no answer to that, so he merely shrugged.

"And if you try to shut it all out," she went on, "you'll also shut out love. And die a sad, lonely man."

"Like our grandpa?" He gritted his teeth. Some words seemed to just come without thought.

She sniffed. "At least Grandma took the chance. We'd not be here, otherwise."

He shrugged again. "Sometimes. . .I feel like I was born twenty years too late. So many people moving west."

Another look. "So go farther."

He wanted to. God help him, he did. But something kept him here on the edge of the frontier, still working with, and for, the very people that made him feel so restless.

The place he felt most alive was in the wilderness. But he still felt a need to be among his sisters, upon occasion, sore weakness though it be.

❦

He stayed for two days, savoring the young'uns chatter and the baby's sweetness and trying not to look when Truth and Micah were openly affectionate, between bantering, just like the old days.

'Twas enough to make a body sick.

Late on the second day, they all sat around the table at supper, talking and laughing. The children ran off to play and finish chores, and only Truth, Micah, and Thomas's sister Mercy remained with him. After a lull in the laughter, Truth lifted her head and gave Thomas a soft smile. " 'Tis so good seeing you. When do you think you'll be home again?"

Something caught him squarely in the chest, and he rose and paced away a few steps. "Reckon it ain't home anymore," he said, finally.

And it hadn't been, not since those two years with the Shawnee.

Mercy blinked and looked away, but pulling at his pipe, Micah made no comment. He understood well enough, Thomas knew.

Truth's gaze held steady. "Nay, I expect not. You always did have more of a restless spirit since Papa died."

She said it without heat, but the implication still stung. "Just haven't found where I'm supposed to be yet."

"Nothing wrong with that," she said, just as soft. The smile returned. "The door's always open either way. You know that. Just don't forget us, you hear?"

His throat thickened unaccountably at that. There was a scrape of chair against the floor, and when he turned back, she was right there, slipping her arms around his waist. "We'll miss you."

He grunted, embracing her in return, cheek against her hair. "Likely not."

A giggle shook her lean frame.

Chapter 3

Mid-April 1794
Bean's Station

The first day of their grand adventure dawned grey and cool, threatening rain.

Kate hoped that did not portend worse things. Or that Papa would delay their departure for another day.

As it was, he and Mama had bickered nearly without ceasing since he'd rejoined them. Perhaps bickered was too strong a word. Spirited discussions might be better, over everything from provisions to mode of transportation to where they planned to settle. Mama was unhappy that Papa had confirmed other travelers' insistence that a wagon could not yet be taken over the Wilderness Road, at least not without great hardship and possibly taking the thing apart in the roughest spots. The road itself had been worn wide enough by twenty years' use, for certain. It was certainly wide enough from Bean's Station to Powell Valley. Mama wanted to try it anyway. Papa doggedly insisted not, shaking his great, shaggy blond head. Yet Papa was the one insisting they make the journey. "A beautiful land," he said, more than once. "You cannot imagine. Richer even than the Shenandoah Valley."

But when Papa said they must take packhorses or nothing, Mama's eyes widened and her nostrils flared.

"But our furnishings and goods," she said.

"New furnishings I can build," Papa said, his German accent becoming thicker as it always did when he was agitated. "And new goods will come to us when the road is improved."

"If the road will be improved with time, then why can we not wait to make the journey?"

"All the best land will be gone if we wait. Our children will not wait to grow, *ja*? We should go now."

"But. . .Indians."

And then Kate realized. Could it be that Mama was secretly afraid?

"Thus why I hire an extra scout," Papa said, his voice dropping back to more even tones.

And at the word *scout*, Kate's thoughts flew back to that day at the tavern. The tall, severe young man who'd risen so abruptly from his chair and walked toward her with a single-minded focus that she couldn't help but be startled by. His pale blue eyes and deep voice.

What had those eyes seen? What stories could that voice tell?

Perhaps there would be opportunity on the journey to find out.

Papa and Mama had traded the same arguments the night before, back and forth, in their room just below Kate's. But this morning they'd arisen, rolled up their bedding, supervised the household in doing the same, and carried on as if none of the spirited discussions had ever happened.

The beds, the tables and chairs, all furniture was to stay behind. Kate folded the last of the linens and laid them in the center of a blanket. Her clothing had already been similarly packed because the trunks would not go. Another thing Mama and Papa had. . .discussed.

Her personal things—brush, pins, journal in progress—were bundled into a haversack to be slung across her body. Papa had warned she'd likely have to walk much of the way and save the horses for their baggage and younger ones. The rest of her belongings were already downstairs, being packed for the journey.

Their journey. After months at Bean's Station, they'd be leaving. Today.

A rap came at the open door, and her brother Johann, tall and gangly at fifteen, leaned into the room. One lock of gold fell over his blue eyes. "Mama says make haste. And that I'm to carry anything extra you have for the packhorses."

"This is the last one." She stood back from the bundle she'd just closed up and laid on the bed. "Is Mama decided yet about the ticks?"

Johann gathered up the packet and somehow mangled it in the process. "Papa has bargained for extra provisions in exchange for leaving them."

Kate was not surprised. For all Mama's strong nature, Papa often had his way. But it would have been nice to have at least a shuck tick for a pallet. Papa said that sleeping in beds had ruined them for travel and they'd all do well to embrace the hardship.

She released a sigh. Sometimes his former soldier habits were a worse hardship than anything else.

The room now lay bare except for furnishings. She turned a slow circle. So many hours, so many words written here. Would she even have opportunity over the next few months? It was bad enough that the bulk of her writings had to be bundled with her clothing, both to keep them safe and because the stack was too thick for the haversack.

She could only pray it truly was the safest place.

The voices downstairs rose to a pitch that could only be called insistent, so with another sigh and a last glance around the tiny attic room, she slung her haversack over her shoulder and around her body, gathered her skirts, and made her way down the narrow stairs.

The rest of the house bore a similarly forlorn air. All that was going had been carried out, it seemed, and all that was left was for Kate to take her woolen shawl and simple straw hat from their pegs by the front door. The hat she tied on at the nape of her neck, beneath the pinned and cap-covered knot of her hair, and the shawl she draped loosely about her shoulders.

Kate stepped aside for Dulsey and Betsy, who carried a basket between them, then followed them outside. A brisk breeze nearly took her hat, and she angled her head against it while tightening the shawl.

Despite the wind, fog obscured all but the nearest buildings. More than a dozen saddle and packhorses stood along the road, in varying states of readiness. Papa stood talking with one of several men in frontiersman dress—oh wait, was that the post rider she'd talked with two weeks ago?

Though his hat brim obscured his face, when he turned, the same dark hair lay in a braided tail down the back of his hunting coat.

It was curious, the differences in appearance and dress among the men she'd seen at their former home in the upper Shenandoah Valley and here at Bean's Station. Papa himself, sporting whiskers now, usually went clean shaven, but Mama told how when she'd met him, he wore a thick mustache, the habit many of his fellow Hessians affected. Many men of fashion still curled and powdered their hair, while some insisted on a neat club and side rolls. Men of the frontier most often either simply tied theirs back, wore it loose, or braided it as this one did.

Even more curious were the changes in ladies' fashion. Mama decried the new high-waisted, short-sleeved styles as hoydenish, but Kate wished she could at least try them on. No arguing, however, that her sensible jacket and petticoats were much more practical for traveling, and Mama said old-style stays offered better support than the new.

Kate tore her thoughts back to the present and surveyed the line of packhorses again. They'd already met the two other families traveling with them. Papa spoke in terms of how many men they had, and how many guns, and she supposed those were important enough, but Kate was more interested in how many children each family had, where they traveled from, and what they hoped to do when they reached their intended destination.

"Kate, is all your baggage ready?" Mama's voice drew her around. "Yes? Then take Stefan, please."

She handed off the shawl-wrapped bundle of Kate's youngest brother—old enough to walk but they daren't let him with all this commotion—and bustled off again in the direction of Papa and the packhorses. Overseeing their family's loads, no doubt.

Kate would rather dandle Stefan and keep him out of harm's way.

The tiny boy grinned at her around a slobbery finger, then took his wet hand out of his mouth and patted her cheek. Laughing, Kate wiped the hand and then her cheek with a corner of her shawl. "Silly child. You'll have us both sodden before we're even properly on our way."

"This is my wife, Jemima Lytton Gruener, and Jemima, this is Thomas Bledsoe, the scout I have hired."

The woman's officious air dissolved momentarily with a flush. "I am most grateful for your services, Mr. Bledsoe. Thank you for agreeing to come along."

Thomas gave a respectful bob. "My pleasure, Mrs. Gruener." It wasn't, but he knew to be civil under the circumstances.

She beamed, nodded again, and turned to her husband. "The packing. . . ?"

This was not his purview. Mr. Gruener excused himself and moved away with his shorter, slightly plump wife, and Thomas took the opportunity to survey the group bustling around him.

A cluster of men conferred about the packing, about half completed, and two young women with babes in arms stood over beyond them. A pair of squealing children, still in skirts, chased each other about, mostly within arms' reach of the women.

A girl, somewhere between childhood and womanhood, stood with a Negro woman near a pile of belongings. And not too far away from them was the young woman he'd met at the tavern, dandling a toddler on her hip.

Her own child or—someone else's? Something between relief and disappointment pricked him, but he shrugged it away. No concern of his whether she was married or not.

'Twould make things much simpler if she were.

His gaze roamed the scene again, skimming past to hilltops draped in mist, but the baby's giggle and the girl's answering chuckle drew him back. Both were completely absorbed in each other, the baby riveted by the silly faces the young woman made in between peals of her own laughter.

His chest tightened, just a little, at the reminder of Truth and her passel of young'uns.

Not for him. Not now, maybe never. *I'll not leave a woman to cry over me.* This was employment, plain and simple, in lieu of the post-rider position. Although if those boys in Danville dragged their feet getting the post running again, maybe he'd just go farther west and volunteer for militia service after all.

In fact, between the chatter of the women, the babble of the young'uns, and the barking of the dogs, militia was sounding better and better. Or rejoining the Shawnee.

A pang struck him. Regret? Longing?

Nudging aside his thoughts and hefting his long rifle, he sauntered toward the packing operations. Setting a load was not one of his stronger skills, but he could lift a bundle well enough, and the more hands that helped, the sooner they could be on their way. Jenkins, the leader of the pack operation, glanced over and gave him a nod. "Bledsoe. You come to lend a hand?"

"I have, that."

With work for his muscles to attend to, the gnawing restlessness abated some. Enough at least for him to tuck it aside and enjoy the prospect of simply being out on the road.

About an hour later, the horses were completely packed, and the party formed up in a line, ready to go. Thomas returned to Ladyslipper and mounted up, then meandered toward the rear while children were tucked into pack saddles, taller ones behind the small, and room was found for the mothers with babes.

He passed Karl Gruener, helping settle onto a saddle the child his oldest daughter had been holding. The young woman glanced up and offered a shy smile, and he nodded in return.

At the rear of the line, he waited, and then the pack masters themselves mounted up. The leader waved his hat for attention. "Before we move out, let us commit this journey to prayer."

Thomas removed his own hat and by habit bowed his head, but he kept his eyes open, periphery alert.

"Sovereign, Almighty Lord, we beseech Thy help and guidance as we take this path before us. Protect us, lead us, overshadow us beneath Thy mighty wings. Grant us Thy peace and Thy presence...."

Just what they needed, a pack master who aspired to preach. Thomas let his thoughts drift and sent discreet glances about. Plenty of others didn't have their eyes devoutly closed either, but they all pretended not to notice each other.

Finally the droning prayer ended, and the party stirred to action once more. The pack leader whooped, and Thomas held Ladyslipper still while the line moved out, segment by segment.

On their way at last. Thomas drew a deep breath and let it out slowly. Impatience would do him no good. Neither would it hurry the traveling party along a whit.

Why again had he agreed to do this?

As the line stretched before him, with folk and beasts finding their stride, he scanned and counted. Ten packhorses, all bearing at least a pair of young'uns as well as baggage, three saddle horses ridden by the pack master and his crew. Ten men, counting the older youths and himself, and at least nine guns. Gruener had mentioned his wife and their colored servant carrying a pistol each as well and both being proficient in reloading.

At least they carried the prospect of being sensible, even if the daughter did tremble like a wild rabbit in his presence.

Said daughter walked alone near the packhorse carrying the child she'd been tending and a slightly older girl. Her head turned this way and that, scanning the mist-cloaked tree line beyond the scattered buildings of Bean's Station—which he ought to be doing, rather than gawking, but part of the task of being scout meant counting how many were in their party and making sure they were all present at any given time.

As they passed, many waved and called a farewell. Thomas kept his response to the occasional nod, and only to those he knew—although those were not a few. The post runs had served to good stead there. Still, the settlers passing through moved too quickly for him to be familiar with all.

He stifled another sigh. Several weeks, a couple of months at most, and he could reasonably expect to be shed of scouting. And hopefully he'd learn something useful for Carrington as well.

CHAPTER 4

At last—the journey had begun.

It wasn't as if this was the first. Close to a year ago, they'd made the journey from the upper Shenandoah Valley, down the Great Road, and eventually to Bean's Station, while Papa went on to find work and land in Kentucky. He'd worked as assistant surveyor for a while and been part of discussions about improving the Wilderness Road to accommodate wagons. Why he'd decided not to wait for those improvements to be made was still largely a mystery to Kate, but even when her papa was most inscrutable, his judgment usually proved sound.

He warned them that only the first part of the road north, from Bean's Station to Powell Valley, would be decent road—in fact, they could easily get a wagon to that point, possibly even trade it to someone coming south out of Kentucky. 'Twas once they crossed the Cumberland Gap that things would be more difficult, and he preferred to use the packhorses at the outset. Kate could see the sense in that, even though Mama argued stridently, because one never knew if the wagon would have to simply be abandoned at the gap.

The first day would be easy, she knew—and it was for the most part, with everyone in high spirits, smiles and greetings from all. Even Jemmy and Stefan chatted as they rode a packhorse together, although it remained to be seen how long that would last.

Probably only until one needed to use the necessary. That should prove to be an adventure all its own. The pack leaders had decided that unless there was an emergency, no one would be slipping off alone, but they'd be stopping for a few minutes at a time. So it was Kate's task, when the little ones began fussing, to keep them diverted until it was time to stop.

On this stretch of the road, everyone knew the precautions were mostly for practice only. They had but a couple of miles until they began their climb of Clinch Mountain in earnest, but for now the party behaved as though they were only strolling out for a picnic. Most of the men loitered up near the front of the line, talking and laughing and paying little attention to the woods surrounding them. Johann, who Mama had tasked with assisting her, was in the thick of them, strutting next to Papa as if he were already a man full grown. Getting to accompany Papa on this last journey up into Kentucky had increased his pride as well as his stature.

The other girls and women kept to a loose cluster as well up ahead. The mothers with babies were riding of course, along with the smallest of the children. Kate didn't mind walking. It was good that they'd enough horses—pack animals notwithstanding—for the ones who'd have more trouble with the journey.

The one who kept drawing her attention was that tall, lean rider bringing up the rear. Unlike the other men, he remained alert, head tipped to scan the country around them, sometimes stopping his horse as if to listen. His worn felt hat, bleached brown by much wear in the sun, boasted a turkey feather as its lone embellishment. Both brim and feather fluttered with the wind.

Someone at least was keeping watch. Kate tucked in her smile from the corners of her mouth and tried not to stare. The man moved as one with his light-footed mount, whose chestnut coat gleamed bright against the grey mist as they wove back and forth behind the rest of the party, up the slope to one side of the road for a short way, and then across and down the other.

He seemed well absorbed in taking in their surroundings but, as if he sensed her attention, turned and met her gaze.

A shiver swept over her. Even across the short distance, she could see the paleness of his eyes, found herself transfixed by the calm directness of his look.

And she'd been caught staring. Face heating, she ducked her head and refocused on the road ahead just in time to avoid stumbling over a stone in the path.

She had to find a way to speak with him, to ask him about himself. Several weeks of travel should provide plenty of opportunity—but she would make her own if none presented itself.

For now, however, as the ground rose and roughened, she should give attention to the path. They approached the foot of Clinch Mountain, which folk had warned would be a steep, hard climb, likely the worst until they made Cumberland Gap itself. But it wasn't the difficulty of crossing Clinch Mountain that unsettled most of them. It was the possible dangers that lay beyond the Clinch River.

Kate nudged those aside. This was a better route, most said, than the old one that led most directly from the Holston River's north fork across to the upper end of Powell Valley, the advantage of Clinch Gap to the north notwithstanding. The new road south along Holston Valley to Bean's Station, they argued, was able to be widened to a wagon road, and it had been mostly improved to such, even on the southern crossing of Clinch Mountain.

She'd noted these and many other details in her journal over the past few weeks—details she longed to verify for herself, and indeed would, on this journey.

Their party had drifted to mostly single-file, and as they made the descent to one of the creek beds, the splashing from the horses' hooves ahead of her grew louder. Fortunately this crossing was made easier for her and other walkers by the placement of stones along the road bed.

Gripping the lead rope in her small hand, Jemmy clucked to the horse to cross the trickle, but when the beast hesitated, she turned wide eyes to Kate. With a small shake of her head, Kate took hold of the halter and tugged to encourage the horse across, while balanced between two stones. The horse tossed its head, then with an odd little hop, scrambled across. Kate scuttled along beside, her hand on the horse's rump to steady herself, in case one of the small ones tumbled off, but all remained well.

She blew out a breath. Too early in the journey to let herself be ruffled by a possible mishap. But hopefully the horse wouldn't prove to shy later at the prospect of a water crossing.

"Kate, don't leave us!"

Jemmy's thready voice hastened her steps and drew her alongside the gelding, who swung its head toward her with a whoosh of breath, as if it too needed her presence for reassurance as the ground grew more rough. Kate reached for a handful of mane and used the horse's bulk to help pull her up the bit of bank.

As she made the short rise, the wind tugged at her hat, but she gripped the crown and tipped her head to catch a glimpse of Clinch Mountain. All remained under a veil of mist beyond the closer, lower ridge forming the foot of the mountain, as if the long ridge still wore a shawl of cloud tucked close about her, over her dress of deep forest and rhododendron.

A shawl that would likely prove to be cold and wet, once they neared the top of the mountain.

Up the smaller ridge they labored, tall oaks and walnut swaying and moaning in the wind. Kate kept one hand tangled in the gelding's mane. As they rounded the top, passing through a small gap in the ridge, Kate peered this way and that, past trees and boulders, for snatches of the misty landscape, but all she could see clearly yet was the valley they'd just departed, with Bean's Station small and forlorn behind them.

Then it was downward again, this time leaning against the shoulder of the packhorse as she picked her way down the trail, stepping on exposed rock for better footing. It was tricky avoiding the smoothest spots, but she managed the entire slope without slipping or sliding too much. Then a narrow, burbling creek—the packhorse stepped more confidently this time—before they began the long incline toward the peak of Clinch Mountain.

The road wasn't a simple matter of going upward, but dipped and climbed through the little hills and valleys forming the mountain's side. They went slowly enough—she didn't feel the least out of breath—but before they reached the edge of thickening mist above, someone called halt. Again leaning on the horse's shoulder, she smiled up at her siblings and stretched this way and that to ease the burn in her leg muscles.

"I need to use the necessary," Jemmy said, a plaintive note in her voice.

Others were making their way into the dense laurel, so with a nod, Kate reached up to take Stefan, then helped the girl down. "Don't go far," she said, and pointed straight downhill to a cluster of bushes just beginning to bloom.

Kate stepped a little off the road to encourage Stefan to make water, and after he happily obliged, she set him back up onto the packhorse. Jemmy returned and climbed up after.

The line was setting out again, the leaders disappearing into the fog that wreathed the mountaintop. The packhorse plodded upward, and Kate took to gripping its mane again.

The fog closed about them, cool and cloying. Damping sound as if their heads were all wrapped in wool. The horse's hoofbeats and her own steps seemed dreamlike, and a breeze still blew, but with palpable moisture. The exertion of the climb, however, kept Kate well warmed, and seeing Jemmy and Stefan huddled together, she took off her shawl and wrapped it about them.

Still they climbed. Stefan and Jemmy both sagged in the saddle, and Kate poked them to wake up. She thought of singing, just softly, so to be in keeping with the pack master's wish that they make as little noise as possible, but the first notes died in her throat, strangled by the almost unearthly quiet.

The plodding of their feet, the soft huff of labored breaths, the drip from bush and tree branch, all these filled her world. Kate thought of the copper-skinned people who must have run this path for long years before white people had come—of a hundred fireside tales of death and capture. Just last year several parties had met a terrible fate on this, the lower end of the road—not on Clinch Mountain but farther on a bit.

She scanned the foggy mountainside both above and below, its folds hidden in mist. This would be as likely a place for ambush as any.

Though her skin still flushed with the heat of their exertion, a deep chill settled into her middle. She leaned harder into the horse's shoulder. The beast's warmth and bulk did little to ease the unfamiliar hollowness yawning inside her, edged by a beating panic.

What was this? She'd not thought herself afraid of the dangers of the road, indeed had turned the matter to prayer so often that it should be as second nature to do so now. But the threat of attack seemed so imminent she fancied she could almost hear rustling in the laurel as they passed, could anticipate the first flying arrow and menacing shriek.

The quiet itself pressed in upon her, breathing its dark threat along her shoulders.

God. . .oh sovereign Lord. . .have mercy.

Warmth settled around her, calming, soothing.

"Yea, though I walk through the valley of the shadow of death, thou art with me."

Not a valley but a mountaintop had her spooked—but God was no less present. Perhaps they'd have to face such dangers farther on in the journey, but for this moment—

Thank You, oh Lord, for being with us. Thank You for the peace.

Behind a cluster of boulders taller than the horses' heads, emerging from the fog, the ground ahead abruptly leveled. They'd reached the top of Clinch Mountain.

Riding through mountaintop fog was always an interesting and slightly unnerving experience. Thomas kept watchful, his ears open, uncomfortable with not being able to see the entire party, much less the lay of the land around them. He'd no real concern about attack—there'd been no sign of Indians, and they tended to not like the cold and damp—but it made him twitchy, nevertheless.

The wagon road wended its way between tree and boulder, so easy at this point, even with the ascent, that the settlers' decision to use packhorses already seemed pointless. Thomas knew otherwise. And even here, the steep ascent and passage across the ridge, followed by a sharp downward pitch, was made far less worrisome than wagon travel would have been.

Below, the mist thinned, and the shapes resolved themselves into traveling folk. Through breaks in the trees, the Clinch Valley spread below them, north and south, with the river just a couple of miles distant as the crow flies. They'd likely camp after crossing the river—give folk time to dry out their footgear before needing to walk a whole day again.

And once more, Thomas felt he could breathe. No sign as far as he could see—or hear—of trouble.

His gaze skimmed along the road as it descended the mountain, then angled away toward the river. It was five, maybe six miles from the top of the mountain to the ford, as the road actually ran. From this distance he couldn't tell how high the river might be. With spring rainfall, it was hard to say.

The party itself seemed to be doing just fine. One or two walkers had the beginnings of being footsore, so that would bear watching.

The journey down from the mountain passed without incident. One more necessary stop near the foot, and a quick dip into provisions to keep the young'uns bellies from grumbling—he was glad enough of a piece of jerky, himself—and they were on their way.

About midafternoon, following the road along the river, they made it to the ford of the Clinch. The river looked a little on the high side, and there was one most likely crossing on this stretch, so the pack leaders were taking their time finding just the right approach. These men knew the road as well as he did—or nearly as well—so he hung back and let them do the picking.

His eyes strayed down the line of travelers, now stopped and waiting for the first ones to start across. A couple of the women who'd been walking were being helped aboard the packhorses—one of those the young Gruener woman. Her father handed her up between the tot and younger girl, and she took the horse's reins with what appeared to be a decent amount of confidence.

Whether she could follow that with experience remained to be seen. But he'd keep watch on all of them.

The first ones in line were headed down into the water now, men on foot wading with rifles and muskets held high, going slow to find their footing in the swift current. Horses snorted and splashed before resigning themselves to the water.

With reasonable caution, the entire party made their way into the river, and the leaders were just emerging on the other bank as the stragglers went in. Thomas nudged Ladyslipper after them. The water was never deeper than chest high on the horses, a bit more than waist high on the men, so with the exception of one young man who lost his footing and got a wetting all over, they made the crossing without incident. The Gruener girl with the two young children had no trouble that he could see, but Thomas bit back a smile at the cursing of the young man at discovering his powder had gotten wet right along with his clothes.

That one had been too cocky, by half. Maybe he'd step a little more careful next time.

CHAPTER 5

Someone said there was an ordinary just a bit down the road where they could stay the night, but those in charge decided it best to find a likely spot to camp near the river rather than count on lodging for all at the inn. Kate waited until her father had helped Jemmy down from the horse before she climbed down as well and took Stefan. Rest would be welcome this night, although a roof might have been even more so. This wasn't her first experience with camping, but they'd always had the wagon for shelter before.

She peered at the scudding mist still rimming the mountaintop across the river and the hills on their side and drew her shawl about her shoulders again before herding Jemmy and Stefan away to the bushes. They'd not be able to lay out bedding and such until the pack master and his crew unloaded the horses.

It had been a good day, all things considered. Even her two youngest siblings had managed the entire day without fussing, except when one needed the necessary, as she'd expected.

Talk of how to lay out camp and who could do what swirled around her. Some helped lead the horses away to be watered, while others began sifting through the unloaded bundles. At the prospect of rest and with their first river crossing behind them, spirits remained high despite the speculation of rain by morning.

Cook fires were started, and provisions brought out. Mama oversaw the boiling of salted beef for supper and water for coffee. With the children's needs tended, Kate let Stefan totter about the camp, keeping a firm hold of his leading strings, while Dulsey and the other girls helped Mama with the cooking.

Papa was busy. . .somewhere. Kate glanced about to see where he might be, but at the moment, he was nowhere in sight. Stefan chose that instant to fling himself in the opposite direction, the sudden tug on his leading strings catching her off guard. Hand tightening on the strips of cloth, she stumbled, recovered, and gasped as Stefan lurched toward the heels of a passing horse.

A lean figure swooped in and caught Stefan out of harm's way. Startled into dropping the leading strings, Kate found herself looking into pale blue eyes before their hired scout turned his attention to the small boy in his arms, now squawking in protest. "Hie now," he said. "You can't be throwing yourself at the back hooves of a horse you don't know."

Popping a finger into the corner of his drooly mouth, Stefan stopped and gazed into the young man's face.

"At least not on the first day," Kate said.

The post-rider-turned-scout glanced between her and Stefan, then smiled, eyes crinkling in genuine humor. "Preferably not any day."

A giggle escaped her, a high-pitched, frivolous bit she was sure made her sound like a child. Cheeks heating, she held out her hands for Stefan. "Thank you for catching him up so quickly."

He passed Stefan back over, his smile fading, but a certain softness remaining as he looked at the boy. "He yours?"

Kate settled him against her hip. "Ah—yes. I mean, no. He's my brother, so he is mine, but—" Oh, confound her tangled tongue and the blush she could feel once more overcoming her face. How was she ever to speak to the man comfortably enough to inquire about his stories?

A chuckle gusted from him, surprising her. He reached to catch Stefan's outstretched fingers and waggle the child's arm. "I was near raised by my oldest sister, so. . .sometimes it's hard to tell who the real mama is."

She gave a rueful laugh as well. "That it is. Mama is often so busy. . . but I don't mind."

His chin tucked, and his mouth flattened a little. "My mama—she died when I was a boy." His throat moved with a heavy swallow. "My papa too. You're fortunate to still have yours."

With that, he put Stefan's hand from him and strode away.

⌘

Now, why in the world had he said that? He'd no reason to be spilling to this girl. . .no reason in the world. Nothing besides the open grin on that baby's face and the reflected innocence in the face of his sister.

Sister. Why couldn't she have been the babe's own mama, in truth, already well claimed by some man? Then he could simply disregard her shy glances, the curiosity in those warm brown eyes instead of being drawn in like the fool he obviously was, blurting things he'd rather not speak of with anyone.

He threw himself back into the work of unloading the packhorses, toting bundles hither and yon as directed by their owners. Resisting the urge to cast a glance about for that fair girl with the dark eyes, and her darling infant brother, no matter how many times he crossed paths with those he knew already were her family members.

It was a relief when the unpacking was done and he could leave Ladyslipper on her tether and retreat to a hillside above camp, both to scout and soak up a bit of quiet.

He took silent, measured steps, slowly circling the camp, breathing in the smell of loam and dogwood. This might be the one thing to save his sanity on this journey. If so, he'd volunteer for watch every night.

Having made two circuits about the camp, he settled on a ridge overlooking it. The aroma of coffee and cooking salt beef drifted on the wind. His belly rumbled, but he refused to move.

He should go down and eat. He should.

"Here you are," a male voice said from not too far away, a little winded. "A hard man to find, you make yourself."

Thomas rose as Karl Gruener stepped into view in the twilight, bearing a pewter plate and a tin mug. His gut gave another growl.

Gruener nodded and smiled. "Hungry, I'm sure you are. I've brought you food and coffee."

Thomas accepted both with a word of thanks. The coffee was decently strong, the beef and bread filling. While he ate, the other man watched him without comment for a few minutes.

"Is there need for watch tonight, truly?" he asked at last.

Thomas flicked him a glance. "P'raps not. But best to be 'ware, just in case."

Gruener nodded. "I trust you in this. But should the others not help you keep watch?"

"I asked Jones to come relieve me after a couple of hours." It was either that or sleep on his post. Not even he could stay awake all night and then again all day.

A brisk nod and the other man sat down beside him.

The quiet wrapped them about as Thomas set aside the empty plate and sipped the coffee. A whip-poor-will started its wistful song, and a second one joined in. Thomas released a long breath.

Peace, at last.

Crouched at the fire, Kate poured coffee, this time into her own cup. Papa had already taken a cup and plate and gone in search of their scout. She swiveled, preparing to rise, but found her way blocked by a pair of large feet and gaiter-covered legs, both shoes and garments a bit worse for the dip in the river. Above a coat that at one time had been blue, a youthful male face offered a grin. "Could I get some of that coffee?"

One of the Hughes boys. About her age, if she didn't miss her guess by the attempt at whiskers on his chin.

"We've a bit left, I think."

Kate picked up the cloth she'd used to lift the pot, then glanced up again in search of the young man's cup. His hands were, predictably, empty. With a suppressed sigh, she considered her own cup, then held it out to him. His grin widened as he scooped the cup out of her grasp. "Many thanks." He drank, humming in appreciation. "I'm Jacob Hughes."

With a tight nod, she rose, stepping back to put space between them and brushing off her petticoat. She looked up to find him staring at her, eyebrows raised.

"And you are?" he prompted.

"You may address me as Miss Gruener," she said crisply.

"Oh. Well. Of course." The smile faltered, then found purchase once again. "The coffee is mighty fine. You make it?"

"Yes. Thank you."

"Some of the best I ever had."

His eyes were shining in the firelight, unrelenting in their admiration. Kate glanced away. She'd been looking forward to that coffee.

She could go borrow Mama's cup, of course, or wait until Papa returned from feeding their scout. . .

Bledsoe, she corrected herself. His name was Mr. Bledsoe.

The Hughes boy was still sipping at his coffee—*her* coffee—and gazing at her, so she squared her shoulders and turned back to him. "So. Is it your elder brother who has a wife and babe, or your father?"

She thought she knew the answer to that, but it was best to get all the connections straight from the outset.

Jacob Hughes likewise straightened, looking inordinately proud that she'd chosen to speak to him. "My brother, James. That's Sarah and aye, their babe, Johnny. My father is John Hughes and our mother died a few years back."

Her thoughts flashed back to Mr. Bledsoe's pronouncement. Loss of any sort was difficult, and he'd spoken correctly, she should be glad to still have both parents. "I'm sorry to hear that," she murmured, with as much sincerity as she could muster. "Any other sisters or brothers?"

"Two sisters, Rebecca and Rachel. A brother, Joseph. He's the one who fell in and ruined his powder." He was nearly preening now. "We came down the Great Road from Philly, wintered at Blue Lick."

Well, this one would have no problem spilling his story. Through a wave of weariness, she forced a smile and let him keep prattling.

She'd sorely miss that coffee.

It was a relief when Mama called her over to their part of the camp to help get the younger children settled. Her feet ached and her eyelids would barely stay up, but helping tuck Stefan and Jemmy in meant she could lie down for a few moments.

Gracious, but that must be how Mama felt.

With clouds still thick and grey and the hilltops heavy with mist, dark fell quickly. The little ones were plenty weary as well, and for once didn't protest bedtime.

Papa came walking out of the gloom, carrying the plate and cup, both empty, and handed them off to Mama. "I've washed these." When she continued to look anxiously into his face, he bobbed his head and continued, "All is well, 'Mima. Let us bed down and sleep."

He'd made them a pair of tents from canvas which during the day wrapped their possessions and were loaded onto the horses. Tonight they'd provide a bit of dryness in case the promise of rain materialized.

Kate hesitated in the opening of the one where Jemmy and Stefan lay. "Do you need me to do aught else, Mama?"

"No. You've helped much tonight. Thank you."

She wavered at the strangeness of Mama's spoken gratitude and crawled back inside. Next to Stefan—for Jemmy lay on his other side—she burrowed under a woolen blanket and a coverlet, and scrunched to get comfortable. Stefan snuggled in against her back and sighed. Kate echoed it, silently.

The sounds of camp settling wrapped them about. Low voices in conversation. The horses stamping and snorting, not far off. A baby crying then hushing. Whip-poor-wills calling out on the ridge above, as they had been since just before dusk.

Somewhere out in the dark was their scout. Would he be able to sleep tonight at all? Kate couldn't imagine anyone standing watch all night. She drew a long breath, held it, released it again with a half-articulated prayer for his well-being and that of the entire party.

"In vain the watchman stayeth awake."

That wasn't the entirety of the verse, nor could she be sure she quoted it correctly, yet the truth remained that it was ultimately the Lord's care that preserved them from harm.

But the sharp ears and eyes of that young man couldn't be amiss if the need arose.

CHAPTER 6

Morning dawned with a bit more edge to the wind and the clouds more thick and grey, spitting definite rain. No choice but to move on, the pack masters said. They'd make the gap tomorrow, if all went well.

They bundled their belongings and loaded them as the day before, set the children and women with babies on horseback, then started out after prayer. Someone murmured there'd be scripture read that night.

Kate drew her shawl closer about her shoulders and tried not to think about the ache in her body from yesterday's exertion. She'd be trail hardened soon enough.

Deeper than the ache was a renewed chill, like the one she'd felt up on the mountain yesterday. The section of road they'd be traveling today took them through a series of narrow passages through the hills below and Big Sycamore Creek—passages that made the perfect place for an ambush by the Cherokee just last year. The Watauga Association had dealt with the threat, but it was still on everyone's minds. She'd heard the whispers while they broke camp that morning but tried not to pay attention because, truly, what could they do but press on? And their journey had barely begun.

God could protect them, as the pack master had reminded them all before prayer—as she had reflected while falling asleep last night. And if they could not put their hope in Him, then—what else was there?

Spring flowers bloomed along the way—nodding bluebells and delicate spring beauties. Tiny white, forked blooms hung in a line on their stalks like so many pairs of breeches hung to dry. The occasional blood-root. They provided welcome spots of color in the morning gloom, though she could not linger to enjoy them.

The streams and hills were beautiful enough in their own right. Dog-woods with their white blooms, redbud in pink, the laurel with their star-shaped clusters. The trees beginning to leaf out. The overall hint of green gracing the forest.

It could still snow, they were told. Not until late April or May would the weather warm enough beyond any danger of that.

Would they see snow, crossing the gap? Today it seemed likely. Kate knew from accounts of others' journeys that such had happened before.

They made it to Big Sycamore Creek with no mishaps, and crossed at a ford that was so lovely, so ideal, it seemed they could almost avoid getting their feet wet. Kate contemplated mounting the packhorse as she had the day before, but led the beast rather than trouble anyone for help. She'd save that for when it was truly needed.

Some removed shoes and stockings before crossing, because of the danger of foot scald. Kate hesitated then did the same, tucking them into one of the packs before stepping down into the water. Its coldness took her breath away, but she kept going, focusing on keeping her footing while hanging on to the horse's lead—yet staying far enough away that the animal wouldn't inadvertently step on her while it too navigated the rocky creek bottom.

They were halfway across and the cold no longer a shock to her feet and legs when her foot failed to find purchase on a muddy, slick patch, and down she went. Scrambling to stay upright, the rocks hard against her toes and ankles though no pain registered, she came up again as quickly as she could, flailing for the horse's lead rope. But her fall startled the animal as well, and it rushed past, yanking the lead from her grasp. The splash of another horse heaving across the knee-deep expanse threw water in her face, and by the time she got her legs under her and stood, dripping and gasping, midstream, their mounted scout had caught up with the pack-horse and snagged the lead.

Again, he'd intervened at her failure.

She stood, trying to regain her breath at the shock of the cold, then grabbing sodden skirts in both hands, waded ungracefully after them.

Both horses gained the creek bank, and Mr. Bledsoe drew them up short and turned to look at her, his eyes a pale glint under the hat brim. Suddenly she did not feel so cold. It was a wonder, in fact, that her clothing did not at that moment put out steam.

"My—gratitude—once again, sir," she gasped, hauling herself up from the water's edge.

He made no reply, nor any move to hand her back the packhorse's lead. "See to your feet," he said finally, and moved his horse farther up the bank before dismounting. The rest of the party was doing the same alongside the road.

She swayed, about to protest—but the prospect of plunking her backside on the nearest boulder for even a short rest didn't seem so undignified after all, under the circumstances. So she sat, her lungs still heaving, and drew back her skirts to peer at her feet.

Two or three toenails were ripped, one torn completely off, and all bleeding. And was that bruising or just mottling from the cold? Some of both, it would appear.

"Those'll bear wrapping," came Mr. Bledsoe's voice, from right at her shoulder. She started upright. His pale eyes met hers for a moment, impassive, and he squinted at her feet again. "You ought to ride, at least for a day or two."

"But—the packhorse is already carrying so much."

"No helping it," he said evenly. "Your feet'll be useless if you keep walking, injured as they are. And you don't weigh that much."

"But—"

Papa came striding down the bank, Johann in tow. "Ach, Daughter, what have you done?"

"I only slipped and fell in the water, Papa—"

"Her feet are cut and bruised. She needs to ride, or later she'll slow us down more," Mr. Bledsoe supplied.

Papa glanced between them and bent to examine her feet more carefully. He clucked his tongue and shook his head. "No help for it then."

"But the horses are already so loaded down," Kate said.

"She can ride mine," Mr. Bledsoe said, almost before she'd completed the sentence. "That is, if she can handle a horse."

Kate could only blink at the beautiful mare tethered just up the bank, and then at Papa, who regarded Mr. Bledsoe with a narrowed gaze. "Thank you, but that is not necessary," he said at last. "Johann and I will take Stefan on our shoulders and let Kate ride with Jemmy. If it comes to that, Jemmy herself can walk a while."

Mr. Bledsoe gave a short nod then stepped away.

"Really, Papa, I'm sure I can walk," Kate murmured.

"Perhaps." He pushed to his feet. "Johann, see if your mother has aught for clean wraps."

Kate bent and pushed at one of the torn toenails. That would bear snipping with her sewing scissors, at least, before it snagged on the wrapping, and before her toes warmed enough to truly hurt.

Thought of her sewing kit, bundled across her back, gave way to thought of—

"Oh no!" She pulled the strap of the sodden haversack from over her shoulder and head, and scrambled to open it.

The contents were damp but not completely soaked, but even so—she drew out the carefully wrapped roll containing her journal pages. The buckskin pocket she'd sewn for it had, for the most part, preserved them, and only the edges were damp—

"Katarina," Papa said, disapprovingly. "Is that what it appears to be?"

Kate froze and stared up at him. "It's—my journal, Papa."

The crinkles around his eyes deepened. "Your journal."

Half a dozen explanations came to her lips then died. She closed her mouth, tucked the pages back inside their pouch, and the pouch back inside the haversack before picking up the completely sodden packet of sewing things she'd laid on the rock beside her.

"Katarina. The expense of parchment and ink—"

"I take in extra mending along with Mama to make up for it," she said quickly.

He blew out a hard breath. "You are not a child, Kate. We have talked of this. You told me you understood."

She blinked away the burn of her eyes so she could better see where to apply the scissors. Her feet were beginning to hurt, but she could still hardly feel it under the weight of Papa's censure.

Then Mama arrived. "We will speak of this later," Papa said quietly but firmly, as Kate snipped the first bit of torn toenail away.

❦

Thomas forced his attention to the rest of the party, leaning to look where others were just putting stockings and shoes back on, conferring with the pack master, Jenkins, on proper foot care. While they might have a bruise or two, none of the others seemed as needful of attention as Miss Gruener—but none of the others had been trying to lead a packhorse while making the crossing with bare feet either. He'd been on his way to relieve her of the horse's lead when she'd fallen, and while the young'uns were in no real danger, he was glad to be as close as he was when the horse got loose.

The young woman was beginning to concern him though. She'd need to look sharp if she was to survive settling the frontier, and this was the second mishap in as many days.

They weren't even to the most difficult part of the trail yet. What would happen once they were?

All he could do was watch, and no more. There was one in every traveling party, he supposed, and it'd been long enough since he'd scouted that he'd forgotten how vexing it could be.

He walked back through the crowd, rested enough and shoes back on, to retrieve Ladyslipper. The Gruener family still clustered, but the oldest daughter was now astride the packhorse, lead rope looped about in place of a rein, both small children dispersed to others.

Thomas untied Ladyslipper and swung into the saddle, then held her back as the others moved out. Miss Gruener did the same, and he edged Ladyslipper closer to her mount. "Might be best if you had a bit and bridle now, instead of halter and lead."

Her head dipped, cheeks coloring. "How likely is he to wander from the back of the line?"

Thomas shook his head a little. "Wandering isn't the concern. Being able to hold him if he startles, is." In fact, he wasn't sure why Jenkins hadn't used a bit and bridle for when the young'uns rode, but maybe he'd counted on the horse being led by someone else. He watched the line moving out, set Ladyslipper into motion beside the packhorse. "You should be fine for now. I'll ask Jenkins at the next stop."

"Thank you," she murmured.

He peered down at her feet, swathed in wrappings. Before he could comment, she said, "Mama was too zealous with the bandages. My shoes won't fit."

"Nothing wrong with that," he muttered. "Keep you from wandering off."

Her head snapped around, her dark eyes wide—then she completely shocked him by bursting into laughter. Honest, genuine laughter, musical and rich, not the annoying titter of so many girls.

A reluctant grin tugged at his own mouth in response.

"It might, at that," she said finally.

CHAPTER 7

The change in perspective was not unwelcome by any means. She'd felt far less anxious about their river crossing the day before, accomplishing it on horseback rather than trying to wade the current—even with having Jemmy and Stefan to contend with as well as guiding the horse through the water. Having a real bridle would make things simpler, but she'd not cause even more trouble by owning it before the next stop. Hopefully the silly horse would not cause any trouble on his own.

Though the guilt still lingered over making Papa carry Stefan, and Jemmy having to walk, her feet were throbbing in earnest now inside Mama's bandages. It was a relief to not be forced to endure putting her shoes on over that.

And the whole landscape seemed different from atop a horse. It reminded her of when she was yet small enough to ride in the wagon during their travels, but without the bone-jarring rattle, and of the times she'd ridden behind Papa. Only this—this was better because, being at the rear, she had a view of the entire traveling party, interesting in its own right.

She peeked over her shoulder at Mr. Bledsoe, who'd finally dropped behind enough to allow her a full breath. Fortunately he was well occupied with scanning the woods around them, trotting that lovely mare up the rise parallel to the road and not peering back at her. She'd need to get over being all a-jitter in his presence, or it would be a very long and tedious journey indeed.

Not to mention she'd never pluck up the courage to ask him about himself. And how difficult could that be, anyway? When the young Hughes boy nearly wouldn't leave the night before, so eager was he to share. It always seemed the more willing a body was to share their story, the more likely that story wasn't worth hearing.

Although, everyone's story was worth hearing. She couldn't let herself be so unkind. But some were more worth hearing a second time than others, for certain. And Jacob Hughes did not fit that category, at least not thus far, not when half of his chatter was merely bragging about what he and his father and brothers planned to accomplish once they reached Kentucky.

A gust of wind drew a shiver from her. 'Twould be nice if the sun would come out. She'd given her shawl to Jemmy that morning, so at least she had that back, dry and warm, but sitting on horseback and not walking on her own meant her wet clothing was especially chilly. She bent and wrapped her arms around the horse's neck, and that helped. And with them merely plodding along this part of the road, she didn't need to pay particularly close attention.

The next thing she knew, someone was shaking her shoulder. "Miss Gruener. . .wake up, Miss Gruener."

A persistent rocking motion lulled her nearly into not responding, but the shaking of her shoulder was so at odds with comfort that she dragged her eyelids open just to see who dared disturbed her.

The tight-lipped face of Mr. Bledsoe hovered near. She started and sat up, rubbing her eyes, and he moved away. "Are you well? You shouldn't be falling asleep on horseback."

"I—so tired." She covered a yawn and drew the shawl more tightly about her shoulders. Another shiver overtook her. "And cold."

The movement made her cap and pins slip, and she reached up to catch the mass before it tumbled completely down. Gracious, she was a mess.

She'd truly fallen asleep on horseback?

Mr. Bledsoe's expression went a little less severe. Edging his mount closer to hers again, he reached over and rummaged in one of the packs, then pulled out a woven wool blanket. "Here. Wrap this around you. No sense in coming down sick from the wetting you got."

An unaccountable thickness swelled her throat as she pulled the edges up over her shoulders, the back of her head, and under her chin. She'd deal with her cap and hair later. "Thank you."

He bobbed a nod, tucked the pack edges back under, and flipped a corner of the blanket higher so it wouldn't drag the ground.

"How many sisters do you have?" she blurted.

He stilled, eyes widening a little. "Four," he answered slowly, then finished arranging everything and made to move his horse away again.

"How many older, how many younger?" The words tumbled out of her before she could think.

"Two each." His hands twitched on the reins then relaxed.

"Any brothers?"

He shook his head, gaze scanning the woods around them. She smoothed a hand across her face again and also looked around. More lovely spring woods, and a few laurel among the rocks but—otherwise unremarkable. An abandoned-looking cabin stood along the road behind them.

"Do your sisters have names?" she asked.

He snorted, a corner of his mouth lifting. "They do." He hesitated so long that she thought he wouldn't reply, but then, "My parents were partial to good, solid Puritan names. My older sister is Truth, then came Patience, and the younger are Thankful and Mercy." With a sudden, full grin that did something strange to her insides, he added, "And me they named Thomas, after my grandfather."

"Oh!" She winced a little at the tone of her exclamation, and tried to modulate her voice. "Those are lovely. And—there's no shame in sharing the name of one of Christ's disciples."

"The doubting disciple," he said too quickly, some of the humor fading from his expression.

"Still." She found herself determined to tease the smile back to his face. "It could be worse—much worse. You could have been named Steadfast, or Comfort, or—like my own grandfather, Goodwill."

She was rewarded with a quick glance and a silent laugh, then a shake of the head. "Or Troublesome."

"Persistence," she said, also laughing now. "Worthwhile."

The smile fled again, as if that suggestion sent him into deep thought. "Tribulation. 'Tis close enough that they named me Doubtful."

She shifted on the horse's back so she could better watch his face. The blanket and her hair were slipping, but she ignored it. "No. Thomas became most worthy, later."

His gaze came to hers and held. "Did he?"

"Yes. He traveled into Asia, all the way to India, where he preached the Lord and later died an honorable martyr's death."

The pale eyes rounded. "You know this, how?"

She smiled a little. "My papa entertained notions of entering the church in his younger years. He'll tell you he studied overmuch."

His expression was a study, to be sure, but she wished he would say more. Instead he tore his gaze from hers, shook his head again, and fell silent for another short space. "I have an uncle who was given the name Loving," he said, slowly as before, as if he had to chew the words before releasing them. "Most times it gets shortened to Lovin'."

"And—is he? Loving, that is."

He glanced back to her, as if startled she was still there. "He's a good man."

"And where is he now? If I may ask, that is."

His eyes narrowed as he tilted his head to look across a far tree line. "You do ask a lot of questions."

"I like. . .hearing people's stories," she murmured, ducking her head again. "Hearing where they've been, what they've seen. What makes them who they are."

"Mmm."

She peeked at him, and he seemed to be chewing on that as well.

So, she was bookish. In his experience, the bookish ones were often the clumsiest, but that wasn't anything she could help, and he didn't have anything against a good story himself. No harm in telling her a bit about the uncle he loved as well as his own pa.

"Lovin' was at Kings Mountain, where my pa was killed. He and his family, along with one of my older uncles, live up in western Virginia, but they've been talking of going west as far as St. Louis. Two of my older uncles, though, were killed over at Bledsoe's Lick, north of Nashborough—one about six years back and the other just last year."

"I am sorry to hear that," Miss Gruener murmured.

He sneaked her a glance. Those dark eyes just watched him. Her cap and hair were askew, but she appeared not to notice, and he sure wasn't going to point it out.

"I should be scouting the sides of the road and not jawing," he muttered.

"I thought there was less danger this side of the gap."

True enough, but—he leveled her the sternest look he could summon. "Mostly."

"Well." A flush overtook her cheeks again. "Please do not let me detain you."

A chuckle rose in his chest at her sudden stiffness. Miss Gruener turned away and fumbled with the falling cap and coils of hair. Bright, rich gold it was, all unfurled down her back.

He was like to get himself slapped for staring. Yet somehow he couldn't move.

She swiveled toward him, eyes wide, fists full of blanket and cap and pins. "Here, since you have sisters—hold these." She shoved a hand at him, and without thinking, he opened his. Hairpins tumbled into his palm, followed by the wad of linen that was her cap.

Before he could comment, she wrapped the blanket more securely around her waist, and went to work on gathering up the glorious tangle of her hair.

He wasn't sure he'd ever seen that particular color. Not loose and tumbling everywhere. He couldn't breathe, couldn't even move except to hold his hand out closer where she could reach for the pins once the tangle was tamed enough for them.

Her own small hands, now that was a safe focus. They moved, nimble and quick, twisting strands into place. Swept a pair of pins from his palm, tucked those in, returned for more.

He caught her glance as she put the last ones in place and took the cap back. "Thank you," she murmured. Again.

His breath returned in a rush. With a quick nod, he yanked his attention away—back to the line of travelers stretching ahead, to the folded hills on either side, the short meadow spreading off to the left. He could almost wish for some sign of trouble to give him a reason to gallop away.

"So"—her soft voice rose above the horses' plodding hooves—"Loving Bledsoe is the youngest of your uncles?"

Another nod. When he looked back at her, the trailworn cap once more draped her head, all proper-like, and she was tucking the blanket back up over it and around her shoulders.

Much less distracting now. "He was the youngest child of my grandfather, and his mother was our grandfather's second wife. My pa's three older brothers were already grown by the time Loving came along. And then he wasn't much more than a baby when my grandpa disappeared on a long hunt into Kentucky."

Miss Gruener turned to look at him. And once again, he couldn't seem to remember where he was going with that thought.

Only—oh, that was it. The question that had always lingered in his mind of whether Grandpa hadn't perished after all in those deep, forested hills, as they'd surmised, but simply never returned. And all the years that Thomas half expected to run across the old man, near ninety years of age by now, holed up in a cave somewhere, lean but hale, having chosen to never return to civilized society.

The howling deep in his own being yearned to do the same.

Return to the Shawnee.

He dismissed the thought and found himself blinking at Miss Gruener.

"How difficult that must have been for all of them," she said.

He shrugged. " 'Twas no more than what anyone coming into this country should be prepared to face." Both the gesture and the words were more diffident than he felt, of course, but she needed to understand.

"Yes. I've heard the stories." She clutched the blanket closer. "I suppose anytime there is a push into a new land, some lives will be lost. At least, that's what Papa says." She angled him another glance. "Are you one of them? The long hunters, I mean?"

He stared back, and a rusty laugh burst from him. "The time of the long hunter is past, Miss Gruener."

Oddly, she did not laugh or smile in response, but gazed at him thoughtfully. "Do you wish you'd been then?"

Her question caught him by the throat. "Aye."

That was the crux of the matter, precisely.

And just how did this doe-eyed girl manage to wrest that admission from him?

"I must return to my duty," he muttered, and heeled Ladyslipper away into a stand of laurel.

CHAPTER 8

Mr. Bledsoe's abrupt departure left Kate feeling oddly bereft. She watched him lope off into the brush, then straightened to see Papa watching her. She gave him a small wave.

It was a thoughtful thing Mr. Bledsoe had done, pulling out that blanket for her—indeed, of noticing her hurt feet to start with and insisting she ride. And then the way he'd let her prevail upon him to hold her hairpins and cap, for pity's sake. Perhaps he was just being kind and protective because of his own sisters. He certainly seemed reluctant enough to speak of himself. Modesty—or did he simply not enjoy talk? Many folk she'd known did not.

Unfortunately many of those had the most interesting tales to tell, when one could get them talking.

She'd not give up on Mr. Bledsoe yet. Perhaps Papa could persuade him to sup with them this evening before he went off to scout or at least before he went to stand watch, and being with her family would encourage him to unbend a little.

Her gaze went back to him, threading his way up along one of the hillsides parallel to the road. The thought that he'd offered to let her ride that beautiful mare...

Papa's almost disapproving refusal echoed through her memory. Was that because he didn't feel she could handle the horse? She should ask.

Having handed Stefan off to Johann, Papa stepped to the side of the road and waited until Kate reached him, then fell into step beside the packhorse. "Is all well, Daughter?"

"Yes, Papa. Why would it not be?"

His blue eyes strayed to the distant figure of Mr. Bledsoe and his excellent mare. "Does he behave with honor toward you?"

A slight chill swept her. "He does, Papa, thank you."

Though his brow remained knitted beneath the plain, black felt hat, he nodded. "You will say so if he does not, is that understood?"

"Yes, Papa." She hesitated. "Do you—not trust him, Papa? Is that why you refused to let me ride his horse?"

Papa did not answer immediately. He swallowed once or twice, gazed a long time at the rovings of their scout, then said, "We simply do not need to be any more indebted to him than necessary."

She nodded as if she understood—which she did, in part, but not entirely. "He speaks to me but with reluctance. Even inquiring about his family, which he seems to hold in affection, I had to pull every little shred out of him piece by piece. Then when he'd share larger bits, he seemed almost dismayed by the fact that I'd gotten him to speak. So—I'd not worry overmuch. I think he does not like me."

Papa peered at her for a long, hard moment. "I would debate that, *leibchen.*"

Something fluttered in Kate's middle. "What—why would you say that, Papa?"

He shook his head. "Just—let the man have his secrets, Katarina. Stop pestering him."

"Pestering? I am not!"

Papa just smiled and kept walking.

"Papa!"

He reached over and patted her ankle. "Trust me, leibchen, I know you mean well. Perhaps he simply does not enjoy—talk."

Kate thought of his unaccountable nervousness, how one moment he did seem to enjoy conversing with her, and then in the next, making excuses and leaving abruptly. "Unlike Jacob Hughes," she muttered.

Papa's attention snapped back to her. "Pardon?"

She blew out a breath. "It's nothing, Papa." But his sharp gaze would not be refused, so she went on, "Jacob Hughes came by last night, asked for a cup of coffee. And was all too happy to talk, though I was tired and simply in want of a quiet moment by the fire."

The corner of his mouth tweaked upward briefly. "Well. You will say so if he continues to be a bother, yes? Or anyone else, for that matter."

"Of course." A giggle rose in her chest at the disparity between his severity and apparent amusement. "I simply wish that Mr. Bledsoe would speak even half as much as Jacob Hughes. He is far more interesting."

Papa's smile grew. "And that Jacob Hughes would speak only half as much as he does?"

"Precisely."

At midday with a sky beginning to clear, Mr. Jenkins, the pack master, called for a halt. Already aching in places she'd not previously been aware of, Kate was glad to dismount and stretch. Stepping down from the horse, however, brought a sharp reminder of why she'd been instructed to ride. Her feet were not so tender as she supposed they'd be if she had to wear her shoes, but neither dared she wander far in mere bandages.

She handed the packhorse off to Johann and padded away into the laurel. There was talk of stopping that night at an ordinary, more for safety and convenience than need of shelter. They'd all have to accustom themselves to the illusion of privacy in the woods along the way, regardless of where they camped, but being able to use an actual necessary, with walls, would be a welcome change—especially when the rawness of her toes made picking her way among the boulders such a trial.

If not for her sore feet, she could wander all day, the hillside was so beautiful.

On the way back, she looked up long enough to glimpse a view across the hills—not quite as breathtaking as the one from Clinch Mountain, but enchanting nevertheless, with ribbons of mist clinging across the far mountaintops, but lit by the sun peeking through above. She lingered, drinking in the sight. A pity, almost, that they couldn't settle right here.

If not for Papa's promise of Kentucky's richness, she'd be tempted to ask that very thing.

She wasn't sure if where they were headed in Kentucky had hills. She would miss the mountains though.

"Come, Daughter!" Papa's voice floated down the hillside. "We've plenty more views to take in farther up the road."

She plodded back up the way she'd come and emerged from the laurel to find Mr. Bledsoe standing at her packhorse's head, fitting the beast with a real bridle. Her cheeks burned. Of course he'd have heard Papa's call. Everyone would have—and why the thought of his opinion on it mattered was beyond her—but that didn't stop the blush.

He adjusted the headstall and looped the rein over the horse's neck, then turned to her as if he'd known the entire time that she was there. Without a word, he bent and offered a hand for her to step into, elbow braced against his knee.

The heat in her cheeks swept the rest of her and burrowed deep in her chest. Even so, she accepted the offer and placed one foot in his broad palm, then pushed off with the other, ignoring the throb from bruised toes.

He lifted her with what seemed no effort, giving her such extra momentum she nearly pitched over the other side, all the packs notwithstanding. Muffling the squeak threatening to escape her throat, she settled herself then peeked at him. Beneath the brim of his hat, a tiny smile tugged at the corner of his bearded mouth.

"Mind you don't saw on the bit," he said, without looking up. "Makes a horse's mouth tough."

He gave the beast's shoulder a pat and walked away to collect his own mount.

And of course Papa was standing a few paces away, watching with an inscrutable look on his face. Kate swallowed and collected the reins. Papa just nodded and started back down the road.

The afternoon waned by the time they made the tavern and trading post at Tazewell. Camping at inns or taverns along the way, though it meant having to deal with more folk, would lend itself to Thomas's need to hear the latest from up and down the road. And hearing outside news was a welcome distraction. Especially after the events of this day.

How one slip of a girl could upend his attention was beyond him, but Katarina Gruener managed it. Or Kate—likely she preferred that to the longer name, not that it signified anything. He'd best keep it to *Miss Gruener*, even in his own thoughts.

As on the night before, he helped unload and tend the horses, toting packs to this part of camp or another as requested. At one point he found himself face-to-face with the formidable Mrs. Gruener, who fastened him with a searching look before breaking out in an unexpectedly warm smile. "Would you mind terribly, bringing this bundle for me?"

He bobbed a nod and shouldered the pack, then trailed her across the camp to a snug little corner of the tavern yard where Miss Gruener sat upon a section of log, unwrapping her feet. Their black servant knelt beside her with a basin of water.

She was being seen to. 'Twas not his concern. Thomas set down the bundle, accepted Mrs. Gruener's thanks, then made his retreat.

He made sure Ladyslipper was picketed, unsaddled, and had fodder for the evening, then headed for the tavern.

Inside, he elbowed up to the counter, setting the butt of his long rifle on the floor, with the barrel supported in the crook of his arm. The tavernkeep greeted him with a grin. "Bledsoe! Good to see you. What'll it be, man?"

"Ale, please." While the stocky older man drew him a mug, Thomas pulled off his hat and hung it over the rifle barrel. "What news of the road to the north?"

Cole slid the mug into his waiting hand. "Surely you ain't still riding post? I heard tell they stopped that."

Thomas shook his head then sipped at the ale. The bitter, nutty brew rolled across his tongue and went down smoothly. A very decent one, as Cole's always were. "Scouting for a party of settlers headed to Severn's Valley. And aye, Kentucky might be a state now, but Governor Shelby is still sorting things out."

Cole squinted at him. "You going to pick up doing that again when you can? Even after what happened with Ross last year?"

He drew another long swallow. "Thinking to. Have to see."

"Well." The older man swiped a rag over the counter. "Road's pretty quiet from here to just over the gap. Much nonsense happening up around Boone's fort with the whiskey tax. Talk is of getting Daniel Morgan and his boys to crack down on the whiskey makers."

A third draught, and Thomas could feel himself beginning to relax. "I'm interested more in what you hear of the Shawnee and Chickamauga."

"Hmm, well, you know how it is. Always someone finding settlers with their skulls split along the way."

"Cole," Thomas said, warningly.

A dimple flashed, incongruous against the man's jowls, and for some reason Thomas thought of Kate. *Miss Gruener.*

Cole shook his head and leaned both meaty hands on the counter. "Quiet there too, but. . .not. Rumblings from the Cherokee, as always, especially to the west. No one's really sure what the Shawnee are up to. There's talk of a council at Fort Detroit. But I hear tell the woods in Kentucky are still, like before a storm, waiting for trouble to break."

Thomas nodded slowly and sipped. Not truly helpful, but nothing in particular to flag his caution either. Only the gnawing restlessness he knew better than to ignore.

A group of men burst into the tavern—some of his own traveling party, mingled with some he'd never seen before. Thomas took his mug and tucked himself against a wall, as much in shadow as he could get by with. Nursing his ale, he could sift through the various conversations without anyone taking particular notice of him.

Hughes and Gruener and their oldest sons respectively filed up to the counter, Hughes greeting Cole and one of the other men, Gruener looking around the place and giving Thomas a slow nod.

The others were asking after news of the road as well, and of the Cherokees and Chickamaugas. Cole related essentially what he'd told Thomas, to which mostly unhelpful bits and pieces were added by the traders come down from Virginia. The whiskey tax was uppermost on people's minds to the north—not that it was irrelevant here as well, but none of that mattered to the settlers Thomas was hired to scout for, at least not at the moment. Still, 'twas best to listen to the rumors and speculation about it all.

Gruener approached Thomas after a brief conversation with Cole about provisions. "If it please you, we'd be honored to have you sup with our family this evening."

He wasn't sure it pleased him at all, but Mrs. Gruener's cooking had been tasty enough the night before. "Mighty kind of you."

"I appreciate your care of Kate's feet," Gruener went on, dropping his voice for Thomas's ears alone, his accent thickening. "She is stubborn enough to refuse it if someone does not insist."

Thomas peered into his near-empty mug, then tossed back the rest of the ale. He had no reply for that except, "My sisters have their own share of stubborn."

Gruener smiled a little. "I expect they'd need such out here."

"Aye. And so will your daughter." Thomas moved to slide his mug onto the counter. "Is there aught I can lend a hand with, to earn my dinner?"

The older man shook his head. "As if you have not already. You may help carry provisions from the trading post next door."

CHAPTER 9

Kate crumbled pieces of dry bread starter into the bowl of sweetened water and stirred gently until they dissolved. "If I had a pair of Papa's or Johann's shoes, I could at least walk around camp," she muttered.

Dulsey shot her a tight-lipped frown. "You be staying put, now. If Mr. Bledsoe say your feet need rest, then rest you shall have."

"Pushed about by you as well, am I?"

"Surely so. Do you need more flour there?"

"I believe I have a sufficient amount, thank you." The starter was already beginning to bubble, so she scooped in some flour, stirring as she went.

Mama rounded the heap of bundled bedding, a pail of water in each hand. "Katarina Grace, are you arguing with Dulsey?"

"Never, Mama."

"Of course not."

Mama and Dulsey exchanged a quick smile. Kate shook her head. " 'Tisn't fair, Mama. My feet are fine for here in camp—"

"You let me be the judge of that," Mama snapped back.

Kate subsided to a mutter again. "Dulsey did the bandaging."

Mama's fists popped to her hips. "Katarina!"

"You forgot to add 'Grace.'"

Mama's mouth hung open. Kate smiled and scooped more flour into the bowl. An inarticulate sound of exasperation came from Mama, and she threw her hands into the air and turned away. "See to that bread, and do not move unless your petticoats are on fire."

"Yes, Mama."

She held her grin until Mama was well occupied with another task, and even then kept her head down, stirring the dough with a vengeance. It was wrong of her to tease—so wrong, she knew this. At such times the words just popped off her tongue.

Why was it she could speak the wrong words so easily, but not find the right ones when the occasion warranted it?

The dough smooth and ready for rising, she handed the bowl off to Dulsey for covering and setting aside. Too early for brewing the coffee, but Dulsey was quick to pass her the grinder and coffee beans.

'Twas good to keep busy. Better yet, however, if she were allowed to move about.

She sighed and gave attention to measuring the beans. A little extra tonight—especially if Jacob Hughes made an appearance again, or should she be unmannerly and tell him they'd none to spare?

Tonight—and only for tonight—she'd make extra. Then ask Mama about it.

There was the added complication of not wishing to encourage the Hughes boy in. . .whatever he thought he wanted from her, besides coffee. Just the thought of how best to handle that made her pulse race and her palms damp.

She ground the coffee and carefully poured it into the kettle. Dulsey followed that with a small basket of half-dried potatoes and a knife. At least this took less thought—Kate was expert at paring them as thin as Mama liked.

Supper preparation turned to mending—though they'd caught up on that well enough in the days leading up to the journey—and Kate glanced up with surprise to find the meal nearly ready, and Papa walking into their corner of the camp trailed by not only Johann but Mr. Bledsoe, all bearing sacks of provisions. Papa let his slide to the ground and indicated to the others to do the same, then crossed to Kate. "An extra for supper. I thought it easier to feed him here than elsewhere."

Kate bit back a smile. "Very well, Papa."

From the corner of her eye she saw Dulsey's glare, and tucked her head lower over the gown she was sewing for Jemmy. Papa gave only a noncommittal grunt and walked away.

Dulsey put the coffee on the fire and pulled off the pot of stew. The bread came next, already making the air fragrant. Kate's mouth watered.

The family gathered in, seemingly from all corners, and Papa said a short blessing before Mama and Dulsey portioned out the stew and bread.

While others received their plates and settled nearby, Kate folded and laid aside the gown, then tucked the threaded needle, scissors, and thimble back into her still-damp housewife and set it behind her to continue drying next to the other contents of her haversack. Jemmy settled next to her as Mama handed Kate a plate. "And how did you like riding Clover?" Jemmy asked.

"Clover?"

"The packhorse. I asked Mr. Jenkins his name, and he told me."

"Well then. I enjoyed riding him very much. But I'm sorry that meant you had to walk."

"Oh, I enjoyed walking. 'Twas a lovely change."

Kate choked down a laugh. Spoken as if she were a lady full grown, rather than a mere six years. "I'm glad," Kate said, in all seriousness. "Thank you for so graciously letting me ride Clover."

"You're welcome." Jemmy smiled and applied herself to her stew again.

She glanced up and looked right into the pale eyes of Mr. Bledsoe, sitting half across the circle from her, hat on the ground next to him as he downed his supper. His dark hair, still pulled back into a long braid, lay in smooth waves, a high, square forehead framed by a widow's peak and a few loose tendrils. Several days' stubble shadowed his jaw in a way that looked not as unkempt as it should have.

In fact, she'd have said the effect was little short of charming.

The chattering of the rest of her family drew his attention, and cheeks blazing, Kate looked away as well.

As they ate, Dulsey passed out cups of coffee, bringing Kate one as well. She sipped, then set the mug at her feet to finish what was on her plate. Mr. Bledsoe had put his empty plate aside and was leaning back, one hand curled around his cup, watching and listening to the conversation around him. Even at rest he remained alert, his expression intent.

Stew finished, bread crust in one hand and coffee in the other, Kate sneaked glances when she thought he wasn't looking. She'd not be caught staring yet again.

She was saved that fate when Papa turned to Mr. Bledsoe and inquired of news of the road past the gap. Mr. Bledsoe straightened, shaking his head a little, and cradled his cup in both hands. "Nothing yet. Cole said all seems to be quiet, but that could change."

Papa nodded. "And tomorrow we reach the gap?"

"Aye."

"Didn't you say you have family in Kentucky?"

"A cousin, up near Boonesborough. Maybe more by now."

"All others are still here in Tennessee then?"

Was Papa asking these questions for Kate's benefit? If so, he showed no sign of it.

Mr. Bledsoe shifted. "Aye. Well, except for my uncles in Washington County, Virginia. My sisters are all still here."

"And you plan to settle here, or in Kentucky?"

"I've no plans either way, at this juncture."

Another thoughtful nod from Papa, whose gaze wandered about the circle, lingering for just a moment longer on Kate before moving on. "There's need of able men in the Kentucky settlements, as I'm sure you know well."

Mr. Bledsoe took a long sip of his coffee before replying. "There's need of able men all up and down the frontier, I expect."

Papa smiled. "Very true."

The arrival of Jacob Hughes forestalled further conversation. Kate's heart sank. The boy's glance swung between her and the coffee pot on the fire while Papa greeted him, but he turned and gave a proper reply. "Begging your pardon, sir. Mr. Jenkins wishes me to tell everyone that if it please you to come, we'll be having prayer and scripture reading directly."

"Thank you. Jacob, is it?" Papa said.

The boy's head bobbed. "Aye, sir."

Another longing glance toward Kate and then toward the coffee. She kept her head down and pretended to ignore him.

It mattered little though, when she shot her own glance toward Mr. Bledsoe's place and saw him gone.

Blast the security of being near a tavern and trading post, that there was no need of extended scouting this night. Thomas had no excuse to escape the pack master's attempt at holding church, but surely he'd be able to find something to busy himself with.

Giving Ladyslipper a good brushing would do for starters. If he were quiet, perhaps he could get by with grooming the whole herd.

He retrieved a brush and started in on the mare about the time they began singing a hymn. It was an endless thing, with verse after verse about Jesus reigning here and there all over the earth. Thomas gritted his teeth and brushed harder. If God was so great and so merciful, why had He taken Mama? And later Pa? Especially in the way he'd died, with a bullet in his side that didn't actually kill him until days after the battle.

Of course, that had worked out just fine for Truth and Micah. Although he'd caught all his sisters crying without account, more than a time or two. A terrible burn rose from deep in his gut. It was as he'd said to Miss Gruener. The frontier exacted a bitter price. It was best to brace oneself for it and simply move on.

The tune of another hymn flowed over him. This one—he tried so hard not to listen to the words but could hardly help it—spoke of God laying down His glory to take up a crown, for the sake of His great love for humanity.

The burning inside spread until it like to have consumed him. And again—where had that love been for them?

He'd started on a second horse, the one called Clover, when the singing mercifully ended and Mr. Jenkins took up a Bible.

Hearing his attempt at preaching wasn't much better. Thomas tried to let his thoughts wander, but his attention kept being yanked back.

" 'I go to prepare a place for you,' " Jenkins read, in a voice that surely carried all the way to the gap. " 'And if I go and prepare a place for you, I will come again, and receive you unto myself; that where I am, there ye may be also. And whither I go ye know, and the way ye know.

" 'Thomas saith unto him, Lord, we know not whither thou goest; and how can we know the way?

" 'Jesus saith unto him, I am the way, the truth, and the life: no man cometh unto the Father, but by me. If ye had known me, ye should have known my Father also: and from henceforth ye know him, and have seen him.' "

"...and Thomas said unto him, Lord, we know not...how can we know the way?"

The words echoed and re-echoed through his heart. That was it, exactly. How did he know—really know—the truth?

"I am the way, the truth, and the life."

He'd grown up hearing the stories, God sending Jesus to die for the sins of mankind. But how did a man really know?

"From henceforth ye know him."

Well, that was no answer, that from here on he'd know.

Thomas bent to work the brush around Clover's hocks, smoothing one hand across the horse's rump to steady him. The horse shifted but didn't otherwise protest.

What about it, God? Are You there? Do You see? And how do we know?

The horse was brushed to a fine sheen—or as close as he could after a hard day's ride and a coat still shaggy from winter—and suddenly Thomas could not face staying any longer within the sound of the pack master's voice. Tossing the brush back amongst other gear, he grabbed his rifle and set off, straight away from the inn and into the woods.

Not until he'd made it halfway up a hill, deep into the laurel and wrapped in the hush of oak and chestnut, did he pause for breath and bearings.

Leaning on an oak, he forced his breathing to slow and, after a moment or two, felt his heart's pounding ease as well. The tightness of his throat did not lessen though. *God in heaven. . .how can You let a man rattle on like that and yet not answer me all these years? Does it even matter to You?*

Back against the tree, he slid down to a sitting position, knees up, rifle across his lap. He dropped his hat to the ground next to him and tipped his head back.

Oh God.

That moment when Pa had pulled the blanket up over Mama's face and turned away, while Thomas continued to cling to her hand and sob. The desolation of her mountainside grave, where he'd sneak away and whisper to her.

Forward a few years to when Truth broke the news that Pa would not be returning from King's Mountain, along with the terrible revelation that their new friend was a Tory.

He'd run wild a few years after that, ostensibly to learn to hunt and carry his weight, as Truth was encumbered with babies not long after she and Micah married. In truth though, it was to escape the reminder that Micah was there and Pa wasn't, that his sister had found a way not only to forgive and be at peace, but seemed to have genuine happiness.

And then—the day the Cherokee had caught him unawares. Truth told him later how they'd found Grandfather's rifle hidden among the leaves. Thomas hadn't even remembered dropping it, so terrified was he to look up and find them looming over him.

When the terror wore off, days later, it was a shock to realize that they'd actually, all things considered, treated him with kindness. Which was completely at odds with half the stories he'd been told.

When he'd finally come home again, after nearly two years—most of that spent among the Shawnee to the north—his sisters' tears had been only part of his resolve to never leave another woman grieving for him. It was just too hard to face.

The other part—nay, he'd not let himself think of it. Thomas scrubbed his hands across his face and reached for his hat—then stopped.

On the boulder opposite him, about eye level and a little on the other side, were a series of scratchings. He rose, glancing about, then knelt to examine the boulder. Not as fresh as they could be, he'd guess, but fairly recent. Figures of men, and a brace of lines with curlicues in the middle. Braves, and guns. *Attack.* A chill slid across him. It was only last year that a party had been ambushed making their way through the narrows they'd be navigating on the morrow.

Perhaps this meant nothing but. . .perhaps not. There was no way to tell.

He passed a hand across his face again, replaced his hat, reached for his rifle. He stood and this time made a long, slow survey of his surroundings.

Birds twittering, a pair of squirrels chasing around a tree a short distance away. Not a thing out of the ordinary, for the moment anyway. His racing heart slowed to a more normal rhythm, and he considered the Indian sign again. It still bore watchfulness—and at least a brief scout around the area.

CHAPTER 10

His scouting turned up nothing else, and because they'd all agreed not to set watch this evening, so close to the tavern, Thomas returned to the camp as the sun dipped below the hills. He'd take his blanket and bed down near Ladyslipper and watch over the horses at least.

The camp had mostly quieted by now. In the hills above, the whip-poor-wills were matched by the mournful dip of a fiddle from somewhere near the buildings—probably the tavern. Thomas found himself glad that Jenkins had agreed they'd camp outdoors when the weather remained fair, whether near an ordinary or not.

He stretched out, arms bent and hands cradling his head, and peered up at the stars. Tomorrow they'd face the last stretch before the gap, and then—then came the gap itself. Thomas felt a sudden, unaccountable longing for that majestic, white-rock wall, to reach the summit of the gap and then make his way across the path to the overlook.

His eyes slid shut. Thoughts of the overlook brought one of sharing that amazing vista with a certain young woman with golden hair. . . and the memory of all that hair cascading over her back and shoulders, across the packhorse's rump, bright as sunlight even under a grey sky.

Waking thought slipped away into dreams where Kate Gruener rode without packs or saddle or bridle, hair loose, blinding under the sun, her dark eyes laughing. And then her dark eyes became those of another girl, long ago, with dusky skin, laughing and flirting with him, accepting shy kisses, wrapping slender but strong arms around his neck—

Thomas bolted awake with a gasp. The camp lay completely dark and still except for the whuffle of the horses. His cheeks were wet.

Red Flower. That had been her name. He'd not allowed himself to even think of her for many a year, and here he'd gone and dreamed of her.

'Twas the Gruener girl's fault for tearing down that particular barricade. Or maybe more his own for letting his attention be snared by a veritable waterfall of sunlight.

He swiped the wetness off his face and settled back, this time on his side. Closed his eyes. A ripple of laughter came again—the Shawnee girl who was the first to snare his attention. Then later, the mirth replaced by a wounding of the sorest kind, given by the news that he was to be traded back to the whites in exchange for Indian prisoners.

He'd very nearly refused. Nearly. But the memory of his sisters and the sure knowledge that they'd grieved for him. . .

He dragged in a long, ragged breath. *God. . .oh God, please. . .*

What was he praying for? Was God even there? So many sleepless nights he'd begged for mercy, for more sleep, to just be able to forget. . . .

So it's mercy I ask for again. It's one thing to be up, keeping watch—another thing entirely to waste sleep on useless dreams and musings. I can't keep doing this, Lord. I. . .cannot.

Calm settled over him, almost a resignation, bordering on exhaustion. *So. . .weary. . .*

With a sigh, he fell back into a soundless slumber.

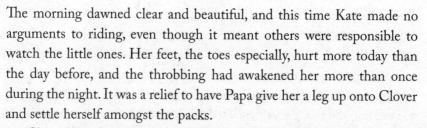

The morning dawned clear and beautiful, and this time Kate made no arguments to riding, even though it meant others were responsible to watch the little ones. Her feet, the toes especially, hurt more today than the day before, and the throbbing had awakened her more than once during the night. It was a relief to have Papa give her a leg up onto Clover and settle herself amongst the packs.

She gathered the reins and looked around. The folded hills surrounding their campsite were breathtaking.

They set out without incident, and the first mile or so was easy. She knew from talk around the fires last night that the pack masters were a bit anxious about the hills they'd be passing through today. But for now, all Kate could think of was the excitement of glimpsing the Cumberland Gap for the first time once they were on the other side and the beauty of the country around her.

Johann carried Stefan on his shoulders up ahead, and Jemmy trotted along beside Dulsey and Betsy and Mama. Papa was—far ahead, talking with Mr. Jenkins, Mr. Bledsoe, and one of the other pack leaders whose name she didn't yet know.

She scanned the rest of the party. Mrs. Hughes and Mrs. Murphy chatted, each mounted on packhorses as well, babes in arms, almost side by side since the road was more than wide enough on this stretch. Neither woman looked much older than Kate herself, but their status as wives and mothers set them apart from her, and neither had spoken even a pair of words to her so far. And the others—

Some sense tugged her attention aside, and she found Jacob Hughes staring at her as he stepped off the road and waited for others to pass. Kate's heart sank. Despite the cheer of the day, she was of no mind to suffer Jacob's puppyish manner.

"Good morning, Miss Gruener," he greeted her as she drew even with him. "I heard tell you hurt your feet yesterday."

"I—a little, yes. I can't yet fit my shoes so—they thought it best that I ride. Otherwise I'd be perfectly capable of walking, I'm sure."

He glanced at the bandaged member peeking out from under her petticoat, his expression still sober. "I might have a pair of old moccasins you could use. With your bandages they might fit fine. Be easier on the hurts."

She swallowed back any tartness she might have spoken. "If it's no trouble. It's very kind of you to offer." She'd not thought him capable of concern, much less generosity—even of a pair of worn footgear.

A smile lit his otherwise plain face. She felt a pang—perhaps she'd judged him too harshly. Boys tended to a little foolishness in the presence of girls they thought well-favored. At least—that's what she'd often read, and her experience certainly bore it out.

Of course by that reasoning, Mr. Bledsoe didn't find her well-favored at all, since he was anything but foolish in his manner with her.

And why shouldn't he be everything that was sensible, as their party's scout? Papa hired him to keep them safe, and that meant having a cool head about him at all times. She'd not want him to be distracted by her, simply to satisfy some vain, girlish longing. As Papa said, she should let the man do his job, unencumbered by her concerns.

But she still craved to hear his story, to know what thoughts flittered behind those pale eyes.

She realized Jacob Hughes had asked her a question and was waiting on a reply. "I beg your pardon."

He laughed shortly, head dropping. "I know I'm poor company, Miss Gruener, especially compared to Mr. Bledsoe. . . ."

Heat washed across her, and she drew a sharp breath. "I—I beg your pardon," she stuttered again. "I meant no discourtesy."

Another wave of laughter gusted from him. She gritted her teeth against a terrible urge to kick him in the chest. "What does Mr. Bledsoe have to do with anything?" she said, trying to keep her voice low.

She knew already, of course, but—

Jacob pulled off his hat and wiped a hand across his face. "Oh, come now, Miss Gruener. Can't hardly miss the special attention he's given you. And then he was at supper with your family last night. . . ."

Her cheeks were on fire. "My papa invited him."

"Ah." That sobered Jacob a bit. "I see."

"No, you don't see. Not at all. Papa hired him as scout for our party, so he feels an obligation to make sure the man is properly fed. Nothing more."

Jacob slanted her a glance, then put his hat back on. "So you're saying Mr. Bledsoe ain't sparkin' you at all?"

Kate's mouth dropped open. Sparking her? Mr. Bledsoe? "Ah. . .no. Most definitely not."

The boy's gaze remained steady for a moment. "Would you want him to?"

Why did it feel as though her tongue was suddenly made of lead? Or that she couldn't seem to lift her jaw from Clover's withers? "I. . .why does it matter?"

Jacob's head dipped again, but not before she saw the deep blush on his cheek.

"If you can't figure that one, Miss Gruener, then I ain't going to explain it to you."

Kate tipped her head to scan the hillsides. The breeze brought a welcome cooling to her own face and neck. "I suppose you needn't explain, at that."

When she turned back, she found Jacob watching her again, shyly, from the corner of his eye. "Would you. . .would you object if anyone else were seekin' your attentions?"

Her heart thudded heavy and painful in her chest. "We've a long journey ahead of us, Mr. Hughes," she got out, finally.

"Jacob," he said, his voice husky.

"Mr. Hughes," she returned, more firmly. "I—I cannot say, this moment. But—but surely the journey affords both of us an opportunity to know each other better—"

He squinted up at her. "You surely do like to talk fancy, don't you?"

She narrowed her own gaze upon him. A smile hung at the corner of his mouth. Was he mocking her or—?

"Yes. I do," she snapped. "And I make no apology for it."

CHAPTER 11

A finer spring day one could not ask for. Clear sky, birds a'twittering in the trees, the hills coming to life in the way Thomas loved at winter's end. A breeze gentle enough to warm rather than chill—although he stayed plenty warm much of the time with just his hunting shirt. But all he felt the farther they journeyed this day was darkness, and cold.

These hills weren't high, not compared to Clinch Mountain and the Cumberland ridge, but they were tangled and twisted. The perfect place for an ambush—and the Cherokee had taken full advantage of the fact, more than once.

'Twas a year ago though. A whole year. And no hint of attack in the area since.

So why couldn't he shake this deep unease? Nay, dread?

After talking with Jenkins and the others, he rode ahead to scout for a bit, then circled around the party as they were coming up into the skirts of those hills. He found nothing to be alarmed at, but the dread would not go away.

He nudged Ladyslipper back through the rhody thicket and onto the road behind the party. Miss Gruener again rode at the rear, but this time young Jacob Hughes walked next to the packhorse, looking up at the girl with a laugh.

Well that was hardly a surprising development. Although, judging by the set of her shoulders, she was not amused by whatever Jacob had said. He couldn't blame her for that—two days on the road and he could already tell that the Hughes boy was a bit of a fool.

Or maybe Thomas was the fool. He should be glad of Miss Gruener having an admirer. And what business was it of his who that might be?

As if she'd heard his thoughts, she turned and looked behind, straight at him. Her eyes widened a little, and even from the short distance, he could see her immediate blush. Something in his chest kindled in response.

Blast it all, anyway. Aye, she was pretty enough. Any man with eyes could hardly fail to see otherwise. But again, why should it make any difference to him?

Besides, she was a distraction he did not need—especially right this minute. Descending a short slope, they were entering the first section of road where almost sheer rock rose close on one side and a burbling creek edged the other. No issue for the horses and walkers, of course. He scanned the steep hillside above them, then the hillside opposite them, across the creek. Nothing to be seen. But they'd an hour or two, maybe more, of this.

God, please. . .mercy.

The echo of last night's prayer flowed through him as easy and soundless as a breath. He didn't know whether to be relieved, chagrined, or—annoyed.

The last. Definitely the last.

Didn't help that young Hughes kept casting sharp, furtive glances his way, as if he were the threat and not whatever it was that Thomas sensed out there. He chewed back the urge to go box the boy's ears and tell him to attend Miss Gruener, that Thomas had no intention of attempting to steal her affections away from him.

In fact, 'twould be most amusing to see the boy's response, despite his determination to stay alert.

His insides tightened until Thomas felt near to doubling over in the saddle.

If You're there. . .I ask mercy. Not for me, but for those I'm tasked with protecting. Protect them, at least. Turn away whatever is out there.

The knot in his gut eased—just a little. He held his position and kept watch, nevertheless.

They were about halfway through the narrows when Hughes fell back. His expression held curiosity now. "Expectin' trouble?"

At least the boy kept his voice down. Thomas gave a short nod. "Maybe. Maybe not. Can't ever tell."

He wouldn't pretend the threat wasn't real, but neither would he send everyone into a panic.

Young Hughes made his own slow survey of the hills, remaining blessedly quiet as he did so. "How would we ever know?" he said at last.

Thomas shook his head slowly. "Just—anything that doesn't look right." He wasn't sure he could explain it. "Shadows that shouldn't be there. Logs that—are not logs. And movement, of any sort."

The boy's gaze sharpened, trained still on the rough slopes stretching away beside them. Thomas bit back a smile. Fire the boy's pride, and perhaps he'd learn to be useful, if he could keep his attention on scouting rather than the Gruener girl. "Tell you what," Thomas said, pitching his voice low. "I could use the extra pair of eyes while we're in the narrows. Mind watching with me?"

Jacob nodded slowly, then realized he was giving the wrong answer and shook his head, eyes widened and chest puffing, as Thomas expected. This time he let himself grin, then waved toward the rocky hillside again. "Look sharp then. Let me know if you see anything amiss. Anything at all."

Another sharp nod and Jacob set to the task with right good attention.

Thomas looked up to see Miss Gruener turned in the saddle, watching both of them. Once she'd caught his eye, she gave a slight nod and smile and faced forward again.

Well. His keeping Jacob Hughes busy apparently pleased her for some reason. And he wasn't sure what to think of that.

Whatever was behind Mr. Bledsoe giving Jacob Hughes a diversion, Kate would be glad of it. She blew out a long breath and resettled herself. This portion of the road was rough but beautiful, with the stream running alongside and the rocky hillsides rising steeply above. Wildflowers grew plentifully here, with more dogwoods and redbud scattered throughout.

No one could fail to be cheered by the view.

She peered back over her shoulder at Jacob and Mr. Bledsoe. Whatever seemed to have alarmed the latter—she could describe it no other way, after observing his almost frantic intensity—seemed to have passed. At least, for the most part.

Her own unease had grown over the past hour, but she'd attributed that to Jacob Hughes deciding he needed to be her particular escort. If, as Mr. Jenkins and the others had discussed, there was yet a real threat of attack here, though the last one here was a year past—

Father, keep us safe. Give Mr. Bledsoe—and the other men too, of course—eyes for any danger, but I ask that You'd turn the peril away before he has opportunity to see it.

Over the next hour, Kate kept praying, staying watchful, and casting the occasional glance back to see that Mr. Bledsoe and Jacob remained the same. At least that terrible fear of the first day climbing Clinch Mountain in the fog never returned.

They crossed the Powell River with little incident. Mr. Bledsoe took Jacob up behind him on his horse for the actual crossing, then let him down again, and they all continued on. A cry went up from the party ahead, out of sight beyond a bend in the road. Kate's breath caught, and her heart leaped into her throat. She pulled Clover to a stop. But then the words became clear—

"It's the gap! We can see Cumberland Gap across the valley!"

She glanced back at Mr. Bledsoe and Jacob. Both their faces reflected her own alarm and relief. She threw them a wry smile, then hurried Clover on to catch up with the others.

Sure enough, as they emerged from the curve of the road, Powell Valley spread before them, a mile or so wide and extending as far as she could see from northeast to southwest.

Shimmering blue in the early afternoon stood the high ridge of the Cumberland.

Kate could not get enough of the sight. A tightness grew in her chest and rose in her throat, and her eyes burned. This—this was the grand gateway into the country that would be her home, perhaps for the rest of her life.

At Patterson Crossroads in a meadow adjacent to a busy ordinary, they made camp. Another traveling party was there as well, on their way down from the old part of the eastern Wilderness Road that crossed over to the upper Powell Valley from Gate City. Kate applied herself to helping Mama and Dulsey with cooking and laying out camp—still mostly seated—but kept her ears open to the snippets of talk exchanged here and there.

The other group was headed straight north to Boonesborough and beyond. They, in fact, were only resting a short while before pressing on over the gap and to an intended stop for the night at the ordinary on the other side. Before long, they moved out, and only Kate's traveling party remained.

A festive mood permeated the camp during supper and after. Mr. Bledsoe ate with them again, while Jacob Hughes was thankfully called away by his own family. Kate waited until everyone's initial hunger was met, then taking both her plate and cup of coffee, sidled around the circle and settled near Mr. Bledsoe. "You were sensing something amiss on the road today?" she asked, without preamble.

He favored her with a silent look—which she ought by now to be used to, but she looked away and gave attention to her plate so she didn't appear overeager for him to reply.

"Aye," he said at last.

She waited for him to elaborate, but he didn't. "Did you see anything?"

He hesitated before shaking his head.

"You did see something."

His eyes widened, just a bit, as he flashed her a quick look, but he took another bite and chewed it. "Naught I could speak of with any certainty," he said, so softly she almost did not hear. "And I'd thank you to hold your tongue about it as well."

"I can be quiet when need be," she murmured. She thought she heard him snort quietly, but decided not to let him bait her into a protest. "It was. . .clever of you, to have Jacob Hughes help you keep watch."

Another bite, and his head bobbed. He seemed to relax slightly. "The boy needs to learn to look sharp if he's to survive the wilderness, of a certain."

"That he does," Kate said, scraping the last of her food together in a mound near the side of her plate. "I was praying."

Mr. Bledsoe's eyes were upon her again, sharply. "I thank you for that as well."

His tone told her those thanks were reluctant at best. "You don't believe God hears our prayers?"

One shoulder lifted. "It's impossible to say either way."

Intriguing response. And not entirely honest. "I asked whether you believe, Mr. Bledsoe. Not whether we can prove His hearing—or responding."

Another look—this one longer. A band of sky-blue rimmed the paler shade of his eyes, which was made so by flecks of almost white. The entire effect was of a sunny winter sky.

An intriguing combination as well.

Then he blinked and broke the spell. "It makes no matter what I believe. God will do whatever He wills, regardless."

Her heart beat with sudden painfulness at his words. What had he suffered, to speak thus?

He set his plate and spoon aside with a firmness that made her flinch. Tossing back the rest of his coffee, he put that in the middle of the plate and rose. "My thanks for the fine supper, Mrs. Gruener. Again."

He strode away without so much as another look in Kate's direction.

CHAPTER 12

Jacob Hughes made good on his word and brought Kate a pair of worn but serviceable moccasins. The next morning, she donned them over fresh bandages and walked across camp to test them. "Very fine," she said.

Jacob's grin would be heartwarming if—if she were not still troubled over other things this morning. But she forced a smile in return. Time to put aside thoughts of Mr. Bledsoe and their conversation from the night before. Today they'd be crossing Cumberland Gap, and she would see Kentucky for the first time.

Mama sniffed. "Proper shoes would be better for walking, but I suppose this is better than nothing for now."

"You also might find yourself wearing moccasins before this journey is done," Papa remarked as he walked past, carrying a bundle of bedding to be packed aboard the horses.

Jacob Hughes continued to hover as if she were infirm, and Kate could feel her smile thinning. "Really, Mr. Hughes, you need not escort me today."

He stammered for a moment, his cheeks coloring. "I—but it would be my honor, Miss Gruener."

She vented a tiny sigh. This one was bound to find himself sorely disappointed if he insisted on presuming upon her good graces. "Do your sisters not need your help? Truly my feet are just fine in these—and 'twas very kind of you to loan them to me."

He gulped. Obviously he was determined to outlast her attempts to courteously fend him off.

Behind him, Mama glanced up with a knowing smile as she packed her cooking utensils. "Perhaps he could walk with you as far as the top of the gap, unless his family calls for him."

"Thank you, Mrs. Gruener," Jacob said too quickly. "That's exactly what I was thinking."

Kate suppressed the rolling of her eyes and, after slinging her haversack across her body, went to help Dulsey with the last of the bedding.

Jemmy and Stefan were settled back onto Clover, and this time Johann was tasked with leading the horse. Papa silenced his protest with a quiet word.

"Nursemaid to all of you," Johann grumbled, waving Kate ahead of him in the procession.

"Doesn't hurt you to take a turn," she shot back.

"'Tisn't like you don't have Jacob there either," he hissed.

She swallowed back a snarl and looked askance to see that one biting his lip, trying unsuccessfully to hide a smirk. "Trade ya," Jacob tossed back to Johann. "You can walk with my sister, and I'll walk with yours."

Johann gave him a withering look, earning a laugh from Jacob. Kate wasn't sure who most annoyed her at the moment.

She adjusted the haversack and settled herself to walk. Her feet were tender, but not nearly as sore as they'd have been with her shoes. And it felt good to walk after two days on horseback. Riding was enjoyable as well, but was a luxury reserved for those less able to make the journey on their own.

And she was nothing if not able.

For the first half mile or so, the road was easy. Papa had said it would remain mostly so up over the gap itself. Kate watched the ridge grow closer, the rippled mountainside becoming more distinct. And beyond, along the far stretch of ridge, lay an expanse of rock, almost blinding white in its starkness. Higher than the near ridge. Breathtaking in its majesty.

And between the two, an opening in the ridge as if some giant had scooped it out.

"Cumberland Gap," Jacob breathed.

Kate nodded. The only opening through the mountains into Kentucky. The only other route west, besides down and across Tennessee, was down the Ohio River, still far too dangerous because of the Indians.

The road grew gradually rougher, and higher, the closer they came to the first ridge. About halfway up, Kate turned and looked back. Already she could survey the valley for several miles in each direction, its ends swallowed in sunlight and haze.

Making his way up the road behind them, steadfastly scouting as always, was Mr. Bledsoe. But he caught her eye, and as he approached, asked, "How fare your feet so far?"

"Much mended, thank you."

He gave the barest nod to her smile. Kate sighed again and applied herself to climbing the hill.

It was true, the bandages inside soft leather made for some of the pleasantest walking she'd ever experienced.

"The moccasins are sensible. Good choice."

She startled at the nearness of his voice, but tilted her head to give him a smile. "They're on loan from Mr. Hughes here. Very comfortable."

Mr. Bledsoe shot a glance at Jacob.

"What's this ridge called again?" Jacob asked.

"Poor Valley Ridge," both Kate and Mr. Bledsoe answered together. They glanced at each other, and Kate ducked her head with a chuckle, letting Mr. Bledsoe continue. "That's Gap Creek beyond. We'll cross the two forks, before heading up the gap itself." He took a breath, then added, "Just yonder, past the saddle of the gap, is a trail leading along the upper ridge to a spot called the overlook. And just below that—can you see it? The cave that the gap was first named for. If we'd time. . ." Mr. Bledsoe cleared his throat and went on. "Anyway, the north fork of Gap Creek is fed by a spring from that cave. Sometimes it's nearly a waterfall, running down into the gorge."

She and Jacob both craned their necks to find the features he'd pointed out, and Kate saw Johann doing the same.

"How far is the overlook from the saddle of the gap?" Jacob asked.

"Oh, half a mile, I'd guess. Rough trail though. Horse could make it, if it's surefooted."

He patted the shoulder of his mare.

"Is yours?" Jacob asked.

Mr. Bledsoe laughed outright, firing surprise through Kate. "Aye, that she is."

He had a warm laugh, deep and rich like his voice. Kate turned her head, pretending to study the high rocky ridge so he wouldn't see the flush on her cheeks.

They all fell silent as they ascended the last bit before the top of the small gap in Poor Valley Ridge. Kate stopped again to look all around.

"There's a better view from farther on," Mr. Bledsoe said.

She nodded and kept going.

The road—or a path wide enough to be one, at this point—wound its way down to one of the forks of the creek, where Kate was able to cross by hopping from rock to rock, and that without the steadying hand Jacob so obviously wished to offer.

At the northern fork, she lingered to peer upstream at the cave entrance just visible through the trees and then at the ridge towering above. The sight wrested a grin from her as she applied herself to crossing once again.

And then it was straight up into the gap itself. Kate made herself go slowly and steadily to avoid becoming breathless. A short distance ahead, Papa walked beside Mama, arm outstretched for her to lean on. Kate could tell she was struggling with the ascent.

For that matter, so was anyone else not on horseback. Even Jacob was puffing a little at her side.

And she'd wager that Mr. Bledsoe wouldn't be, if he weren't riding. He caught her glance and gave her a wry smile. "Everyone has difficulty with the climb," he said. "It's steeper than it looks."

She could only manage a nod in return. Then—abruptly the ground began to level.

"Now," Mr. Bledsoe said, "turn around."

The spring landscape fading miles away into mist took her breath away. The dogwood and redbud, the laurel and tiny dots of wildflowers. . . the muted burble of Gap Creek flowing from the cave, off to the left, and the wind tugging at her hat and clothing, cooling her face. The intoxicating sweetness that swept up to her from the valley floor.

Ah Lord God! The world You made is very fair indeed. Especially from the height!

A laugh gurgled from her chest. Was this how God viewed His creation?

A deep chuckle echoed her own. "Told you."

Both waited, Mr. Bledsoe's horse turned sideways on the road, Jacob at the mare's shoulder. But it was the crooked grin of Thomas Bledsoe that caught her heart in a strange tightness.

She swung away, but she was no longer really seeing the lovely vista before her. "Yes, you did."

What ailed her? Was she truly so foolish?

'Twas only because of Jacob and his blasted questions about the possible affection between her and Mr. Bledsoe. That was the reasonable explanation. All would settle in a day or two. She'd had her heart beat a little faster a time or two before, by others, and knew how quickly one's attention could change.

But Thomas Bledsoe had been a distraction since the first day she'd met him.

Mr. Bledsoe, she reminded herself firmly. There would be—could be— no familiarity between them.

Not that she'd want there to be. He'd not allow it, for one.

Would he?

She wanted to glance at him again, but forced herself to turn, as cool as she could, and keep walking.

He was pointing out features of the landscape to Jacob, the two chatting as amiably as if they'd been companions for far longer than a few days. Kate let herself smile a little. 'Twas very good of Mr. Bledsoe, really. Which made him all kindness as well as everything sensible.

Johann had stopped on the downhill side of the trail and frowned at her from under his hat. Clover lipped the lead rope and tossed his head, and Johann continued on, leading the packhorse.

Kate trudged after him. Her heart beat now with a painful slowness.

'Twas nearly enough to keep her from thinking about the tenderness of her feet. As the road had pitched downward, beginning on the other side of the gorge, the more chafing she felt, especially on her torn and bruised toes—but she'd chew her own tongue to shreds before asking to ride again.

And then, as she rounded a slight bend, it seemed the whole of Kentucky spread before her. A wide basin, thickly forested, lay between her and the rippled, folded hilltops stretching beyond, as far as the eye could see. She stopped, toes throbbing, just for a moment, letting the sight give her strength and determination.

This was her land. She would keep walking, regardless of what it took.

Miss Gruener had gone strangely quiet after they'd reached the saddle of the gap. Dazzled with the height and the view, no doubt, but after her pestering way with questions the last few days, it was a puzzle to be sure.

Not that he wasn't glad for the respite. It left him with less distraction than before.

And the Hughes boy seemed to have simmered down, except that now he was chattering at Thomas rather than the girl, clomping along beside Ladyslipper. Thomas listened with half an ear, but something about the girl's gait, as the traveling party made its way down from the gap, caught his attention. And then he realized—her torn-up feet. Walking downhill likely put more pressure on those toes.

"A minute," he said to Jacob Hughes. "Miss Gruener, hold up," he called. She turned, her expression bemused, as Ladyslipper caught up to her. "Are your feet giving you trouble?"

She hesitated on the reply. "I—am well enough."

The flush gave her away. He dismounted. "Let me see."

"I promise you, I'm not infirm—"

His look cut off her protest, and with a huff, she perched on the edge of a boulder and slipped the moccasin off the foot he'd remembered was the most injured. Blood soaked through the bandages over her toes.

"As I thought," he murmured.

"I'll be fine," she muttered.

"You'll ride until we make camp. And then you'll soak that in the creek."

Her face was crimson now. "I'm otherwise able-bodied. Why such a fuss over this?"

He bent until their eyes were on a level. Not that he didn't already have her full attention. "I've seen men get foot scald from a simple wetting in the creek, and then have to walk until the flesh was fair to rotting. Hate to see that happen to you, Miss Gruener."

Those coffee-dark eyes widened, her pink lips parted. She shut her mouth with a snap and gave a quick nod.

"Now. I'm well able to walk in your place. Can you handle my mare, do you think, or would you rather I lead? She's a spirited one."

"You—are welcome to lead."

That was more like it. While she slipped the moccasin back on, he led Ladyslipper around until she stood angled to the hill, giving the better advantage to mounting. Then he knelt, one hand cupped for her to step into. Without a word, she accepted the leg up and was shortly settled on the mare. A slender calf peeked from the hem of her petticoats before she covered it with a tug and a twitch. Her face remained set in stone.

"You could sit aside if you prefer," he said. "She's a smooth enough stepper."

"Astride is fine," she answered. "I've plenty of years riding my Papa's wagon horses."

And likely until not too long ago. Thomas turned back downhill to hide his smile.

"Something amusing, Mr. Bledsoe?"

Not quickly enough, apparently. He shook his head. "Just remembering the rides my sisters and I would steal. Not just on saddle and wagon horses, but on my uncle's oxen as well."

"Oxen?" She chuckled, and the laugh chased all the former tightness from her face.

Best he keep his eyes on the path.

"I've ridden an ox," Jacob chimed in.

Miss Gruener laughed again, and Jacob threw her a scowl. "I have! 'Twas our neighbor's. I rode it on a dare."

"Did you stay on?" she asked, still chuckling.

"I did," he answered with pride.

"And you?" She looked at Thomas this time.

He couldn't help his grin. "Nay. Not often."

She laughed so hard she doubled over in the saddle.

By this time, of course, they'd drawn the attention of Karl Gruener, who was standing in the road waiting for them, his mouth creased in worry. "Is something amiss?"

"I'm fine, Papa," his daughter said, at the same time Thomas explained, "Her toes started up bleeding again."

Mr. Gruener's gaze went from his daughter to Thomas, and the frown deepened. "Did she fall again?"

"No, Papa, just that—apparently just the walking downhill and chafing inside the bandages. I don't mean to worry you."

The man's eyes softened when he looked at the girl. He glanced back at Thomas after a moment. "So she simply needs to ride for a few days longer."

"Aye."

"Well then."

Gruener looked as if he were not happy with his daughter up there on Ladyslipper, but Thomas couldn't think of any reason why he'd give serious objection to that. "It's no trouble for her to use my mare today. Tomorrow she can go back to the packhorse. I can scout just as well without riding—maybe better."

And it was the truth. The only advantage a horse gave him while scouting was being able to cover more ground, and then speed of flight if he ran into trouble.

In case of the latter, he'd likely need to fight his way out of it anyway, rather than run.

Gruener still looked reluctant but nodded. "Very well. If 'tis truly no trouble."

" 'Tisn't."

Thomas felt the weight of all their eyes in that moment—Gruener, his oldest son, and the Hughes boy. In the absence of anything else to say, he clicked his tongue to Ladyslipper and kept walking.

It was just another few miles—three or so, maybe—to the ordinary on Yellow Creek where they'd talked of stopping for the night. And where he just might have more word for Carrington.

CHAPTER 13

As it turned out, their traveling party stopped briefly at the ordinary for a rest and news, then pressed on a few more miles. Papa took over leading Mr. Bledsoe's beautiful mare and was the one to help her down and give her a leg back up when they set off again.

He said little more about the whole thing, but Kate knew he was unhappy about it. She'd truly tried to be careful—obviously the wounds on her toes were more severe than she'd thought. And if the road were not so steeply pitched, or if she'd stepped in a different way, perhaps they'd not have chafed so—

She'd have to ask Dulsey if there were another way to wrap her toes, perhaps cushion them better. And maybe if she weren't allowed to walk tomorrow, she'd be mended well enough to do so the day after.

"What more should be done to make this a road, Papa?" she asked, seeking to break the strained silence between them.

He gave her a look, which she could not quite decipher. "You see that they've cut trees and brush and widened the way, at least in part. Next would come the work of shifting rocks, digging ditches on either side, making it smooth and level where possible. It is greatly improved already, but much work remains. Thus why we are not waiting before we make the journey."

"Yes." He'd explained that before, but she didn't mind hearing it again. Not if it took his mind off her injury and whatever displeased him about it all.

"But you see how rough the path is, this side of the gap. Why it would have been useless to bring a wagon."

He was absolutely correct about that.

She angled her head and peered up at the forest canopy, the oak and chestnut arched high above them, just now putting forth their leaves. In another few days, no doubt they'd wake one morning and find the forest completely leafed out. It always amazed her every spring how that happened.

And the laurel and rhododendron were now in bloom, where they lay along the steep hillside, both above and below, extending to the edge of the creek and beyond. It cheered her heart just to watch the wind ruffle the pale pink clusters—

"Daughter." Papa's voice was soft, but grave, startling her back to immediate anxiety.

"Yes, Papa?"

"You—will have a care, will you not? With our Mr. Bledsoe?"

"Why would I not?"

But he only gave her a long look from beneath his hat, the blue eyes almost sad. "Surely you are not so unknowing?"

"I—I know not to be a coquette, or—do anything else that might be improper, Papa."

He returned to regarding the path ahead of them. "You are a comely young woman, Kate, ripe for the picking. Or you shall be soon," he said, while she felt the heat rising in her cheeks and would have protested. "And he, a young man who I imagine is not unappealing and who seems to have no attachment elsewhere. I'd not be opposed to one forming between the two of you, but—I'd not see you have your heart broken. Or his."

"Papa," was all she could get out. He'd never been so direct with her about such matters before.

And here she'd been trying not to think of this particular subject, at least not from this perspective, and Papa himself seemed determined to make things more difficult.

"First Jacob, and now you," she murmured.

His gaze was sharp again. "Jacob Hughes?"

"Yes." Too late she realized the more-familiar use of his first name. "He was asking me yesterday whether or not—whether there was interest on my part for Mr. Bledsoe. I told him no." Beyond curiosity about his story, that is. She swallowed. "And now you—you seem to presume there is."

Papa's mouth quirked at the corners. "I'm more surprised your Mama or sisters have not mentioned it."

Upon reflection, so was she, truth be told. "Perhaps they've both been too busy."

"Not too busy to notice, I wager," he said.

"Likely not," Kate said with a short, bitter laugh. So it was only a matter of time before they too were hounding her about it.

So how was she to escape? They'd weeks yet on this journey, and Mr. Bledsoe was going nowhere except with them.

Yet that did not answer—

"Why, Papa? Why do you think it would only end in. . .heartbreak?"

He shook his head, slowly at first, then more firmly. "Perhaps I am wrong," he said at last. "I cannot explain why I feel uneasy about it." He angled her a smile, but it was strained. "Do not trouble yourself about it overmuch. Just—be cautious. As you have already assured me you will."

His words did not convince her, however.

As if she could simply *not trouble herself.*

They made camp just a few more miles down Yellow Creek. Thomas retrieved Ladyslipper from the Grueners and set about scouting in earnest around the campsite.

Plenty of Indian sign, but none of it new enough to concern him. Circling the campsite a second time, farther out, uncovered no more. No matter. He needed to return to camp and plan the night's watch.

The two elder Hughes men, John and Jim, and Pat Murphy, all readily agreed. That would be plenty. Jacob Hughes wanted a turn, but Thomas told him he'd better serve staying in camp and helping there. The boy put on an obvious pout but didn't argue.

Thomas sympathized. At Jacob's age, he was still trying to figure out how to live with his natural family again after returning from the Shawnee. But he wasn't willing to voice that in their hearing.

Kate Gruener was, as he had told her to, sitting on a boulder at the creek's edge, soaking her feet. And looking completely enthralled with her surroundings. Thomas forced himself to look away and keep moving.

At least she'd heeded his warnings. Or appeared to.

❧

It had been a long day, and Kate was glad, all things considered, that she'd gotten to ride the last half of it. Mr. Bledsoe's mare truly was as smooth a stepper as he'd said. And the creek water felt so good on her feet, even though the initial shock of the cold had made her yelp.

She could not get Papa's words, or Jacob's, out of her thoughts, however. Perhaps that was the nature of the journey itself, that she'd too much time for reflection.

Or perhaps she needed to just come out with it and ask Mr. Bledsoe the questions she longed to. Then she could satisfy her curiosity and move on to getting to know the rest of the traveling party.

Which she had been doing already, but with having to sit in camp the last few days. . .not that the other women weren't kind in coming to inquire after her health, but still.

And there was plenty to do in camp—she couldn't argue that.

Dulsey made her way down the bank to where Kate was sitting. "You done soaked enough for now, I reckon. Let me wrap them again. Although, Lordy, how you think to get back up that bank—"

"I'll manage, Dulsey."

The Negro woman gave her a long look. "You tired enough, for sure. Not even givin' me your usual sass."

Kate could think of no reply to that. She lifted her feet out of the water and turned so Dulsey could reach them. "I was wondering if there's any way to bandage them differently so they don't chafe so much."

"Hmm, p'raps." Dulsey bent, considering. "P'raps if I wrap each toe separately first. . ."

Kate let her work, glad her feet were still mostly numb from the cold water. At last she sat back with a firm nod. "There. Now get those mocca-sins back on, and I'll help you up the bank."

She went carefully, using stones and tree roots as stepping places, Dulsey steadying her and giving her a hand up when she needed it. The new way of bandaging did seem to help.

Back at camp, she settled in to help Mama. Supper was speedily fin-ished, but neither Papa nor Johann were back. "Well," Mama said. "I was thinking to send a plate up to Mr. Bledsoe—"

"I can take it," Kate said and hopped up.

Mama and Dulsey both rounded on her. "Your feet—"

"Dulsey wrapped them a new way, and how better to put it to the test?"

Dulsey rolled her eyes, and Mama shook her head but dished out a plate, folded the spoon inside a scrap of napkin, and poured the coffee. "Do you know where Mr. Bledsoe went? And can you manage it all?"

"I did, and I can." Kate took the napkin and spoon, the plate on top of that, the coffee in her other hand, and set off before anyone could say her nay. Or before the pounding of her heart could make her reconsider.

Fortunately she had indeed seen the direction Mr. Bledsoe took, up a slope far less steep than the creek bank, and one that afforded places to step easily.

Lord God, help me find him. Help me know the right words to say. And— help him see You and know that You are with him. Even if he thinks You are not.

Please help me ask the right questions.

As the way pitched more steeply, however, she had to stop to balance the plate over the mug so she had a hand free to lift her skirts.

And please, please let me not trip and spill everything!

She made it to the crest of the hill without mishap and stopped to catch her breath and look around. Now, which way had he—

"What are you doing out here?"

Her head snapped up, and just in time she caught the plate in her other hand. She swung to face him, seated on a giant log. "Oh—there you are. Papa was nowhere to be found, so—"

The ice in his eyes fair stole the breath from her lungs. 'Twas a wonder his coffee didn't freeze right there in the cup. Without another word, she stepped toward him, lifting the cup and plate.

He'd laid aside both hat and hunting frock, and as he set his rifle against the fallen tree and rose to accept her offering, the loose, faded blue shirt half covered his thighs but didn't completely obscure what she'd not noticed before—that it was not the usual breeches he wore beneath, but buckskin leggings and a breechclout. Not unusual attire for a frontiersman but—why did she find it so startling?

She passed off his supper, then withdrew to a small boulder and perched herself upon it while he seated himself again and dug in.

He eyed her feet.

"Dulsey wrapped them again, a new way," she supplied, before he could ask. "So far they feel much improved."

He shook his head, gaze dropping to his plate. Gracious, but he put the food away quickly. Fully a third of his portion was gone already. He swallowed, took a swig of the coffee, then fastened a severe look upon her once more. "You should not be here."

That blasted burn spread through her again. How was it he could so quickly make her feel thus? "You needed your supper while 'twas hot."

Another shake of his head.

"And. . .I hoped you'd share more about your family."

He hesitated, finished chewing, and cleared his mouth. "Why?"

"I enjoy hearing about them." The frost in his gaze had not abated. "Your sisters must be—remarkable. Your uncles as well, since you saw fit to mention them." *What sort of family produces a man as intriguing as you?* was on the tip of her tongue, but she bit it back.

"You truly are a nosy sort, aren't you?"

Kate's throat dried, but a tendril of indignation fired her resolve. "I find it intriguing, as I told you before"—there, she'd managed to use the word in a safe manner—"to hear folks' stories."

Huzzah, she'd managed that more gracefully than she could have.

But Mr. Bledsoe had gone too still, eyes narrowed. "Aye. Nosy." He shoveled the last third of the plate into his mouth in two bites, then chased it with another gulp of coffee. Standing, he set the cup aside, and held the plate and spoon out to her. "My thanks. I'll bring the mug later, make sure it's washed. Now if you'll pardon me—I'm here to keep watch. For that I need quiet, not some chattering squirrel of a female who can't keep her attention away from where it doesn't belong. The safety of this entire traveling party may depend upon it."

Kate reeled as if slapped, then took the plate and spoon in numb hands. She closed her mouth and, with a slight curtsy, made her retreat with as much dignity as she could muster.

Heart pounding, head and neck aching, ears burning, how she managed to not slide and stumble and roll right back down into camp, she was not sure. But somehow she made it back down the hill, without falling, without causing more hurt to her toes—although she might not have felt any pain, regardless.

The entire family was gathered to sup when she got there, including Papa and Johann. Most kept talking and eating, but something of her expression must have betrayed her because Mama stopped to give her a searching look. "Kate? Are you well?"

"Yes, Mama."

She deposited the plate and spoon into the dishpan already sitting near the fire, and took up one of the small wooden bowls. Was there any supper left after the rest of the family had descended? She peered into the pot. Not much. She scraped the ladle through it, considered her brother's appetite, then dropped the handle back against the side. Set down the bowl. Strode away toward the creek.

Quiet, was it? She could be quiet. And other folk in the camp had stories to tell. It was high time she gave them attention.

The last of the burn trickled away, leaving only a sense of shame—and sadness. She glanced back over her shoulder. Her entire family was comprised of chattering squirrels. A wonder that he tolerated any of them.

Chapter 14

During the night, the clouds gathered and the heavens opened. By the time they'd broken camp and were ready to set out, everyone was half sodden.

The weather matched the state of Kate's mood. Of course, the entire camp was much subdued, but her heart and mind held an ache beyond the day's gloominess. As Johann gave her a leg up onto Clover, she dared not look around for—for the lean scout who had so claimed her fascination these past days. She'd not even let herself think his name.

There was nowhere to stow her straw hat out of the wet, so Kate hung it from one of the packs once she was settled on Clover, and pulled the hood of her cloak up over her head. The wool, though damp, would keep most of the rain off of her head and upper body at least.

She was about to gather the reins when Papa approached, Stefan swaddled in a blanket. "Can you manage him and the horse as well?"

At her nod, he set Stefan in front of her, and Kate tucked her cloak about them both. "There, all snug," she whispered. The child's warmth lent a comfort she'd not expected this grey morn.

Mr. Jenkins offered a prayer then gave the call to move out.

The going was hard and much slower than it had been, with the packed dirt of the trail—because at this point it was little more than that, since so much brush had grown back up in the year and more since they'd cleared the way for a real road to be built—turned to mud, making ordinary twists and turns up the creek bank and back down, and around the rocks and across hillsides a thing of true peril. Clover slipped a time or two, bringing Kate's heart to her throat, but for the most part, the pack-horse pressed valiantly on and carried them without incident.

The rain continued, and the path worsened. Yellow Creek swelled to a foaming, ugly stream, coming to the horse's breast at the deepest cross-ings. At midday, they stopped under the shelter of spreading oaks and chestnuts for a cold repast of jerked meat and dried biscuit. Kate heard discussion of an ordinary a few miles farther on, where they might take shelter for the night and dry their shoes and stockings at least. She wig-gled her toes inside the moccasins. Dulsey's new way of wrapping seemed to have helped, but again, Kate would not complain of riding, along with the mothers with babies. Everyone on foot bore mud spatters clear to the knee, or well up the hems of their skirts.

Several slipped and went down in the rushing creek waters, but to no lasting ill effect besides the wetting of their clothing. The men on foot helped where they could, and they all trudged on.

Kate's gut gnawed, and her head ached. Even after missing supper completely last night, she'd not been able to eat much at breakfast. It was silly of her, she knew—she needed her strength on this journey the same as anyone. And in the hours of mulling the events of the past evening, she could do naught but admit that Mr. Bledsoe was right—to divert the attention of a man on watch was surely endangering the camp, regardless of her intent. And she was a very silly female indeed for not recognizing that on her own.

She closed her eyes, and a sigh escaped her. If only she had time for at least a little journaling. Scratching out her thoughts with ink and paper always helped her sort them out and move on. It had been days and days since the last time she was able to do so. She'd known already that likely there'd be no opportunity, let alone privacy, for such a thing on the jour-ney, but—she'd not expected to miss it so much.

Perhaps if she approached Papa with proper humility this evening, he'd let her steal a half hour—

Clover jolted beneath her, and her arms tightened around Stefan. Then, too quickly for response, the horse lurched again, hooves scrambling for footing on the bit of steep bank they traversed, and they were tumbling, down the slope and into the water.

Thomas had crossed the creek and was scouting high on the other side, a little ahead of the party, when the cries of dismay and the squeal of a horse came to his ears. Without a thought, he reined Ladyslipper about and hurried her back.

One of the packhorses had slipped and fallen into the creek, dumping its burden amid rocks and foaming water, scrambling to right itself. Its squeals attested to more than simple distress, but Thomas gave his attention to the cargo being swept downriver. Every one of those horses carried women and young'uns—

There, amongst the bundles swinging and bobbing downstream, a larger figure clutching a smaller one, flailing against the rocks.

Was that—

It didn't matter. They needed help, and quickly. He'd sort out his conflicted feelings on their possible identity later.

He swung off of Ladyslipper, tossed aside his rifle, shed powder horn and haversack, and threw himself down the bank, sliding, the point of his descent calculated to intersect with their tumble downstream. They'd not much time—the creek here had widened enough to be deep and treacherous. He hopped from rock to rock, then ran down the trunk of an overhanging sycamore to crouch in the branches that trailed in the water. He gripped one branch and leaned down, reaching—

Two pale faces, eyes and mouths wide in shock, bobbed in the current. Definitely Miss Gruener and her youngest brother, almost unrecognizable for their panic. Miss Gruener scrabbled at a boulder but slid past it.

"Miss Gruener!" he shouted above the noise of the waters. No response. "*Kate!*"

That brought her head around.

He stretched as far as he could. "Grab hold!"

More shock, dismay—a dozen emotions flashed in her eyes, but she gulped a breath and, grimacing, did her best to angle toward him, the now-wailing child still clasped in one arm. She flailed at the same time he got a handful of her sodden cloak.

"Grab hold of the tree," he told her. Her free arm came out, wrapped around one of the limbs as he hauled her upward. Her body remained submerged from the waist down, but she seemed secure for the moment. "Now hand me the baby."

She gave the boy into his care without hesitation. Hooking his leg amongst the branches, he tucked the child against his side, then reached to help her crawl up into the branches until she lay across the larger part of the tree, panting.

Across the creek, the other men were busy retrieving the packhorse and its bundles. As the horse gained a section of low bank, between rocks, and scrambled for ground, Thomas could see one foreleg dangling uselessly.

Blast. The creature would have to be shot and put out of its misery.

He gave his attention back to the girl and the baby in his arms. The young'un burrowed against his shoulder, its cries already subsiding to hiccups. Thomas shifted him to a better position, still cradling him close. "Are you well, Miss Gruener? Is aught broken?"

Still gulping air, she shook her head. "I. . .think. . ." She turned her head and peered at him through a curtain of loose, wet hair, then turned away again. "I am well."

He winced. It was likely useless to ask and expect a clear answer this instant.

Everything hurt. She was vaguely sensible of having hit something very hard in their initial tumble, before the cold water had closed over her and stolen all breath. They'd rolled over and over, and the only thought she had was to keep hold of Stefan. . . .

She peeked again at the lean man holding her brother with such obvious ease and tenderness, cupping Stefan's head against his shoulder before running a hand across the baby's extremities, even going so far as to lift Stefan's skirts to examine the boy's legs. "Is he—"

"He appears to be well enough, just shaken." His voice rumbled in a pitch just above the water's rush. "I ask again, what of yourself?"

Kate seized a branch to aid in shifting herself to a sitting position, and a groan escaped through clenched teeth. Mr. Bledsoe's gaze was upon her at that. "Simply. . .tumbled about. . ."

"Bend each of your limbs, carefully," he said, and watched as she did.

"Bruised, perhaps, but unbroken," she said. Her head set to throbbing so sharply she felt the urge to vomit. She reached up to push her sodden hair aside and winced at the sting her fingers drew as she dragged them across her forehead.

"Let me see that," Mr. Bledsoe said, quick and stern. He brushed her hand out of the way and gripping her chin, angled her face so he could look. She could discern no clue as to the severity of her injuries from his expression, but then he looked stern at nearly everything.

Especially in regards to her.

She closed her eyes against his examination and did not open them again until he blew out a breath and let go. "Right knocked about, you were. It'll have to be looked at later. You'll likely have a headache for a while."

He rose then and stepped lightly along the tree trunk, toward the bank. She made to follow him but found she still had no strength. "Stay there till I can fetch you," he said without looking back.

She'd no strength for arguing either, it seemed.

Leaning back against a stout limb, she focused on drawing breaths into lungs that still burned and watching the men as they climbed up and down the opposite bank, fishing bundles out of the water. Clover was nowhere in sight—oh there, just upstream, between a clump of laurel and a rocky outcropping. Head up, then down, breathing heavily but otherwise unmoving. One of the pack masters stood at his head but there was no effort to get the horse to higher ground.

She turned back to watching the recovery of the baggage. All but one bundle had been retrieved, and someone had run downstream after that one.

Far upstream, Mr. Bledsoe was crossing, Stefan in his arms, where the water came to his thighs but no higher. Papa waited on the opposite side, Mama on the ridge of the bank, hands covering her face. Once Mr. Bledsoe gained the other side, Papa reaching to steady him, Kate let her head fall back and her eyelids droop again.

All sound hollowed, and her limbs grew heavy. She was so very weary. . . .

"Miss Gruener. Wake up."

A deep, rich voice, but insistent. She tried to move, but could not, even though something shook her.

So. . .weary. . .

"Kate, wake up. Please. You only need get so far as my mare. I'll help you." The voice pitched lower, almost—intimate. "Come on, Kate. Don't do this."

With a deep, painful intake of breath, she dragged her eyelids open. Mr. Bledsoe knelt beside her on the fallen tree, hands on her shoulders. His already serious face seemed troubled, but when she made herself focus on him, his gaze cleared somewhat. The ghost of a smile curved his mouth.

"That's it," he said, this time with definite tenderness. "Don't give up. I know you've more strength in you than that."

He slid one arm behind her back and half hoisted her to her feet. Her moan became a muffled cry.

"I'm sorry, Kate. Nothing for it but to keep moving. I promise you'll have rest soon."

Somehow, allowing her to lean on him, he guided her along the tree trunk and to solid creek bank, where he seated her on a rock. "Stay here while I get Ladyslipper."

She shivered as the warm press of his hands left hers.

He brought the mare and drew her up next to the rock. With care, he helped her stand and climb over to the saddle, then without hesitation, swung up behind her. "Easy now," he soothed, whether to her or the horse, she did not know.

"Ladyslipper," she murmured as he set the horse in motion. " 'Tis your mare's name?"

"Aye." She felt rather than heard the rumble of his voice at her back.

"Like—the flower?"

"Aye," he said again with a small laugh.

"Quite the fanciful name," she said. "But she's lovely."

Another short laugh as he angled the mare down the bank. His arms braced her on either side as the horse made her descent into the water, and when an unsteady step drew a gasp from her lips—it was too much like the first step of Clover's final stumble—those arms pressed closer. "Easy," he murmured, this time nearly in her ear.

At least she wasn't completely insensible. And she didn't panic or lose her balance or otherwise make things more difficult as they crossed back over the creek.

The baby was already in his mama's arms, and Gruener was ready, arms outstretched, the moment all four of Ladyslipper's hooves cleared the creek, to receive his daughter. She swayed but remained mounted while Thomas swung off, then Gruener practically brushed him aside to get to her, crooning much as Thomas had just minutes ago.

Despite being half soaked himself, Thomas flushed hot at the thought. But in the moment, she'd seemed to need it. And no one had heard but her.

He stood back, let Gruener guide her to a rock to sit and begin assessing her. The older man threw Thomas a questioning look. "She looks to have hit her head, but more than that remains to be seen."

Gruener grimaced and glanced about. "Can we make camp anywhere near?"

"We're close enough to Cumberland Ford," Jenkins spoke up. "We should press on and then lodge at the ordinary there. Take a day or so to dry out and rest up, if she needs it."

Gruener's brow lowered even more. "I dislike forcing travel upon her before we know how badly she is hurt. And we are down a horse—" He glanced at the injured packhorse, still panting, then looked away.

"You're welcome to mine, sir," Thomas said quietly.

When the older man hesitated, Jenkins said, "Take it, man. We've no better option. It's cold, the rain shows no sign of letting up, and the ordinary will be snug even if a bit crowded."

With a sigh, Gruener's shoulders slumped. "Very well." He swiped a hand over the unbruised side of his daughter's face. "Katarina. Do you think you can face riding a little farther?"

Her unfocused eyes searched her father's face. "I—am well enough, Papa."

The man dropped a kiss on the girl's forehead, more roughly than he intended, Thomas was sure, seeing her wince. "My brave girl. Of course you are."

With Thomas's help, they packed her back up onto Ladyslipper, and after some hesitation, her father looked Thomas in the eye. " 'Tis your mare, and a fine one she is. I trust you both to carry my daughter a little farther."

Thomas nodded and made to mount, but Gruener clasped his forearm. "I thank you for the lives of both my children this day. It was God's own mercy that you reached them in time."

An unaccustomed thickness rose in Thomas's throat as he swung up behind the girl.

CHAPTER 15

'Twas all Kate could do to grip the saddlebow and the mare's mane, and stay upright until Mr. Bledsoe had mounted and braced her again. Papa's face remained upturned, his face pale, his blue eyes full of worry. He said something, patting her knee, but sounds were fading again and the world around her blurring—or was that Mr. Bledsoe urging the horse on?

She was vaguely aware of someone taking her wet cloak and wrapping her in a dry blanket, of a child crying and being hushed.

"Stefan," she said, and the low, soothing murmur of before reassured her he was safe.

Then men's voices—and Mama's—in lively debate. A gunshot, and Jemmy crying, with Johann telling her to stop blubbering. " *'Tis just a horse,*" he said. *"No, but it was Clover,"* Jemmy retorted.

The sensation of riding uphill, then down. A pillow against her head, firm but warm, that smelled of tobacco, wood smoke, gunpowder, and a teasingly spicy scent she could not identify.

"Stay with us, Kate," the pillow rumbled. "Your family needs you."

She sighed. Where was she to stay? She was simply—so weary.

She opened her eyes, and the forest floor drew into sharp focus, with moss and ferns and curious fan-shaped fungi growing on fallen trees. The pillow resolved itself into a hunting-frock-clad shoulder and arm. Something told her she should find this situation disconcerting, but she did not. She did, however, make the attempt to sit up, only to be rewarded with another wave of that sickening pain through her head and neck.

"Shh, all's well, don't startle now," the rumble said.

Mr. Bledsoe. She was riding with Mr. Bledsoe. After—after Clover had fallen down a creek bank and—

"Stefan?"

"He's well. Strapped to your papa's back, sleeping."

"And—why are you saddled with me?"

He huffed a quick laugh. "Because you thumped your head right good, and we're down a horse."

"Ah." For some reason his explanation did not satisfy, but she could find no words to express what was swirling through her mind. Except—

"We're—down a horse?"

He cleared his throat. "The packhorse's leg broke."

"So—" The gunshot. Jemmy's crying. "Ohh. . .poor Clover."

"Aye." The single word, though spoken firmly with the terrible necessity of the horse having to be put down, held a note of regret.

Kate shifted in the saddle. Now she was beginning to feel disconcerted about the predicament of riding Mr. Bledsoe's lovely mare with him just behind her. "I didn't realize he would slip. Was there anything else I could have done? That stretch of path seemed most treacherous."

"Nay. Jenkins and I looked at it, and likely there was nothing else to be done. Portions of the road are like that—folk can travel across it a hundred times, and then the next time someone walks across—" She felt rather than saw his shrug, and somehow the motion made her face burn. "And figure too how wet the ground is after a few hours' steady rain."

She blinked and looked around, slowly. The rain seemed to have stopped, but the hilltops were swathed in mist again. Drawing the blanket more tightly about herself, she shivered. "I am very much undone here."

He said nothing for a moment, then made a sound that might also have been of amusement. "I've seen worse."

A wave of sleepiness overcame her again, and she yawned. "Oh yes, your sisters."

A definite chuckle this time. "Aye."

She tried valiantly to stay awake, but by the time they emerged at Cumberland Ford, the girl was slumped insensible in his arms again. As relieved as he'd been to have her waken and speaking to him—coherently, for the most part—he was very glad to have her asleep again.

Far less complicated that way. Except for the obscure comfort of her slight form leaning against him.

'Twould be something he'd have to chase from his thoughts later, he was sure.

The party wound its way out of the forest, down a slight hill and into the inn's yard. Jenkins and the others began dismounting while Gruener headed inside, probably to inquire about accommodations. Thomas held his seat until the man could return for his daughter. Best not to disturb her until he knew whether they'd be lodging indoors.

He felt the looks from the other travelers, most sympathetic and concerned, some less than charitable. They could think what they liked. He'd have done the same for any member of the party. The fact that it was Miss Gruener, who happened to be young and—aye, he'd admit it—comely, had naught to do with the matter.

Mrs. Gruener approached, her face drawn and pale, brow creased with worry. "How is she faring?"

"She woke for a bit, held conversation with me," Thomas said.

"Any sign of injury besides the blow to her head?"

He shook his head, but reluctantly. "I think not, but 'tis too soon to tell."

The older woman's expression did not lighten as she considered her sleeping daughter. After a moment, she looked at Thomas and said more softly, "Thank you for all you've done today."

"You're welcome, of course." Nothing more he could say.

She gave a tiny shake of her head. "You weren't even with us when it happened. How did you manage to reach them in time?"

"Not sure, ma'am, but I'm glad I was." Nothing else he could say there either.

"Well. I thank you again." Her earnest brown eyes lifted—he could see where Miss Gruener inherited hers from. "Please know you are always welcome at our table. Or campfire." She smiled. "Or wherever we happen to be."

He nodded, his need for a reply forestalled by the return of Mr. Gruener. " 'Tis all settled. They are able to accommodate our entire party and might be able to find a small room for tending Kate." He glanced about, his gaze settling at last on Thomas and then his daughter. "I will take her now, thank you."

Miss Gruener stirred but did not rouse completely, and Thomas helped ease her down off Ladyslipper and into her father's embrace. "Easy now," Thomas said as a whimper broke from the girl. "She's had a powerful bad headache."

Gruener nodded, and murmuring over her as before, he swooped her up, one arm behind her back and the other beneath her knees, then strode away, Mrs. Gruener trailing after.

Thomas found himself reminded of Truth, and of the special bond she'd always enjoyed with their pa as eldest. At least to his memory she had. But Pa—he'd not ever seemed whole again after Mama's death. How might their family have looked had both Mama and Pa lived?

He shook off the thought and nudged Ladyslipper toward the stable. Useless to be thinking of these things after so many years.

❧

Kate came awake again to warmth and a room that was blessedly dark except for a small fire—somehow they'd made it indoors, and she could not remember arriving. Baggage was brought in, and Mama shooed everyone out but Dulsey, and they helped her out of all her wet things. "Where's the worst of the hurt?" Mama asked, turning Kate's arms this way and that to look for signs of injury.

Kate had to think about it. "My. . .head and neck. But everything aches."

"Well." Mama had her sit forward, half swathed in blanket, so she could examine her shoulders and back. "You'll likely ache for a few days, but 'tis no small mercy if you've escaped worse harm."

Dulsey set down a bowl and wrung out a cloth in the steaming water, then set to bathing Kate's face. "Oh, miraculous hot water," Kate murmured.

Mama chuckled, while Dulsey just snorted softly. "Child, you and your fanciful way of talking."

"Fanciful, is it? I'm not the only one. Mr. Bledsoe's horse is named Ladyslipper, like the flower."

"Huh. Well, she's a pretty enough mare for it."

Mama turned away and came back with a clean, dry shift. "Slip this on, and we'll wrap you back up in the blanket and find you something to eat." Her dark eyes sparkled in the firelight. "You hardly needed a blow to the head to make you more fanciful."

Kate saw the quirk of her mouth despite the sharpness of the words. "Likely not," she answered with a sigh.

"She is as God made her to be," Dulsey said. "You'd not want to change her even if you could."

Dulsey, defending her whimsy?

"As long as she retains some good sense," Mama said firmly. A knock came at the door, and she went to answer it, then returned with a bowl of broth. "Here, drink this. Then to bed with you."

As the salty richness rolled across her tongue, a ragged breath shuddered through her. Just hours ago life's uncertainty had seized her in its rough, relentless embrace, and now, here she sat, warm and dry and comforted with a bowl of broth.

She might have been knocked completely insensible and then drowned. She could be—

On the other side of eternity, in heaven, with the pair of children her parents had already relinquished into God's hands.

Her head throbbed, and that sharp ache still stabbed every time she moved too quickly, but—for whatever reason, God had seen fit to leave her here.

Would she ever know why, during this life?

Chapter 16

Thomas left Ladyslipper tethered and fed and headed for the trading post. He'd more likely hear news there as at the ordinary.

The post was busy as he'd ever seen it, with hunters both white and Indian coming in with their winter harvest of furs. Two men wearing fancy garb from back East elbowed up to the counter with a trio of frontiersmen and two Indians. Mingo, by the looks of them. One wore a blue regimental coat, threadbare but brass buttons still bright, and the other a hunting frock heavy with beading and quillwork. Both wore their hair gathered into a spike at the back, with the sides shaved. While the head trader, Aaron Clark, dickered with half the group, Thomas sidled around the room, pretending to examine the wares stacked high and tucked into every corner, but Clark spied him almost immediately. "Bledsoe! Good to see you. What can I do you for?"

He smirked at the man's turn of phrase and stepped closer as the others made room for him, offering their own greetings. "Here mostly for news today. I'm leadin' a party of settlers up the road, so whatever you all might be hearing about doings north and west of here. . ."

He let his gaze sweep the men's faces, lingering on the features of the two Indians. They seemed familiar—likely he'd met them here a time or two, at least—but neither acknowledged him. Thomas gave a mental nod and moved on.

"Well," Clark said, slowly, "we've had more pass through on the way north than coming back for a long time. But there's word of a passel of renegade Creek and Cherokee savaging the trails to the west, particularly around the Shawanoe River. Sounds like y'all might be safe enough from that though."

"Might." Thomas grunted. His gaze flicked to the Mingos again. "Nat Carrington been through recently?"

Clark leaned meaty fists on the counter. "Aye. He was headed north to Boonesborough. I told him they were more afeared of the whiskey tax there than anything else, but he was determined to go."

Thomas nodded as if that were news.

Conversation between the other men picked up again, so Thomas moved away and kept listening. The Indians took their turns, dickering over price of goods compared to quality of furs. They spoke English at first but after a few minutes, Clark broke into their native tongue. "What do you think of the question from that one over there? Anything of use you might be able to offer?"

"What business is it of ours whether the white settlers live or die?" the older one spoke—definitely Mingo, which Thomas followed well enough, even now. "We do our best to share the hunting grounds, as the white fathers have persuaded us to do, but if they are foolish enough to go where they should not. . ." He gave an expressive shrug.

Clark seemed not to be disturbed by the man's attitude, and Thomas held himself still as well, as if he could not understand.

"And you, Thunder Speaks?"

The other man hesitated. "The elders speak wisdom as they see best, but the young warriors will do what they will. Their blood runs hot, no matter what the white father Wayne might say, and they crave honor. Scalps taken is the old way."

Thomas knew all this to be fact. Treaties without number had been negotiated, signed, then violated on one side or the other for decades—indeed since the time of William Penn, still renowned for his fairness toward the Indian peoples. There were things Thomas could not agree with in the teaching of Penn and his Society of Friends—down to this day—but his endeavors to not rob the peoples already living on these shores Thomas could not fault.

Still, none of their words held any comfort or safety for his traveling party, and since it was his job to save their scalps—

He made to turn and leave the trading post, but a shelf with beaded and quilled moccasins caught his eye. A lovely thing, with flower designs encrusting the top of the toe. Picking up one, he measured it with his eye against the length of his hand—might be just the size for Miss Gruener's foot, and these would be better than her own shoes for a good long while—

Thomas blinked. What was he doing? He set the moccasin down, nudged it even with its mate, and left the building as quickly as he could.

He stepped out and glanced about the settlement that had grown up at the banks of the river crossing and shared its name. The ordinary was just a piece up the road, but frankly he dreaded having to enter what would undoubtedly be a smelly, crowded, noisy space.

Behind him, the door to the trading post swung open, and the two Mingos emerged. They eyed Thomas and would have moved on, but he decided to chance asking them directly. "Brothers. Long have I been away from the land of the Shawnee, yet I remember their kindness. I wish no trouble between them and the people I am leading into Kentucky."

As he'd hoped, the attempt at their tongue brought them up short. "How long were you with them?"

"Nearly two years. I was known as Eyes-of-Sky."

Amusement gleamed in both men's gazes, but only the younger let his mouth curve. "Hardly a name of renown."

Thomas smiled in response. "I was not allowed to stay long enough to gain any."

The older one's head angled a little. "So you wish to know what we hear on the path. Long it has been since the Warrior's Trail knew more of our people's feet than of the whites."

"True, yet your people still know the ancient paths. The people I lead wish for peace, and I would help them not cause offense, if it were possible."

The younger, the one Clark called Thunder Speaks, said, "Then they should return to their own lands."

"Yet you are here trading," Thomas said.

The older made an impatient gesture. "The time is past for such foolish talk. You, Eyes-of-Sky, tell me what sort of men these are you lead. The white man has already overrun our hunting grounds. Why should we allow yet more to come?"

"These men only wish to feed their families, the same as the Mingo and the Shawnee."

Thunder Speaks merely grunted, but the other gave a bare nod. "Fair enough. Very well. I can tell you, the Mingo and the Shawnee are not happy to deal with the white father General Wayne. The elders are for peace, but the young warriors, as we already said, are for war. They speak of gathering to push the white father back. The Mingo and Shawnee have given too much already. They continue to seek opportunity everywhere. You and the people you lead should watch the path. More I cannot say, for I am not an eagle to see afar as it flies."

"Your words are well spoken, and I will take them to the people I lead. My thanks for sharing them with me."

He took his leave of the two and went on. Now he could not avoid the crowded ordinary. Or perhaps that was word he could pass privately to Jenkins, although he felt an obligation to inform Gruener as well. Still nothing specific, but the threat was enough to not take lightly.

As it turned out, several of the men he needed to talk with were standing outside the building, under the covered porch, each with a mug or pipe in hand. With the rain having let off, the yard was full of young'uns chasing each other or playing games. Thomas smiled a little. Sometimes he missed being so free from care.

"Bledsoe! There you are. We were just discussing whether or not we can make it to Elizabethtown by the end of May."

"I don't see any reason why not," Thomas said.

"Well, here we are," John Hughes said, "only at Cumberland Ford, and Gruener is insisting we stay an extra day or so to let his children recover. Are we going to stop and make camp every time someone falls in the water?"

Thomas found himself gritting his teeth, but Jenkins spoke up for him. " 'Tis more than that, and you know it. The Gruener girl was hurt right bad—might not have survived that fall."

"Is that so?" Hughes spoke it as a challenge, and looked right at Thomas.

"It is so," he said. "And I say we see how she fares come morning. If naught else, she can ride again."

An ugly smile curled the man's mouth. "Well, I can see how you might not mind that."

A terrible urge rose up in Thomas to thump that look right off the man's face, but he forced himself to remain still.

"Enough, Hughes," Jenkins said. "I'll be finding another horse by then, maybe two. Have to talk to Gruener about it."

Thomas did not move, and neither did John Hughes. "She'll ride if she needs to," Thomas said, quietly but firmly. "And we'll take as long as necessary for the journey. Unless you'd prefer to risk losing one of your own family."

Hughes relented at that. "Of course not," he muttered and turned away.

The man's manner soured Thomas's gut. What was eating at him, any-way? If this was what they'd have to contend with the rest of the way. . .

"Did you have news, Bledsoe?" Jenkins said.

Thomas unclenched his jaw and refocused on the pack master. "Aye. Just that we need to stay alert for Indian trouble—which we already knew. Once we leave here, might be best to set double watches. Keep an eye out for trouble, and don't go lookin' for any. Things seem to be quiet enough where we're going though, for now."

Sobered, Jenkins nodded, the others with him. Hughes looked only slightly mollified.

"We'll talk again come morning, decide what we're doing."

Thomas nodded and walked away. It was not raining, the stable was as warm and dry as the ordinary, and he would not subject himself to the press of a crowd if he could help it.

CHAPTER 17

My father used to tell the story...

Kate came awake from a swirl of dream, her fingers curled as if it were a quill she held and not a rough wool blanket. She'd fallen asleep rehearsing words, wishing she could write them in truth and not just whisper them in her own mind, and now—

Her journal. Where had her journal gone?

She made to sit up, but a wave of dizziness overwhelmed her. One breath, then two, and it passed enough for her to squint about the room. Mama was up, poking at the fire, but bundled forms here and there, foot to shoulder, attested that some of her family had bedded down in the meager space and slept on. Except for Dulsey, who stirred and rose even as Kate watched.

The woman padded over and peered into Kate's face. "Law, child. I hope you feel better than you look."

She opened her mouth to speak, but only a croak came out. She cleared her throat and tried again. "Likely not."

"Let me get you some tea, and we'll see if that helps mend you a bit."

"I—need the necessary first."

Dulsey helped her up and into a petticoat and bedgown, then rebraided her bedraggled hair. Kate regarded her feet for a moment before deciding to forego shoes a bit longer. Weaving her way between the sleepers, she made it to the door, then looked back to find Dulsey shadowing her.

The dizziness threatened only once more on their way down the stairs, then again as they threaded their way to the back door, through the common room, where the floor was littered with more snoring sleepers.

Outside, she stopped to breathe in the cool morning air, her gaze tracing the barely lightening sky over the hills to the east, then padded the rest of the way to the necessary.

It felt like an indulgence, a real necessary, after even a few days tramping out among the laurel.

Back inside, Dulsey stopped at the kitchen and procured a bit of breakfast. By the time she'd eaten, sipped a cup of tea, and the others had awakened, she was feeling much improved. Papa returned from downstairs and came to crouch beside where Kate was seated by the hearth. He stared into the fire for a moment, then turned to Mama. "They wish to know if Kate is recovered enough to travel today. What say you, 'Mima?"

Mama turned to consider Kate, and Papa's gaze followed. Kate winced. The dizziness still came and went, but— "If you wish me to try, I'm willing."

Papa gave another sigh and rubbed his face. "Jenkins found another horse to replace that which we lost yesterday. He and I have spoken about purchasing an extra, so you have your own mount for a longer time without borrowing Mr. Bledsoe's. I would not press you though. We've time enough, and money enough, to afford staying an extra night. I think, however, that they'll insist on seeing you for themselves before deciding either way."

She nodded. "Let's go downstairs and speak with them. But as I said—"

"And what of your feet?" Papa said, peering downward. "You lost those borrowed moccasins as well."

She swallowed. "I suppose, then, I'll simply have to endure my shoes." She offered a smile.

He wagged his head then pushed to his feet. "Very well. For now, let me escort you downstairs."

"Wait—Papa." She glanced about the room, but could not see the item she'd abruptly, and belatedly, remembered. "Where is my haversack?"

He too looked around, exchanging a glance with Mama, who shook her head. "It will turn up sooner or late," she said.

"But—" She cast about for a solid reason to wish it sooner. "My sewing kit. The needles will rust."

Mama shrugged, but Papa frowned. He knew. He alone knew. Would he keep her secret?

"We'll find it when we find it," he said at last.

Thomas had waited as long as he possibly could justify before crossing to the ordinary. The sun was just peeping above the eastern rim of the mountains, and his belly grumbled the delay.

Best he get over there and claim his share of breakfast, at least. If the Hughes boys hadn't gotten it all by now.

He stepped inside the ordinary and found his traveling party and others in the middle of packing up their belongings. Nodding to the few that looked up to acknowledge him, he crossed to the sideboard holding what remained of the morning meal.

While he loaded bread, sausage, and cheese into a wooden bowl, he glanced around. The Murphys, the Hugheses, and the pack team all more or less clustered in their own areas, bundling belongings and stacking them. Except for Jacob Hughes, standing at a trestle table near the front, poking about in his haversack.

Looking for something, or unpacking it. He had half its contents lying on the tabletop, and was just pulling out a long roll of what looked like buckskin—wet, at that.

Curiosity nudged Thomas closer as he dipped into his bowl. "Whatcha doing?"

Jacob either didn't hear him, or chose not to answer, but instead gave his attention to working loose the wrappings of the buckskin-covered roll. By the look on his face, and his manner of handling it, this wasn't Jacob's haversack after all.

The buckskin bundle gave up its secret in that moment, and proved to be a tightly rolled stack of parchment, curled at the edges from the wet. As Jacob spread the stack flat, Thomas glimpsed script, in an even hand, blurred at the edges but still mostly legible:

Was that—Kate Gruener's?

"Hey, what's this?" Jacob's brother leaned over his other shoulder and plucked the pages out of the younger boy's hands.

"Give it back!" Jacob said, but the elder Hughes twitched away and held the first page up.

"My father used to—to—*tell* the story," he read, "of how he and his fellow—ah, I can't make out the word—sailed down the Hudson with the British, preparing to attack Washington and—" His head came up and his gaze snapped around. "Is that talking about Gruener? Was he a redcoat?"

In the moment of silence that reigned after, Gruener—and the daughter who doubtlessly had penned those words—stepped into the room, his face guarded and severe. Then the place exploded in questions.

⦅❧⦆

In one second, Kate was trailing her father down the stairs, and in the next, a rough western Virginia voice echoed those words she'd just heard in her dreams. Her breath caught. Was she yet dreaming, or—

No. Her haversack had been found.

Gripping Papa's arm, suddenly gone rigid, she stared helplessly at Jacob Hughes's older brother, holding the sheets of her journal in his meaty hands with no more care than if he held a hatchet.

And then the entire common room turned upon her, upon Papa, their expressions awash in disbelief and outrage. "Is it true? You fought with the British? Were you a Tory, or—"

"La, man, that was nearly twenty years ago—"

"Gruener is a good man, he'd not—"

His face as angry as she'd ever seen, Papa raised his hand for silence. "That is my daughter's. I'll thank you to give it over, please."

The parchment crumpled a little more in Hughes's hands as he shook it for emphasis. "Not until you tell us the truth of this. I'll not travel with a bloody Tory—"

Mr. Bledsoe strode up from somewhere off to the left and snatched the bundle out of Hughes's grasp. "That doesn't belong to you," he growled—also as angry as Kate had ever seen.

Something inside her quailed and shriveled. This was her doing—hers and no one else's. If she'd not written those words, then no one would be finding them.

And Papa had sworn her to silence, for this very reason.

"But it begs the question," Hughes said. "We'd already talked of going on without them—this just proves that we should."

"If you go, it'll be without me as well," Mr. Bledsoe said, his voice a quiet but terrible rumble. "I signed on to scout for Gruener and his family. I answer to none of the rest of you."

The entire room held its breath, and stepping back, Mr. Bledsoe nodded at Papa—and her.

Though Kate still stood frozen, Papa nodded back. "I will explain." He laid his hand over hers, in the crook of his arm, his touch all comfort and gentleness. "In my youth I was a rifleman from Hesse-Cassel, in Germany," he said, the words clear and precise despite the slight lisp of his accent—which seemed especially pronounced at the moment. "We were in the employ of the British Crown, aye, but I'd hardly had opportunity to fire in the Battle of Trenton before I and my fellow Hessians were captured. They paraded us through the streets of New York before sending us out to the countryside to labor in farms. I was already disenchanted with the British by that time, but there I met Jemima, who would become my wife, and found myself fully won over to the cause of American independence." He drew a long breath, seeming to grow before Kate's eyes. "I am as much a patriot as any of you, though I was born across the ocean."

A murmur rose like a wave. "I've no issue with that," came Mr. Murphy's voice, above all. "Many of us, or our fathers, were in like circumstance, one way or another."

"I can vouch for Gruener's trustworthiness," said one of the pack masters.

The eldest of the Hughes men—Jacob's father—spat into the middle of the floor. "I'm not sure I want to be waiting around for his daughter to decide she's well enough for travel."

"I'm fully well enough," she said, though even to her own ear, her voice sounded thin and weak. Several pairs of eyes swung toward her as if seeing her for the first time, many of them startled and dismayed.

"See?" Mr. Jenkins said. "Those are some very genuine bruises. She took more than a wetting yesterday."

Is that what they were saying had happened to her? Did they think she'd been insensible most of the day simply for the attention it garnered?

Young Mrs. Murphy stepped near, peering closer. "Ach, it looks a wonder that you're yet living and breathing."

"It is a wonder," came that deep voice she now knew so well, even without looking this time. "They very nearly lost her, and the young'un. So have a little heart and let the girl rest another day if she needs it."

Her chest tightened until she could hardly breathe. She'd caused them such trouble—caused him such trouble. Why would he defend her?

She darted a glance in his direction. He stood at a table, back to her, shoving things into—her haversack.

Lifting the bag, he wheeled and strode toward her, then held it out without a word. "Thank you," she managed to murmur, and this time his nod was for her only. His pale gaze skimmed her face, assessing. Warming where it touched.

"This is nonsense," Mr. Jenkins said. "Miss Gruener, consider yourself at liberty to return to bed. We ain't going nowhere today. And Hughes—if you want to leave, then do so, but it'll be without me and my boys. Or our horses, unless you're paying a fair price."

Mr. Bledsoe's mouth gave a sharp uptick, and with a glance to the side, he turned and walked away.

Kate could suddenly breathe again.

CHAPTER 18

Back upstairs, while Kate unpacked the sodden haversack and laid it all to dry on the hearth, Papa drew Mama out of the room with a quiet word, shutting the door.

Hoping to contain the storm of her disapproval for as long as possible, no doubt. Kate vented a sigh. The entirety of their traveling party knew—what matter was it now, what Mama thought? Oh, she'd be upset enough, but it was naught compared to what had happened below. To Papa being faced with it, like this.

Her haversack lay crumpled beside all its contents. She smoothed it flat, then reached for the sheaf of parchment pages, which she'd left until last. The buckskin cover had done an astonishing job of preserving it, all things considered, but it was not without a wrench of her heart to see where ink had blurred. Still, it could have been a complete ruin.

Dulsey knelt beside her. "I came down. Heard what happened."

Kate tucked her chin and choked back the rising thickness in her throat. "It was. . .most foolish of me to write it."

"Mm." Dulsey lifted the first page and angled it so she could read for herself. "Foolish, perhaps. But perhaps you are only proud of your papa."

The tears overflowed. That, for certain. But it mattered little—if at all—when Papa had been humiliated before everyone because of it.

"Come, child." Dulsey rose to her feet and tugged at Kate. "You need sleep more than aught else right now."

She was only too happy to let herself be tucked back into bed.

Thomas finished the food in his bowl, watching the rest of the traveling party stash their bundles against the walls instead of packing them outside, all the while ignoring the still-bickering Hughes boys. Frankly, he wasn't sure how he felt about the delay. But he sure would do everything he could to make sure the Gruener girl had at least a day to recover.

He returned to the sideboard to fill his bowl for the second time and caught the whisper of voices in the stairwell.

"A completely foolish thing to do! And I'll march right down there and tell them all I think so—"

"Do not be so hasty, Jemima." Thomas could recognize the odd cadence of Karl Gruener's voice, even without his mention of his wife's name. "Think—would you cast your own daughter to the wolves? She is chastened enough by what has happened. Do not add misery to it."

Thomas finished heaping his bowl and hesitated.

"You spoil her, Karl—"

"No, but she understands the gravity of what she has done. Give her time, see what comes of it. . ."

The voices dropped to a murmur he could not distinguish, and having no more reason to linger, he went and tucked himself into a corner.

With a chunk of bread, he scooped bacon-flavored mush into his mouth. As he chewed, Gruener reentered the common room, his wife at his heels.

Gruener crossed the room to speak with Jenkins first, while Mrs. Gruener made a beeline for Mrs. Murphy. Then looking around, the older man spied Thomas and weaved his way between the tables toward him. "You did not have to speak up for us," Gruener said. "Thank you."

Thomas thought for a minute before he spoke. "My brother-in-law was a loyalist fresh from King's Mountain when he came to us. But he was a good man. Helped our family when he didn't have to."

Understanding shone in Gruener's gaze. "As Murphy said, many were in a similar condition."

Thomas snorted, chewed another bite, then swallowed. "Just some are less forgiving than others. Our over-the-mountain folk, now, they were already tetchy about ignoring Crown law, then to have such a one as Ferguson threaten to come over and burn us out—" He shook his head. "That's all some remember. Or that their kin got tarred and feathered. But both sides did that, especially in the backcountry."

Thomas remembered the stories Micah would tell, some of them terrible enough to curl a man's hair.

Gruener was nodding. "Yes, we saw it as well. 'Tis why I've tried so to keep quiet about—this." His blue eyes narrowed. "Foolish though it might have been, Kate meant no harm."

Thomas stilled and narrowed his eyes right back. In truth, he wasn't sure what he thought about that either. But—"And why would that matter to me?"

The older man folded his arms over his beefy chest. "No reason, I suppose. Besides wondering precisely what your intentions are toward my daughter."

What his—

Thomas went hot all over. Surely the man did not think—but aye, the man surely did. Or he'd not be asking. Thomas sat back, slowly and carefully, and laid his hands flat on the table. "To see her and her family safely to western Kentucky. Naught else, of course."

Gruener let out a long breath and finally glanced away, but only for a second. "You will forgive me for being clumsy at this. She is my eldest, and I've never had cause to face such a situation before. But many years ago I had a question posed me, much like that one, and I gave a response much like yours. I did not want to admit to this girl's father that I felt a far deeper attachment than I'd a right to under the circumstances." He hesitated, still taking Thomas apart with his eyes, then continued, more softly, "Her father was most unhappy when shortly thereafter my actions gave lie to my words. I am very aware that I could also be made unhappy in a similar circumstance."

Thomas measured the weathering of the man's features. He was not old by any means—both face and frame were yet hale and strong. Much like Pa when he rode off to help wreak havoc upon Ferguson. And what might Pa's reaction have been had he been the one to come back and find Truth and Micah carrying on as they did?

For that matter, what was Thomas's own gut feeling, especially once he knew who Micah was and where he'd been?

"Then I hold you no blame for asking," Thomas said, as evenly as he could. "And I promise you, I mean no dishonor toward her."

There was more, on the tip of his tongue—*she's a winsome girl, and would do any man proud, even if she is a little cotton-headed*—but he bit the words back. The situation didn't call for that much honesty.

"Very well," Gruener said. "See that it remains so."

The man walked away, and Thomas blinked at the remainder of his breakfast. What kind of a fool answer had he just given? *I mean no dishonor toward her.* Like he'd ever let it come even close to that.

⚜

Kate slept most of that day, but toward evening, she rose and felt well enough to venture downstairs for supper. Besides, she needed the necessary as well, and the room felt close and stuffy, even with the rest of the family away and occupied with other things, and only Mama there to help her dress.

They were contemplating the difficulty of her shoes, which still felt uncomfortably tight. "I could simply go barefoot again," Kate said.

Mama sighed and looked thoughtful. She'd already surrendered on the point of Kate braiding her hair rather than pinning it up, or the need to wear a cap. "I suppose," she began when Papa entered, one hand behind his back.

The expression on his face caught her attention—half expectant, half abashed. He hesitated with both Kate's and Mama's eyes upon him, then with a wry smile, brought his arm around to reveal a pair of moccasins. More delicate than the ones Jacob had lent her, they were beaded and quilled in a beautiful flower pattern across the top of the toe. "Here, Daughter. Try these on."

She unlaced them and slid the supple buckskin over her feet. "Perfect," she breathed, "or as near to perfect as you could get. Wherever did you find them?"

"Well." He rubbed the back of his neck, under the thick but mussed blond tail. It must have been a day, for his hair to look so. His sudden outrush of breath seemed to confirm this. "The trading post had several pairs for sale," he said finally. "We—I—thought them more suitable for the time being than your shoes."

"Thank you so much, Papa." She rose and with an arm about his neck to draw him down, lightly kissed his cheek. "My shoes are still very much chafing."

He smiled into her eyes and nodded. "Now then, are you ready for supper?"

Downstairs, the other women greeted her immediately—Mrs. Murphy with especial warmth, and Mrs. Hughes slightly less so, but surprisingly cordial. Papa muttered his astonishment that the Hughes family was still present. Kate admitted to a goodly share of that herself.

Mr. Bledsoe was nowhere in sight. Not that she was looking for him. Kate sat with her family and applied herself to her food, head down, her cheeks and neck still burning from the morning's events. Afterward, Mama sent her outside with Betsy to take a turn around the yard, insisting that the fresh air would do her good.

Kate stepped out the back door and stopped, craning her neck at the hills rimming the settlement. It seemed they'd turned green—or greener—overnight. Betsy tugged at her elbow. "Let's walk down to the ford. The river is lovely."

"I think I've quite enough of creeks and rivers," Kate said, laughing, but went along willingly enough.

They'd not gone far before Jacob Hughes fell into step on Kate's other side. Before she even had time for a proper greeting, he said, "You probably don't wish to speak with me, but. . .I had to come tell you how sorry I am. I never meant you or your dad any trouble. Didn't even know it was your haversack until—"

"Jacob," she murmured. " 'Tis all right. Truly."

"Nay. 'Tisn't." He kept his head down and kicked at a stone in the path. "If my dad had made good on his threat to leave—I'd not have had a chance to tell you."

It might have made things less complicated had the Hughes family gone on without them, but there was yet safety in numbers. At least that was what Papa said.

She gritted her teeth for a moment. How had her haversack gotten misplaced to start with? Perhaps someone had taken it off of her when they removed her cloak—it seemed the most likely explanation. And the family's name was stitched into the underside of the flap, if one knew where to look. . .perhaps Jacob had missed that.

Regardless. . .at least the haversack was found. . .and her journal not a complete loss. If she ever brought herself to return to writing in it and did not instead simply burn it, as she was strongly tempted to do. . . .

"Kate? Do you forgive me?"

"Of course."

Betsy gave her a sharp look, but made no comment.

There was no other answer. She couldn't even find it in her to be piqued that they were using each other's names so familiarly.

They were at the river now, picking their way down the bank, but away from the road, so to avoid what traffic there was. Kate sighed a little, looking out over the water, her gaze tracing the ripples and shoals. "We crossed here yesterday?"

"Yes," Betsy said.

Kate nodded, trying to remember—but she could not recall that part of the journey. Only that it had been Mr. Bledsoe riding with her on that lovely chestnut mare.

And was it her imagination that he'd called her by her given name, and not—

"Kate?" Jacob's hesitant voice again. "Are you—are you well?"

She opened her mouth, started to reassure him, but what came out was, "I do not know."

Jacob shifted but said nothing this time. With Betsy a few paces off, picking flowers, Kate drew a deep breath of the river air, thick with the smell of mud and downed trees, and tipped her head to scan the hills surrounding them. Above the mountain, the sky flushed a vivid orange-pink and purple, reflected in the surface of the river, broken into ever-moving fragments. Away over on the far side, a pair of whip-poor-wills called.

Another breath, which she let out slowly, and some of the dull pounding in her head began to subside. "I could almost stay here forever," she murmured.

"Pa says the land ain't very good here," Jacob said, but his voice held little of its usual authoritative tone.

"Likely not." Her gaze traced the steep slopes of the pass through Pine Mountain, just across the river. Judging by the direction of the sunset, she was looking south. "Did we come through that already?"

Jacob nodded. "You don't remember much since taking that tumble, do you?"

"Some. Although I couldn't seem to keep from sleeping after it happened. I missed our arrival completely."

He eyed her face, especially the forehead. "You still look a sight."

A laugh forced itself from her. "Thank you for that."

His ears reddened, but she only laughed again. Lifting her skirts, she turned to climb the bank and follow Betsy on her quest for more flowers.

"Where'd you get those moccasins?" Jacob asked, sharply enough to draw her gaze.

He looked—startled. Dismayed, even.

"Papa brought them to me before supper. Why?"

His mouth opened then closed. He shook his head, glanced up, and met her eyes.

What was the matter with folk tonight? First Papa, then Jacob. Kate turned and picked her way over mossy boulders, through a thicket of glossy-leafed rhododendron. Betsy was still within sight, but far enough ahead to send a feather of alarm skimming across her shoulders. "Don't go too far," she called.

Betsy waved a hand and bent to pick what looked like trillium, a splash of deep red against the leaf mold.

"I saw Bledsoe with a pair of those a little while ago," Jacob said, so quietly she almost missed the words.

That did bring her completely around. Under the trees, the growing shadow cast Jacob's face in harder lines than she was used to seeing there.

"Can you think of anywhere else they might have wound up, besides on your feet?" he went on, with not a little belligerence.

"He has sisters," Kate said, her thoughts floundering.

Had Mr. Bledsoe been the one to procure these for her? Is that why Papa seemed so odd as well?

Jacob gave a short laugh and shook his head, then trudged past her. "You hit your noggin harder than I thought."

She peered at her feet. Wiggled her toes inside the butter-soft buckskin. The thought still gripped her throat and made it hard to breathe.

Pale blue eyes looking into hers, as if he were reading all her secrets. . .

It was a foolish thought, that he meant anything but to guide her family to better decisions while navigating the wilderness. Best not to think of his winter-sky gaze—or his chest, pillowing her head while they rode.

She sucked in a hard breath to dispel the sudden warmth infusing her, and hurried on up the riverbank after Jacob and Betsy.

Thomas sat on a ridge overlooking the settlement, falling into shadow under the slow sunset. Ladyslipper stood tethered in the thicket behind him, nibbling at the tender young grass and leaves. The greening forest was almost too densely leafed out for scouting like this, but he'd combed Pine Mountain today and many of the hills surrounding the settlement, and right now he was just plain tired.

And still that gnawing restlessness inside him would not be silent.

This time, it drove him back to the trading post for those moccasins he'd seen the night before, not just to look at them but—actually lay down coin for them. And then carry them to Karl Gruener, so he could be the one to present them to his daughter and not—not himself. It didn't count as a gift if he handed it off to her father, did it?

He leaned back, and for the umpteenth time, scanned the line of the river, curling away to the northwest, and the folded edges of the hills surrounding the hollows where the Wilderness Road unfurled into the heart of Kentucky. Where, Lord willing, they'd be heading again tomorrow.

Just a few more weeks. Then he'd deliver these folk to their intended home—and be on his way. Maybe never agree to ride scout again, for all the trouble this party had been. He'd gladly go back to carrying the post—well, once they decided to start that up again. People would be fussing too much for them not to, had already been fussing, even before that final run.

His gaze strayed back to the settlement. The tiny figures of people and horses moved to and fro, cast in shadow by the setting sun. He should be getting back before darkness caught him out here alone. A chill touched him. All these years and having lived with the Shawnee—of becoming one of them—and the eeriness of the hills never failed to catch him a bit by surprise. For that matter, the Shawnee felt it as well—perhaps even more deeply than he did.

He rose and looking about, brushed off his clothing, and returned to Ladyslipper. 'Twas a sore temptation to simply stay out here this night, wrap himself in a blanket, and fall asleep under the stars. 'Twould be his last night of peace for a while.

CHAPTER 19

Kate was surprised the next morning to find they'd purchased not just another packhorse, but an extra saddle horse as well—for her. A dark bay, which Papa said she or her sisters could name.

"Jack," Johann said.

"Clover," Jemmy chimed in.

Betsy looked thoughtful but just shook her head.

Kate thought of splashes of red on a wooded hillside. "Trillium," she said. She decided against mentioning the similarly fanciful name of their scout's horse and resisted the impulse to look for him.

She'd definitely not show any sign of suspicion that he'd had anything to do with her beautiful new moccasins either.

They traveled the next several days without incident, or at least that Kate could remember. The first few were exhausting, difficult, and she could only be grateful for being on horseback as they traversed the hills, rocks, and creeks, sometimes having to find a way around mud holes or sand pits. At times she could hardly hold herself upright, despite her fascination with the changing landscape.

'Twas three days, through mud flats and canebrakes, and over steep, rocky hillsides, to the settlement of Barboursville, and then another four to Hazel Patch, where there was a great fork in the road. North continued through rough country, up Boone's Trace to Boonesborough. At this point their party would head northwest on what had been known as Logan's Trace, toward Crab Orchard and Danville. Folk they met along the way talked like these were grand places. Anywhere there were four walls and a room with a straw tick seemed grand, she was sure, after the privations of the road.

Somewhere along the way, however, Kate ceased thinking of them as hardships and was simply grateful for each night's stop. The aches of the fall with Clover and Stefan faded a little more each day, but the headaches lingered, with the dizziness sometimes forcing her to lie down along Trillium's neck, tangling her hands in his mane so she'd not fall. She shut her eyes to the concern in Papa's, Mama's, and Dulsey's gazes, murmured the appropriate thanks to Mrs. Murphy's and Mrs. Hughes's trying-to-be-helpful suggestions and sympathies, and prayed for strength.

Please, merciful God, let us reach our new home safely.

Jacob likewise tried to be helpful, but for the most part held his silence or kept his distance.

The gaiety of the early days was definitely gone, and the air of the group more subdued. How much of that was because of what happened to Kate and Stefan? She could not say. She wasn't sure she even properly cared.

Small settlements and way stations came and went, tucked into the rugged countryside like the wildflowers growing from niches in the rocks. Even more curious was the occasional settler—she counted not more than a dozen—who somehow had chosen to not go any farther up the road and stayed to build cabins, carve a living out of the wilderness, rather than go on to better land where they could clear and farm. Mr. Jenkins and sometimes Papa stopped to greet folk if they came out to watch their passing, but most often they'd simply wave to those standing in yards or doorways. 'Twas impossible to linger everywhere they might want to, and some of these folk appeared so rough they seemed as wild creatures of the forest themselves.

Somewhere about the third day, Mr. Bledsoe edged closer and inquired on how the new horse was doing. Half a dozen replies were on the tip of her tongue. "Not as smooth a stepper as your Ladyslipper," she said at last. "But I'm grateful to be riding."

He offered a nod, and the ghost of a smile, and withdrew without another word.

'Twas a trial to watch the girl try to stay in the saddle as the day wore on, most days, but to give her credit, he never heard a word of complaint cross her lips. And the one time Thomas let himself get close enough to ask after her welfare, he couldn't bear staying long enough for a whole conversation.

It was either put distance between them, or haul her over onto Ladyslipper, where he could ensure she'd stay put and get the rest she still so obviously needed after her injury. He didn't think he could find enough words to justify such a thing to her father. Not without finding himself far more obligated than he wished at this point.

Why did he feel such a fool thing anyway? She'd survive this journey, or not. He'd been hired to guide and scout, nothing more. If she survived, then good—spare her family the grief, and some man down the road would be thrilled to have her as wife. And if she didn't—well, the world would lose some of its brightness. Not to mention it would reflect badly on him.

What he couldn't figure was this gnawing ache that surfaced at the thought of her coming to harm again. Or even at the thought of getting to the end of this journey. The growing fact that he couldn't see anything of his own future beyond delivering them to their intended new home. He wasn't superstitious, not the way some were, but—it was right unsettling.

Add to that—and here was where he truly needed to put his thinking—he'd seen some fresher Indian sign, and heard more rumblings at the taverns they passed about the doings of that renegade Chickamauga band to the west of them. Mostly they'd harassed settlers along the Cumberland, but there was word they might be setting their sights to the north as well.

Right where Thomas and his party were headed.

CHAPTER 20

K ate lost track of the days, but by her best reckoning it had been a bit over a week since the accident at Yellow Creek. It seemed one morning, after they'd been through the settlement called Crab Orchard and were well down the road, that she sat up from leaning over Trillium's withers and came awake for the first time in days.

Around her, the forest had turned a deep, lush green. Wildflowers still peeped here and there from the forest floor, but the dogwood were past their peak, with leaf replacing the delicate white petals. The trees around them were full of birdsong. A more exquisite day, Kate could not imagine.

She breathed in deeply. The loamy woods smell was a sharper, richer one than on the other side of the mountains in Virginia. But then there was a whiff of—

Someone shouted from the front, and Kate drew Trillium to a halt, holding the reins tight as the horse snorted and tossed. She couldn't blame the animal. A terrible stench filled her nostrils.

Another shout, then cursing, breathless and furious. One of the women ahead cried out, then started sobbing. Word swept down the line, "Travelers—dead!" And everywhere, adults turned children away, covering their faces, bending over the small ones as if to shield them from the same fate.

The beauty of the day turned into a mockery. Trillium continued to fidget until a strong, capable hand took the horse by the bridle, and Mr. Bledsoe's face, upturned, appeared beside her. "Get down. Lead the horse away a bit, and sit."

He offered his other hand to assist in her dismounting, then nudged her toward a moss-covered boulder, off the path several paces. "Sit," he said again, "and don't move. Put your head to your knees if you feel faint."

She could think of no reason to do anything else, and leading Trillium by the reins, plunked herself down on the rock. Breathe in, breathe out—the wind was at such an angle as to make the air here a bit sweeter. A wave of dizziness swept over her, and she bent, cradling her head in her hands. Trillium nudged her shoulder with his muzzle and blew noisily against her hair.

The tales were common enough of travelers massacred on the road and the ones who came behind left to find them. But all that kept pounding through her with every beat of her heart was the thought that it could have been them. Or the Hughes family, had they gone on ahead that day Papa insisted they wait and let Kate recover a little. Jacob's father and brother were not the best of men, but she wished them no ill—not such as this.

Thank You, merciful God.

Yet why? What profit was it that they had been spared? What good had she accomplished? To what purpose did the Almighty place her and her family on this journey, only to allow her to be struck down by this blasted injury? She was but a hindrance, someone to slow them down. Perhaps better that she had perished. . . .

But no, that was foolish thinking. She pushed upright again and rubbed Trillium's head under the bridle. The horse nodded its head as if in vigorous agreement, eyelids lowering and lips going slack. A chuckle rose in her chest. She should go help Mama with Stefan and Jemmy, but she could find no strength in her limbs to rise.

Mama shortly came to her, however, face still pale under the flush of the walk's exertion, leading the two youngest by the hand. Dulsey and Betsy trailed after, looking similarly shaken. "Those poor people," Mama said, then shook her head, apparently unable to say more.

Stefan climbed up into Kate's lap, and she hugged him close. Circumstances could so easily be different, and every breath was precious.

Thomas tethered Ladyslipper and got to work helping the other men.

It wasn't his first time witnessing the aftermath of such an attack, but no less easy to face it. Three men, one with grey hair, two women who were likewise older, and three small children, a boy and one that might be a girl. The women and young'uns were always the hardest. Even after living with the Shawnee—granted, it had been a relatively short time—Thomas could never quite reconcile the kindness he'd been shown with the brutality of such slaughter.

But he knew in the eyes of the Shawnee and others, these people were little more than invaders, no matter what their intent.

It had been at least a day or two, and the stench was terrific, but he shed hat, hunting shirt, and gear—leaving all lying within handy reach—and joined the other men still lingering at the edges of the scene. The slain party's belongings were still strewn about, ruined rather than taken, although Thomas doubted not that the Indians had plundered first. A pair of hounds also lay dead, but any horses had gone with the attackers.

Gruener looked stricken and pale, but he was the first to move, taking a torn and mostly empty feather tick, and draping it over one of the women lying sprawled, facedown, at the side of the road. Hughes the elder and Murphy stood at the edge of the scene, cursing softly, and Jacob Hughes stared, unmoving, but Jenkins and his team were in motion after Gruener, fetching petticoats or other garments to likewise cover the dead. Thomas found a flowered gown, half scorched in the fire, and wrapped it tenderly around the smallest form, still in skirts and unrecognizable after the scalping as either boy or girl.

The youngest Gruener child. . .this could have been him. Or either of the littlest Hughes young'uns.

The pack team fetched a pair of shovels, chose a site on the downhill side of the road, and commenced to digging. The ground here was at least softer than farther back in the mountains, but it was still slow going. Thomas helped gather up what was left of the ruined goods and set them in a pile off to the side, then once the graves were ready, returned to wrapping the bodies more carefully and helping carry them to their final resting place. By this time, some of the women had edged closer, and when the burial was finished, and they'd gathered rocks enough to cover the loose dirt to keep wolves out, they stood back, wiping their brows, while Jenkins gathered his thoughts.

" 'The Lord is my shepherd,' " the pack master began, and many joined in. " 'I shall not want. He maketh me to lie down in green pastures. . . .' "

Thomas glanced off through the woods, where meadows broke the thick timber here and there, and thought of the land many had worked to clear while settling here. Twenty years and more, and the flow of travelers was thicker than ever. Twenty years, and there was yet the threat of Indians.

" 'Thy rod and thy staff they comfort me. Thou preparest a table before me in the presence of mine enemies. . . .' "

Was it not true, that in the midst of danger, there was still provision?

" 'And I will dwell in the house of the Lord forever.' " Jenkins cleared his throat, as the others fell silent. "May they all find their place in the Lord's house, to sup at His table forever. Amen."

As they turned away, heading back to horses and baggage and their places in line, Thomas looked across and caught the dark gaze of Miss Gruener. Beneath the shadow of her straw hat, her face was etched in pale, sorrowful lines.

It could have been her, bloody and lifeless, those glorious golden locks a trophy on some warrior's belt. His heart twisted at the thought he'd kept turning aside for the past hour and now could not avoid facing. And just as quickly, a deep burn followed. She was too delicate for the frontier—hadn't she already proved that? This journey was by no means over. They'd still so many miles to travel before she was safely to their new home—and even then, unless General Wayne managed to put down the Shawnee once and for all, the threat of Indian attack remained. He should harden himself right now to the probability of her not surviving.

It was no business of his, regardless.

The safety of the entire party was, however, and he'd best keep that in mind. Thomas poked around the edges of the slain folk's campsite. Those who'd taken their lives had vanished into the forest with very little sign—just enough that Thomas knew they'd been there, could guess well enough which direction they'd be headed, and that they did indeed carry away one or more members of the traveling party they'd attacked.

It made his gut burn to know he dared not leave his own to track them down. These were the people he was obligated to. And he knew well enough that most who survived being carried away likely would be treated well enough after.

They were now less than a day from Danville. A few miles down the road from where they'd found the hapless travelers, they made camp. Everyone was tired and a little disheartened.

The men sat around the fire, pipes dangling from between their teeth, discussing the change of the terrain since leaving Hazel Patch and what they hoped to do once they reached Danville. At last, as the fire burned down and the sun sank lower with a matching red-and-orange glow through the trees, talk turned to the folk they'd found slain. Who they were, whether there were more who had been taken captive—and whether the Indians who had done this were still anywhere nearby. Mr. Bledsoe had thoroughly scouted the area, both back at the site of the attack and where they camped, and said he didn't think there was any immediate threat, but they were all nevertheless subdued and watchful.

Kate sat, a shift to be mended in her hands, the stitching half done, but she could only stare off into the distance as the words swirled about her. The prospect of seeing their first large settlement—properly a town, this one—had seemed exciting enough days ago, but now dulled at the thought of those still, wrapped forms so freshly laid in the earth. Feet that would never walk again. Voices that would never again speak. Plans that would never come to fruition. Travel that ended far short of where they intended, if the few papers scattered about were any indication. Papa had gathered and rolled them, then tucked it all into his shirt for later. She'd seen him afterward, at the fire, pulling them out and slowly perusing them, offering bits of what he'd gleaned to the others before putting them away again.

Papa loomed over her suddenly, startling her. "Daughter," he said softly, then hesitated. He reached inside his waistcoat and drew out the very roll she'd been thinking of. "I want you to take these. And—your journal. Begin writing again. Record what you can of these people and their travels, and of our own."

She nearly dropped her sewing, so complete was her surprise. Had she heard him aright? "I—what? Are you sure, Papa?"

He crouched next to her, swallowing heavily, and held the tied roll out to her. "I am. Life is too short, too—fragile—and we leave so little behind. If it is in your heart to say something of our own story, for others to perhaps better understand our lives, then I shall not say you nay."

She tucked her needle into the mending and folded the garment neatly aside, then accepted the bundle from him. "Thank you." Truly, he was giving her free rein to continue her journal? She slid her hands around the roll of papers as if they were a treasure. The thought of pulling out ink and quill and all, however, right there in full view of everyone, felt so odd. "I should. . .finish mending this shift."

Papa chuckled. "Of course."

"And"—she angled a quick look at Mama—"will she approve?"

"I'll speak to your mama." He rose. "Anything you should need, beyond what you brought with us, perhaps we can purchase in Danville."

She hardly knew how to respond. "Thank you—again."

With a nod, he smiled and moved away. She tucked the papers into her haversack, lying on the ground next to her, then sat staring at it for a moment before gathering up the mending and applying herself with a fresh will.

She'd so much to catch up on.

CHAPTER 21

They'd agreed in advance to stay three days in Danville, partly to rest and give folk a chance to attend a real church, and partly to provision up again. Thomas spent most of it in disappointing conversations with officials who were still undecided on whether or not to start up the post again, despite complaints from settlers. He had equally unproductive conversations in the taverns—partly because of the slain Grant party they'd come across that day before their arrival and partly because no one could tell him anything besides the fact that the Shawnee were determined to take up the hatchet up north. He was more than half tempted, once they reached Springfield or Baird's Town, to go find a side to join.

Sometime in the afternoon on that third day, he could no longer avoid his own party and made his way to the ordinary, through a steady and soaking rain, to make sure all was still as planned.

Inside, most of the women sat near the fire, occupied with mending and other tasks, as he expected on the eve of setting out again. The younger girls had the young'uns off in a corner, playing some game, but—he saw none of the men, which was who he was looking for. Thomas hesitated, about to duck out the door again, as the women lifted their heads and greeted him, smiling. On the other side of their group, the face of Miss Gruener appeared, and he saw now she sat at a small table, papers and ink bottle spread before her, a quill in hand. Her cheeks colored, and with the barest smile, she returned her attention to the papers.

Jacob Hughes and Johann Gruener came in from the back, their arms full of sacks, which they left on the floor near the women. Jacob crossed the room toward Thomas. "Mr. Bledsoe! We was taking bets on whether or not you'd show today."

The familiar burn, which he'd been fighting back for days, rose in his chest again. "Why wouldn't I?"

But Jacob only smiled ruefully and shook his head. The other men were filing in, bellying up to the counter, so Thomas left the youth and sidled up as well. He nodded to the offer of a watered ale, although it was his third that afternoon.

"So," Gruener asked softly, "what news?"

Thomas shrugged, sipping. The ale here was no worse than at the other establishments—in fact, it might be a mite better. "The Grant party, as we knew, were headed for north of Harrodsburg. No one knew aught of them, more than what you read in their papers, of course. And"—Thomas shook his head—"no one knew aught of who might have killed them."

"That renegade bunch?" John Hughes piped, leaning from Gruener's other side.

"I think not," Thomas said slowly. "Been thinking on it, and we all agreed it looked like some were taken. Renegades ain't likely to take captives. Unless"—and he sipped again—"unless they intend to sell them somewhere. But that's a lot of trouble to go to if they're just looking to harass settlers."

Gruener stared into his mug. Thomas wondered if he was seeing again those bloodied bodies. It was a hard enough thing for someone used to battle or the frontier—harder still for those who were not.

"Is there anything we can do, beyond what we already are?"

"Nay. Simply keep watching."

"And pray."

Thomas held his tongue at that. He felt the weight of Gruener's gaze.

"Are you not a man of faith then? I reckoned you as such."

He rubbed his thumb around the rim of his mug. "Might have been at one point."

Gruener leaned back a bit to consider him. "What changed?"

What didn't change, more like. "God will do as He wills," he said finally.

"I wondered why we did not see you at church yesterday," the older man said softly.

Another sip. "There are other churches."

Gruener snickered. "I did not figure you for a Baptist either."

Thomas had to laugh at that. The sect had gained quite the reputation for feeling and sentiment, with extravagant displays of affection toward their Creator. Like as not, that had settled little now that many boasted an actual meeting house.

"In all seriousness," the other man went on, "I greatly doubt your journey is yet over or that the Almighty's grace to you has been thwarted as much as you seem to think it has. I will pray that you're able to see it more clearly in days to come."

Thomas gave him a long look. The man's blue gaze held only kindness, and none of the reproach others' eyes often contained. "Your daughter did tell me you had once aspirations to ministry," Thomas said.

Gruener was the one to laugh this time, but ruefully. " 'Tis true. But truth is truth, no matter who speaks it. And God's mercies are new every morning."

"Well," Thomas answered at last. "May His mercy on you and your family continue, at least."

He made to push away from the counter, but Gruener caught him by the shoulder, firmly but kindly. "His mercy is toward you as well," he said, his gaze gone suddenly sober. "Regardless of what has happened."

And how should he answer—

"Hey, Bledsoe," Jenkins said. "Have you heard whether they've found Harrod yet?"

Grateful for the distraction, he took a better grip on his mug and stepped away from Gruener. "Nay. And it's going on two years now."

"What is this?" Gruener asked.

"James Harrod—who founded Harrodsburg. He left on a hunt or some such year before last, never returned. Nobody knows whether Indians got 'im or—" Jenkins shrugged and tossed back a drink.

All the men winced, or shook their heads. Gruener looked grave. "But that was—you say two years past?"

"Aye," Jenkins went on. "But there've been other incidents up and down the road. Like the post rider, murdered and cut to pieces just a year ago." His gaze flicked to Thomas.

"More like a year and a half now," Thomas said. "He was the first post rider, Thomas Ross." He cleared his throat. "I replaced him."

"Aye," Jenkins said. "No part of the road has been exempt from ambush at some time or another. We've been fortunate, at the least."

"God's own mercy," Gruener murmured, flicking Thomas a glance.

He'd not admit that the thought had occurred to him as well.

Supper was served, and Thomas made the decision to stay and eat. While they were all finding tables, Jacob edged up to him and nodded toward the women. "Has she asked you yet about your story?"

The familiarity of the words tugged at him, and without thought, his attention was pulled straight across the room to Kate Gruener. "What?" he asked. "And—who?"

Although he knew. . .

"Kate, of course. Her dad's set her to writing what she can of our journey so far. Haven't you been here at all the last few days? She's hardly left her quill and ink, even to eat. And has taken to asking each of us to sit and tell her about ourselves—our 'story,' as she puts it, so she can write it down." Jacob huffed. "Right queer, 'tis."

Thomas watched her, just now capping her ink and wiping the quill, offering what looked a strained and weary smile in response to a comment from her father. The ink stains on her hands were visible even from this distance as she spread out the pages and blew gently on them.

What was that she'd said to him? *"Each person has their own story. . . ."* He'd been too irked with her in the moment to recall the rest.

"What makes folk who they are." Aye, that was it.

And why had Gruener suddenly given his daughter such a task?

She looked—different, somehow. In the next moment he realized—it was her hair being pinned up, covered with a clean cap. Looking all proper and composed and—sweet and fresh, despite the shadows beneath her eyes and the tightness between her brows.

The last of the bruises from her tumble seemed to have faded. But after spending all day and more writing, she must have a powerful headache.

"Mr. Bledsoe?"

An accompanying nudge at his elbow made him startle, just as Miss Gruener rose and discreetly stretched. Beside him, Jacob sported a sly grin. "She's right purdy, ain't she, when she's all cleaned up?"

Thomas chewed back a snarl. Truth was, she was right pretty even soaked to the skin, with her hair in sodden strings around her face. And somehow, even as he forced himself to turn away completely, he couldn't quite keep his gaze from sliding back toward her, or his thoughts from the memory of her slender weight in his arms.

She'd nearly died, and he was in the right place at the right time to prevent that. Nothing more.

The ache under his breastbone sharpened.

He plunked himself in a chair at a table, not paying too close attention to where or with whom. Jacob somehow landed next to him, and the pack team in the other chairs surrounding, with the Grueners and other families safely at separate tables.

Supper passed uneventfully, and afterward he went back to look in on the horses and make his own last-minute preparations, including a quick jaunt to the mercantile.

This time, at least he'd no need of stray items for vexing females. Or as the case might be, one in particular who now managed to tie his thoughts in knots just by her presence across a room. There could be no other explanation to his lingering urge, through supper, to ask her about her work—which she'd applied herself to, again, the moment she was finished eating. The girl had focus, he'd give her that.

At the mercantile, he stopped to examine a display of rifles. One in particular caught his eye, a double-triggered. Though he'd no need of a new rifle, it was a tempting piece—two shots either at once or in quick succession. Would reloading be faster since he could do both at once as well? And the stock held a beautiful burl, polished to a deep sheen.

He gave the piece a last, longing touch, then swung away. A group of

Indians was just leaving, and the dress and manner of two in particular—

He followed them out quietly, and once they were a short distance away from the building, he called, "Brothers!"

They halted and turned, the two he'd marked as Shawnee looking most interested at his greeting in their tongue.

"Greetings, brothers. Long I have been away from the kindness of your people. How fare the towns of Shannoah?"

They went so still, he was afraid for a long, agonizing moment, that somehow he didn't remember the words aright, or that he'd otherwise spoken amiss, but one of the two with the distinctively cut, drooping earlobes stepped forward and peered closely at him. Thomas took off his hat, and recognition flared in the other man's gaze. "It is you, Eyes-of-Sky! Long have been the years, and your father has given up ever seeing you again."

Memory kindled, as he hoped it would, and they grasped each other's forearms. "Crying Bird. The years have been long indeed."

Quick introductions were made all around, between Thomas and the four companions of the man who had been Thomas's closest friend over that year and more. Then dark eyes searched his face, intent. "What became of you after the white soldiers took you away? We thought you might have found a way to return to us."

For a moment, Thomas's throat closed, and he could not speak. His Shawnee family had missed him so greatly? "I have thought much upon it. My white sisters, however—it was a sore sorrow to them when I was first taken and became Shawnee. They wept many tears because of the death of our parents, and I could not again break their hearts."

Something in Crying Bird's face closed and hardened. "You were given to us. The white soldiers should not have taken all our new family away. Your white family had grieved already. There was no need to open the wound again by your return."

"Nay, but their wounds were healed by my return." Thomas flailed for words. He'd not expected this. "Would my Shawnee father welcome a visit?" he asked softly.

Crying Bird's nostrils flared, and his mouth pressed thin for a moment.

"He would welcome it indeed."

"Then I will come when my present task is finished."

Interest sharpened their gazes again. "What is your present task?" another of the braves asked.

"I will tell you, if you will tell me yours and answer my other question."

They exchanged glances, and the taller Shawnee, Grey Hawk, folded his arms over his chest. "The towns on the Spelewathiipi and Scioto are in great distress. The white father Wayne tells us we must bend to the white man's way and find new homes. You know, since you lived among us, that we do not wish for war, but if the white father brings war to us—"

He stopped, as if he'd spoken too much.

"It is said that the Shawnee and others are ready to take the hatchet to Wayne," Thomas went on, still quietly, "because of all the promises the white fathers have broken."

Nods all around.

"That is very true, my brothers," Thomas said, "and a grave wrong. But as I have said to others, understand that many of the white men, perhaps those whose word has no weight with the white fathers, wish only for what my Shawnee brothers seek, a place to dwell and feed their children. They too wish for peace. Many do not understand the way of the Shawnee, the Cherokee, and others. But there are also many in the Shawnee who have no wish to understand."

The tall Shawnee rolled a shoulder. "Why should we seek to understand when our ways are the ancient ones? Our people have prospered under them for longer than the land has memory."

One of the other men spoke, his voice slow and deep, but thick with scorn. "Perhaps Eyes-of-Sky follows the white Christ, and thinks his way is more ancient and that he has no need of understanding."

Thomas fought to contain his rising anger. "All peoples need understanding of one another," he said at last.

Grey Hawk leaned in. "Then understand this, little brother. The people are weary of being taken from and taken from, without end. It is time we put a stop to it."

Thomas forced himself to not move, not blink. "I hear your words, brother. But answer me this. Are you the ones who left a party of travelers slain, two days ago?"

He watched for small signs that might betray the truth, whatever their words might be, but all five held his gaze steadily for a long, tightly wound minute.

"What matter are a few dead white settlers?" Grey Hawk said at last.

CHAPTER 22

The next day brought a mist-wreathed dawn, much like the morning they'd left Bean's Station, with hints of gold glimmering on the eastern horizon through the trees. Here, strangely enough, Kate loved the fog in all its mysteriousness, and today was warm enough for her to dispense with the cloak and simply keep her shawl to hand.

She'd suggested to Papa that she walk and let someone else have Trillium, but he was firm about her continuing to ride. Though she felt guilty doing so, she enjoyed it.

Danville, she supposed, had been neither more nor less grand than other settlements they'd passed through, except that more of the houses were built or faced in stone. The settlement boasted a courthouse, three taverns, and two mercantiles, and Betsy had been anxious to visit both. Kate let her sister lead her out the first morning, but afterward preferred to settle in, interviewing various members of their party to share specifics about where they'd been and where they were going. And now she simply longed for more of the countryside.

Mr. Jenkins had explained that they'd be following a trace westward from Danville, leaving the Wilderness Road which continued north to Harrodsburg. This one was nearly as good as a wagon road, through gently rolling hills rather than harsh mountains and rocks. They still encountered the occasional canebrake, but instead of laurel and rhododendron, she observed a curious thorny, scrubby tree with knobby green balls called Osage orange. Grasslands broke up the lush, green forest. If their chosen homestead was half as beautiful as this, it would be a wonder indeed. Just as Papa had promised.

Mr. Bledsoe and Ladyslipper trotted past, through the woods a short distance away. The usual flutter went through her middle. She'd not been able to quite shake from her thoughts the way he'd stopped to stare at her the night before, from the other side of the common room. What in heaven's name had Jacob said to him?

He'd been all business this morning, however, and even more abrupt than when the journey had first started if that were possible. Which helped but didn't entirely squelch the lingering wish, after three days of being not only allowed to ask others about their stories, but actually encouraged to record those events as well, to finally hear Thomas Bledsoe's story in full.

And their journey would be done in another week or so, with the hard work of building their homestead taking its place. Little enough time then for her journal, even if Mr. Bledsoe were to stay around. 'Twould be a wonder if he stayed with them past Baird's Town.

Which meant if she wanted the opportunity to speak with him. . . she'd have to make it for herself. And she'd already failed at that once.

Just to contemplate doing so again soured her stomach and slicked the palms of her hands. She dried one, then the other on her skirts. Could she even bring herself to do this, with how unhappy he'd been the last time?

But if she didn't and lost her chance to even try—could she live with that?

There was staying alert, and then there was feeling every nerve stretched to its limit. To his very bones, Thomas could feel something brewing, like the heaviness of the air with thunder rumbling in the distance before a particularly fierce storm.

He was fairly certain that Crying Bird and the others weren't responsible for the slain settlers they'd found a few days ago, despite their dismissive answer to his question. But the exchange with Crying Bird left him with no peace at all, and worse, there was nothing of the conversation he could relate with any helpfulness to Carrington, even if the man weren't busy somewhere up the north fork of the Wilderness Road. At this point, he also didn't know who he could trust of the patrols back at Danville and farther south. He knew their impatience with the situation—that the militia did little more than bury the dead after the fact, rather than fulfill their intended purpose of keeping travelers safer—but whether that impatience would wind up adding to the tensions and only provide the spark in a too-dry heap of tinder, Thomas could not say.

And he was no longer sure whether it was his to even try to say.

His desperation to get these people to their homestead site and hopefully settled rose to the point of pain.

With the weather fairing up, they pushed as hard as they could and made it nearly to Springfield and to a station willing enough to let their party camp close by, even if they'd not enough supper to share for the night. It should have been a comfort, but Thomas's restlessness would not ease.

After supper, he crept away into the woods, found a likely spot from which to watch the camp, and hunkered down to listen. The usual calling of the whip-poor-will and bobwhite faded after full dark into owls' hoots, and even then he kept as still as he could. His patience was rewarded when, an hour and more after sundown, footsteps and murmurs warned him of their approach. And just as he suspected, the figures of five Indians came slipping through the woods.

Keeping his distance, he crept along behind them. A short distance away from the camp, they crouched, just as he had, and waited.

And watched.

Should he go closer and make his presence known? Likely that was a quick way to get tomahawked. Fire a warning shot then hurry away?

He reached down, searched the forest floor with one hand while bracing himself with his rifle stock. There—what folk hereabouts called a hedge apple, those knobby green balls that fell from the Osage orange trees. He hefted it, gave an experimental swing, then tossed it as far as he could to the left.

As he hoped, all five figures startled, whipping about to scan the forest. Thomas held still until all backs were once again turned, then he was ready with another throw. This time, the Indians filed away, toward the right.

Dared he reapproach the camp himself? Thomas waited, slowed his breathing, until the forest had grown quiet again. Though he had to get back and let the others know to keep extra watch, he stayed hidden until reasonably sure the Indians were well and truly gone. With a grip on his rifle, he eased up and crept toward the camp.

A lone figure detached itself from the rear of a tent and headed out into the dark—a figure with skirts. Thomas bit back a growl. Headed for the necessary, or—? He halted, easing back against a tree, and waited once again. But the skirted figure kept up her stealthy trek into the woods, stopping and listening every few steps.

And somehow he could not mistake that particular silhouette, or the way she moved.

He huffed, as silently as he could, and angled toward her, moving only when she moved. Ten paces away, while she tried unsuccessfully to hold her breath and listen, he spoke. "What do you think you're doing, Miss Gruener?"

She yelped and jumped, slapping a hand over her mouth to hold back a scream, he was sure. He could not keep the ferocious grin from his own—but it was no matter for laughter.

"You shouldn't be here," he added.

She lowered the hand, focusing on him in the darkness. "Mr. Bledsoe. What—"

He closed the space between them and put his own hand over her mouth. "Shhh. Not a word. Take yourself back to camp, right this minute. If it's the necessary you need, use the station's. But I mean it when I say you *should not* be out here."

Dark gaze riveted to his, she drew a long, slow breath, but did not move away. And in that moment, something inside him sparked and kindled—

Aware suddenly of her warmth, of the softness of her cheek and lips under his palm, he snatched his hand back.

"Why?" she whispered.

He let himself lean a little closer, but she did not flinch. "Because your life may depend upon it."

Those lips parted, her eyes widening. Gathering starlight, it seemed. A fraction closer, and the tips of their noses would brush, or—

"And what about your life?" she asked.

Her breath fanned his cheek. The words, his soul.

Her nearness, scrambling his thoughts in ways he'd been sure he was long past susceptible to.

He yanked his attention back to the matter at hand. "Your life, and that of others," he said. "Is that so—"

The blow fell from behind. Rough hands seized him, rendering him half insensible before he could react.

CHAPTER 23

One moment there was only Mr. Bledsoe, looming over her in the dark, his presence so strangely irresistible that even after the horrible fright he'd given her and those dire words, she could not find it in her to flee back to camp. Not until she'd spoken as well. And then the way he'd hovered, as if—as if—

And *then* the snatching grasp, a hard embrace, and the suffocating warmth of wool wrapping her about before she was tossed over a shoulder and carried, jostling. No time for outcry or to fight off her assailant.

And Mr. Bledsoe! Was he taken as well? Or worse?

Oh Thomas. . .

Beyond his name, Kate could not think, could hardly breathe. She tried struggling, stiffening her body, and kicking against her captor, but when she'd nearly slid free, a rough voice growled something and tossed her back into place, held more firmly than before. She tried not to cry but could hardly help it for pain seizing her middle or the way her stays dug into her skin.

Gracious God, help!

She was going to perish from lack of air before her captor even got her very far. . . .

A jolt brought her back to herself, and the parting of the blanket around her head. Cool night air rushed over her, filling her lungs with a desperate gasp.

"God—oh God—"

A heavy hand covered her mouth for the second time that night, silencing the equally desperate prayer. A hissed word followed, the tongue unintelligible but its tone commanding. The hand started to move, but a whimper escaped her, and it pressed harder. The word was repeated, also with more force.

Oh—God—please help.

She blinked furiously, trying to resolve the dark shape hovering over her into something she recognized. The smell—it reminded her of men coming in from a long hunt, tangy with the woods and smoke and acrid bear grease.

Indians?

When she did not move, the hand eased away, and she bit her lip to keep from crying out. It was indeed an Indian outlined against a rising moon. And he was not alone. Behind and beside, at least three other figures, or—two, and two others carrying another between them.

Could that be—Mr. Bledsoe? Was he still alive and captive as well?

Her mind almost refused to accept that word—*captive.* All the fears of the frontier wrapped there. The horrors told over a hundred campfires. There'd been rumors too of some being treated well, but one never knew which it would be—and those not cared for didn't return to tell of it. Some of those who did return, changed beyond recognition, in soul and spirit more than body.

Oh God!

They dumped the form they'd been half carrying in an unceremonious heap beside her. A faint groan was the only response. "Mr. Bledsoe?" she whispered, but he did not move. She reached over to touch his shoulder—the hunting frock seemed right—and then the head, now bare of its hat. Her fingers encountered stickiness.

A blow to the head then? Her own throbbed as if in sympathy. "Mr. Bledsoe? Thomas?"

Another groan and she crawled closer to peer at him. "Thomas—are you well?"

She touched his head again, trying to gauge the size of the wound, and he flinched and sucked in a breath. She sat back, still frantic for his well-being but suddenly conscious of their closeness. "Oh thank the Lord they did not kill you."

"Yet," he moaned and tried to sit up, but one of the Indian braves put a foot in the middle of his chest to push him back down. The action was followed by a long string of words she could not understand.

Mr. Bledsoe must have, however, because he lay still, staring at the man—then answered him in what sounded like the Indian's native tongue.

Kate's surprise could not have been more complete.

Another exchange, which turned obviously angry, and the two Indians hauled Thomas to his feet and, despite a struggle, bound his hands behind him. She was also yanked upward, and a cord of some sort tied tight around one wrist, then tugged forward. She stumbled, choking back her own cry as they hurried on through the forest. Gathering her skirts in her free hand, she did her best to run along behind her captor, while glancing occasionally to catch a glimpse of Mr. Bledsoe.

Please, merciful God. . .

The next hours were a nightmarish blur of fleeing through the forest, the burn of the cord around her wrist, the ache of her feet and legs, the chafe of stays that had been hopelessly rearranged when she was tossed over the Indian's shoulder. . .the litany of prayer that seemed to go no further than the canopy of leaves above. . .and a searing fear mingled with stabs of hope that somehow this would all prove to be simply a dream. The moon was much higher in the sky before the Indians halted, and she was shoved toward a thicket, yet not untethered—presumably so she could relieve herself. A growled command accompanied the motion. She shifted from one foot to the other, then, in too much discomfort to hesitate any longer, she turned her back, found a likely spot, and squatted, skirts hiked to shield herself from the men.

She was too weary as well, and too numb to feel proper shame.

Afterward, her captor pointed to another patch of ground and grunted yet another command. Heat flashed through her. Surely he did not intend—but he gave her no choice, pushing her down, and repeating the word. She drew her knees up, hugging them, tucking her skirts tightly around her feet. Her captor glared at her, then turned away, still holding her tether, and took up a conversation with the other men.

Mr. Bledsoe was once again pushed down next to her. "He says to sleep," came his voice, thick with pain and fatigue.

"Sleep? Here?"

"Aye. And you best take advantage of it."

The conversation rose suddenly into what sounded like an argument, then settled after a few sharp exchanges. The men surrounded her and Mr. Bledsoe, each finding his own place on the ground. Kate's captor threw the woolen blanket roughly over her. She seized the edges, watching as they all stretched and made themselves comfortable—except for one, standing guard.

With a ragged breath, Kate straightened the blanket and stretched herself next to the unmoving Mr. Bledsoe. She hesitated, then reached out to brush his sleeve. "Are you," she whispered, haltingly, "are you—well?"

It took him a minute to answer. "Not dead yet, as you already said." Another moment, then, "And you?"

"I'm—unhurt."

A soft snort was his only reply, and in the gathering moonlight, she could see his eyelids close.

Sleep. How was she expected to do that, under such conditions? And not even an arm's length from any of these men.

Morning came with brutal suddenness. Thomas felt rather than heard when, seconds after he came to full, head-throbbing wakefulness, Kate woke beside him with a start and a gasp.

Three of the Indians were on their feet, two just stirring. Kate's skirts rustled as she sat up, but he stayed where he was, arm across his face, for a few more precious moments.

He'd never before experienced the like—at least two or three of the Indians getting the drop on him. The girl had distracted him, plain and simple, and it had nearly cost both of them their scalps. Still might.

And those of the others.

Crying Bird and the others didn't seem much of a mind to negotiate either. Thomas was baffled at how he and Kate—*Miss Gruener*, for heaven's sake, and why could he not keep his thoughts straight?—had been taken, with naught said about why. Their argument last night betrayed a division of purpose, to be sure. And how might Thomas use that to best advantage?

Muffling a groan, he gave up and pushed himself to a sitting position, or as close as he could manage without stopping to breathe hard. Seemed they'd stopped just short of actually tomahawking him.

He peered over at Miss Gruener. She sat huddled, skirts bunched about her knees, cap completely gone and the length of her hair in a twisted coil across her shoulder. Her dark eyes were shadowed, but she seemed well, otherwise.

Before he could say a word, her brows knitted, and she unfolded to kneel beside him. "Is your head the only injury? Will they allow me to tend it?"

You've done quite enough already, he wanted to say, but clenched his teeth against the words. "I'm sure it'll mend with time," he muttered and turned away. He could not afford to be distracted by her again—not right now.

And as he'd already admitted to himself, she was more than comely enough to distract him under any circumstances.

He felt for the edges of the cut. Not bad. About two fingers wide—

"I'm so sorry," she murmured. "I seem to only ever cause you trouble, wherever I am."

The mournful admission tugged at him, but he held on to his ire. As much as she'd suffered through no fault of her own, she brought just as much upon herself. "Aye," he said at last, "you do."

And immediately regretted the words, for the way she withdrew and folded in on herself again.

He rubbed his face, working loose the bits of dried blood that had trickled down the side. If only he could similarly free himself of the sharp words that kept working their way to the surface.

"What do they plan to do with us?" she asked, her voice very small.

The edges of his heart crumbled. She must be terrified, yet here she was, not in the least given to hysterics, as many he'd witnessed in similar circumstances.

He looked around. All five were up now, busy at various tasks, Crying Bird engaged in an argument just out of earshot with a tall one Thomas decided must be Cherokee. "Well," he said, keeping his voice low. "If they don't at some point decide to just kill us, then generally things shouldn't be too bad. I'm not sure what they'll do with me, seeing as how—"

He stopped and gulped a breath. Was he ready to tell her all that?

Was she not going to find out sooner or late anyway?

"You, now," he went on, "you'll have a better chance. They just might want to adopt you."

She stared at him as if he were speaking Shawnee and not English. Which he was likely about to, because here came Crying Bird, stomping toward him, the black eyes glittering and face set in granite. "You both, get up. Time to go."

Thomas eased to his feet and motioned for Miss Gruener to do the same.

CHAPTER 24

They traveled fast nearly the entire day, on foot, their only long stop around noon for water and a few bites of jerky. Kate found herself unreasonably grateful for it. And well it might have served her had she walked most of the way into Kentucky and not ridden, because her body sore protested both the mode and the pace.

By now, Papa and Mama and the others must be frantic at her disappearance. Her eyes burned. At least it was just her gone, and not her brothers and sisters. But with no warning, possibly no sign of her being taken—would that be more of a grief to them than if they'd found her slain? If, as Mr. Bledsoe said, these men decided to keep her captive, with the eventuality of her being adopted, would that give her family hope to know she possibly lived, somewhere?

Adopted. She shivered. *Oh blessed Lord, have mercy.*

And what had Mr. Bledsoe not told her during that too-brief conversation? He'd kept silent the rest of the day, talking only a little with their captors and with much anger.

Perhaps this evening, they'd have opportunity to speak again.

In the meantime, all she wished was to just stop, curl up, and go back to sleep. Yet all the stories she'd ever heard warned that if she did that, the Indians would lose patience with her and take her scalp on the spot.

That would be the easy way out. The coward's way. At one point, as if he guessed the tenor of her thoughts, Mr. Bledsoe turned and looked right into her eyes, as much emotion in his as she'd ever seen, before his captor cuffed him on the head and shoved him back around.

The resounding pang in her own breast brought a fresh burn to her throat and tears she could hardly blink back—though she dared not shed those either.

"I'm not sure what they'll do with me, seeing as how. . ."

What had he been about to say? And where had he gotten his command of their tongue?

She knew. In her heart, she knew. This was not the first time he'd been taken captive.

She'd looked ready to faint.

Be brave, Kate. Just a little longer.

He couldn't say the words aloud but hoped she'd see it in his face.

His own spirits were falling fast. He'd heard enough of the arguments between Crying Bird and the others to know that a couple of them had wanted to just hit the Grueners' traveling party hard and fast, take scalps, and move on. Instead, Crying Bird had somehow persuaded them with his own bitter sense of justice to take Thomas and Kate captive, with the intent to deliver them to the town where Thomas had lived years ago.

The dissension now was over whether Crying Bird and the other Shawnee would take the captives north and let the others go back to taking scalps. Or whether he and Kate would simply wind up dead as well, leaving them all free to continue harassing the settlers.

If only Thomas could get them away. . .

Would Kate be able to endure another flight on so little sleep? He thought not. And he'd not leave her. No matter how vexing he found her at times.

"I only ever cause you trouble."

More of his heart crumbled.

Another echo, this time from weeks ago. *"You know where I go, and the way I know. And Thomas saith unto him, Lord, we do not know the way."*

The frustration rose up in him, dark and bitter. That seemed the story of his entire life.

Lord, I do not know the way here. And I know I likely have no right to ask, but—please, if You are there, show me.

Dusk was falling before they stopped for the night. Once again, after tending to the necessary, Kate was shoved rudely down, the rawhide tether attached to her wrist simply dropped. Mr. Bledsoe, however, was made to kneel, hands still bound behind him, and his captor made the other side fast to a sapling.

Apparently they were more concerned about him getting away than her.

An argument ensued almost immediately among their captors. Mr. Bledsoe cocked his head, listening but almost as if pretending not to care, and after a few moments, Kate could tell he was working his bonds behind his back.

"What are they saying?" she whispered.

He shook his head at first, then with a furtive glance at them, looked at her. "Might as well not hide it from you. We're in a tight spot, and no mistake. They're talking about separating the two of us—taking you to one town, me to another, if they bother to keep me alive—and go back for the traveling party. Likely join up with enough others to mount a strike all up and down the trace."

She sat back, suddenly winded. "Thank you," she managed at last, "for being honest." She watched him struggle for a moment, then, "I could help with that."

He stilled and just looked at her.

"Is there anything you can do?" she murmured.

Another glance away again. "Maybe. But it would mean I leave you."

The Indians' voices rose then fell, and despite not understanding their words, she felt the urgency of the moment well enough. A great calm came over her. "Then leave me you should."

Mr. Bledsoe knelt closer, his face but a pair of handspans away from hers. Very like the night before. In the dying light, his eyes searched hers. "Are you sure?" he asked softly.

She nodded before she had a chance to change her mind.

"I don't do this willingly."

An ache rose in her throat, but she choked it back. "No. If it's our best chance—my family's best chance—then you absolutely should go." Bother, but the tears were threatening again.

"Understand, they're not likely to harm you. Indians don't tend to ravish women captives, whatever the stories you've heard. And you—you're pretty enough—" As a wave of heat washed through her, his voice caught, his gaze flickered, but he swallowed and went on, "Let's just say, you've a good chance of being kept and adopted. That would be—a good thing. They'll treat you reasonably well."

Her breath caught. He thought her pretty? She pushed aside the thought and focused instead on her family. Little Stefan and Jemmy. Betsy and Johann. "Even if they do not, it—it would be worth it for you to be able to go warn them." The tears welled up and overflowed, and dropping her head, she swiped them away with the back of a hand.

"Kate." His voice was suddenly low and rich, in a way that tickled a memory she didn't want to think too hard about, but it was his use of her first name that startled and drew her attention back. His eyes were shimmering. "Listen. Whatever I might have said to you before, whatever trouble you think you've caused, this is a brave thing you've decided."

Was it? There was hardly any other choice available to them.

"Here." Mr. Bledsoe turned, offering his bound hands. "If you can't do anything with the knots, I believe I still have a small knife in my leggings."

Her cheeks burned at the thought of having to search him so familiarly, so she applied herself to his bonds. Her own hands ached so fiercely, making any headway seemed nigh on impossible, but the first layer was just coming loose when he hissed over his shoulder, "They're coming."

She turned, putting a mild look on her face—or her best attempt at one. Two of the Indians stomped away, muttering something, but Thomas leaned over and said, "They're going hunting. We'll see what the others do."

Two of the others, the one he'd told her was named Crying Bird, and one of the tall ones whose hair and dress was different, began debating again. Kate took the moment to reach behind and continue working loose the knot. "Will you go now?"

"As soon as it's full dark. I'll hold the loops between my hands—there, like so—and make them think I'm still bound. Then I'll sneak away."

"Perhaps. . .you should go now, while they're quarrelling."

He nodded slowly.

"But you've not eaten."

"I've endured worse."

The tightness came back to her chest, and she looked away. If this went wrong, he'd likely be killed before her eyes. She wasn't sure she could bear that.

"Kate."

Unthinking, she turned her head. Once again, he was so close, she could see the flecks in his eyes. One hand came up to brush across her cheek, and the touch was startling.

"Sweet, lovely Kate," he murmured, and then he angled his head and kissed her.

A heartbeat's stillness, and her lips parted in surprise. He seized the moment, taking the kiss deeper, and she found herself leaning in, savoring the salty warmth there, her hands coming up to touch his bearded jaw—

He broke away, his breath as ragged as hers. "Be brave, sweet Kate. I will come for you when I can." Then he was gone.

Miraculously, no one noticed.

A sob tore itself free of her chest, and she slumped to her side, curled as much as her stays would allow. Thomas Bledsoe had just kissed her—most thoroughly at that—and then left her, as he had so many times before, but this time to hopefully warn her family.

She'd never felt so exalted, and then bereft, in her life.

CHAPTER 25

He could run for miles on the strength of that one kiss, if not for the agony of having to leave her behind in such uncertain hands.

Please, Lord. . .protect her where I cannot! And let this not be in vain.

He'd not told Kate everything. She'd grasped well enough the overall danger—thank heaven for that—although her sudden decision to sacrifice herself, in effect, was not what he'd expected. He'd not even planned it all out in his own mind completely up to that point, but as soon as she'd suggested he escape and leave her, he knew that was what had to be done.

Yet the doing of it might kill them both, one way or another.

And—Lord, what had he been thinking, to kiss her like that? Except that he was not thinking. It was pure impulse, watching her fight to hold back tears and flailing for something, anything, that would convey the depth of his own feeling in that moment.

And then the way she'd leaned into him—

He was already running all out, jumping over logs, sliding down a creek bank, trying to make as little noise as possible. Knowing speed was the thing now, a fresh energy flowed through his limbs. Dusk had faded into twilight, the gathering stars his only companion, yet he felt no alarm but that he might not reach the Grueners' party in time, or that his warning them might not make a difference.

The fact of having to leave Kate in the hands of five already-furious Shawnee and Cherokee completely aside, of course.

At a run, could he make it back to that station by daylight. He knew well enough where it was located on the trace and could navigate if the stars stayed out.

And once he got there, he'd need to send others up and down the trace to warn them, so he could set out immediately to fetch Kate back. Which would be its own trial, and he'd only the slightest idea how to accomplish. . .

Kate. . .oh Kate, how could I have left you?

※

She'd not the luxury of weeping alone for long. Firm footsteps and an indignant voice dragged her out of her huddle on the forest floor, although at first she could not stem the flow of tears. Another torrent of angry words only pressed another sob from her—as if it were her chest being stepped upon, as Thomas's had been just hours before. Then a huff, and the one Thomas called Crying Bird shoved the other man aside and crouched before her. "Where is Eyes-of-Sky gone?"

He spoke English? Kate gulped and scrubbed a forearm across her eyes. Despite the distraction of his hair and oddly ornamented ears, she made herself focus on the lean features that seemed carved of dark, polished wood. Deep-set eyes glittered at her from above high, full cheekbones and beneath a wide forehead with dark, slashing brows. His lips were set in a hard line.

"Where is Eyes-of-Sky?" he asked again, seeming to lower his voice, whether for her benefit or the others, she could not say.

Kate shook her head a little, but held herself steady under his gaze.

"Are you his woman?" the Shawnee asked.

His woman? That was hardly a question she knew how to answer. Kate swallowed, her thoughts going unbidden to that kiss and the sudden intimacy in his use of her name. Though she could hardly hide the heating of her cheeks, she lifted her head and straightened her shoulders.

Crying Bird huffed again. "If you are his woman, why would he leave you?"

Why indeed. Except that kiss. . .

He shoved to his feet, then stood looking down at her as if she were an insect he should squash or merely flick away. Finally, he pointed to the ground. "Lie down. Sleep. We leave early."

Kate exhaled. For once she was glad to do just that. She curled up and closed her eyes.

Lord, protect Thomas! And my family and the others. Turn these men away from more killing, and let there be peace between their people and ours.

At the least, let there be peace here, tonight.

The way the men had quarreled was frightening enough.

The stars were fading before Thomas came across a trace he reckoned would take him in the right direction. He stopped, breathing deeply against the burn in his side that came and went throughout the night, and glanced at the trees. Moss on the north. Aye, that way. And disregarding the weariness of his body, he set out again.

He'd gotten a plan mostly worked out, but 'twould depend upon who'd be willing to ride up—and back down—the trace to warn the militia. And how willing the rest of the party was to help him stock provisions for his plan.

Fear gripped his throat, slowing his stride. It was a terrible plan. Just terrible. And the worst thing about it: part of him wanted what he was planning to be for real.

He pushed the thought away and kept running.

"One of these days, you're going to meet a girl, get so attached to her that you won't want to be without her."

Truth's words echoed so loudly in his head that it was like she was right there with him, running alongside. He slid to a stop and bent, heaving for breath, hands on his knees.

It was his eyes that burned this time.

He was only feeling this way because he knew all too well what the possibilities were for Kate's future. And how her family would mourn if she weren't returned—how they must already be mourning. And if he could save one family that kind of grief, especially one as solid as the Grueners, then. . .

He coughed, straightened, and kept going, walking at first, then forcing himself into a trot.

Nay, this was Kate who had kissed him back with heartbreaking sweetness. Maybe it was just the desperation of the moment, knowing she was laying down her life to give her family a chance, but—

In his heart, Thomas knew it was more. Or would be, if they also had even half a chance.

He drew a deep breath then pushed himself faster. Could he afford to let himself think that way at this point? There was too much yet to resolve.

And what did he even have to offer a girl? This settler's daughter?

Around the next bend of the trace, a blockhouse came into view, with people and horses milling about the yard, and a camp tucked up in the edge of the woods. Familiar people and horses, a familiar camp. His knees nearly buckled at the sight, and his mouth dried completely.

Someone turned, spied him, and gave a shout. Soon the entire camp was in full cry and surrounding him. He dropped to his knees, and then a cup of water was thrust at him, which he accepted gratefully.

Karl Gruener shoved to the front of the crowd, and likewise kneeling, seized Thomas's shoulder. "Kate," he gasped. "Where is she? What happened?"

Thomas could still not find the breath, or the words. He held up a hand, shaking, and Gruener took the now-empty cup and passed it to someone behind him, who refilled it and handed it back. Thomas downed that as well and swiped his forearm across his mouth before forcing himself to look the man in the face.

This was not the time or the place to dissolve into hysterics himself.

"She—I—we were taken. Indians. Had to come back and warn you, they're planning an attack all up and down the trace—"

Gruener's hands were hard now, shaking him. "Where is she?"

"She—was too weary to run the whole way back. Insisted I leave her."

A tearing wail rose, somewhere back in the crowd. Kate's mama, likely. Her pa's blue eyes narrowed. "You left her? You left my daughter in the hands of—"

The glancing blow felled him, landing well enough before two or three men pulled Gruener away, but Thomas pushed himself back up. The world spun around him.

While Gruener lunged against the other men's hands, Thomas shook his head, trying to sort out the words. "Nay. Listen. She has—a chance, since they'd not yet killed either one of us. And once we get word to the militia, get the warning out, I'm going after her."

Gruener stopped struggling, but still glared, his blue eyes feral, teeth gleaming against his beard.

"I am going after her," Thomas repeated. "I'll not leave her. And I've reason to believe they'll not hurt her." Holding the man's gaze, he dragged another breath deep into his lungs. Everything ached. "I promise, if there's any way to accomplish it, I'll fetch your daughter back. I have—a plan. But I need your help."

The older man gradually relented, then shrugged off the other men's hands. "Come along," he said. "We'll talk."

Amazing how sweet sleep could be on the bare ground, with naught but a blanket for warmth or comfort. Kate woke before dawn to the chorus of the forest birds and, trying to be as still as she could, lay watching the sky lighten.

I give You this day, Lord. Help me—help all of us. Help me be strong. Help Thomas reach my family in time. Lord, look upon all of us and have pity on where we are.

She felt cradled by peace—strange, considering the circumstances.

Around her, the men stirred and rolled to their feet, their conversation a bare murmur against the sounds of the woods. Crying Bird threw her a glare as she sat up. Disgusted to still find her here, perhaps? Kate squelched a smile at the thought.

And in the next moment, a wave of fear swept over her, stealing her breath. There was no guarantee that they'd not take her life at any moment. The thought of her family—or Thomas—never knowing her fate. . .

Be brave, sweet Kate.

She was trying. . .oh, she was trying.

Lord. . .please.

But her prayers seemed exhausted for the moment. And God either held her life, and held it more securely than any man ever could, or He did not. Nothing she could do, or say, would alter that. Only He could sustain her in this.

Karl Gruener sat heavily on a piece of log that served as a chair. He motioned to Thomas to do the same across from him, then dragged both hands through his hair. Mrs. Gruener handed Thomas a bowl of mush, and while he ate, Kate's papa watched him. Jenkins and his team, Murphy, and the Hughes men all trickled closer.

"It started in Danville," Thomas said, once he'd gulped down the first bowl. Mrs. Gruener took it away empty and brought it back full again. "I ran into a Shawnee brave I once knew—and you all know how the Shawnee are full of anger right now. He and his companions questioned me right hard about where we were going, and I didn't give them a straight answer, but their interest didn't set easy with me. So that first night out, I watched, and sure enough, they showed up. I was in the process of making my way back to camp to warn y'all, and Kate—Miss Gruener—came wandering out from camp. I tried to tell her to go back, but—too late. We were both taken."

He went on to explain how the braves had argued and he had overheard their plans, and how he and Kate had decided that him going back was their best chance of everyone surviving—or of the most folk surviving, at least. Gruener dropped his head at that, and Jenkins only gave Thomas a searching look. "I'll go on up the trace, if someone'll ride with me," one of his team said, and the oldest of the Hughes boys said that he'd go as well, back down the trace toward Danville.

Jacob gave Thomas a last baleful glare and said that he'd ride with his brother.

"Tell the militia to send word to Nat Carrington in particular," Thomas said. "Tell them to pass the word down the trace and then up as far as Boonesborough and back down to the gap and beyond, if necessary."

"We'll do that," Jim Hughes said, and turned away to begin preparations.

Most of the men left to do the same, gathering ammunition, going to talk to the ones who owned the station to see whether they could stay or needed to hurry on to the next fort up the trace. Only Jenkins and the Gruener family lingered.

"Were you a captive before?" Jenkins asked softly. There was no accusation in his voice, only curiosity.

Gruener's head came up for Thomas's answer, and he could see the wetness on the man's bearded face. His wife—Kate's mama—knelt beside him, her face still half hidden in her husband's shoulder as she peered at him, also still weeping.

"I was, aye," Thomas said. "With the Shawnee for nigh on two years. I still speak the language fairly well."

Jenkins nodded. "I thought I recollected someone saying you'd been one of those. Too many in that situation."

Thomas gave a quick nod, then turned to Kate's pa and mama. "It's why I can say with some confidence that they'll treat Kate well enough, should they decide to keep her. But it's getting her back that might be tricky. Unless—unless they somehow grant me favor as an adopted member of their people. But even then—" He drew a breath then blew it out. "I need—some provisions. Things the Indians would value."

"You mean to trade for her," Gruener said, slowly.

Thomas winced a little. "Mm. . .bride price, more like."

The camp went absolutely still.

"If I appeal to them on behalf of her family here," Thomas rushed on, " 'twill make no difference. They see the adoption of captives as their rightful due, after a loss of their own family members. Once adopted, that person is no longer considered white but is Shawnee or whatever tribe they're adopted into. But if I go in, asking for her as—as my own—"

He faltered, heart pounding more at the moment than when he and Kate were actually taken.

Jenkins was rubbing the back of his neck, looking half amused, half thoughtful. Gruener's gaze was like to bore a burning hole through Thomas again, and Kate's mama had risen, one hand over her mouth, eyes closed.

Gruener waved a hand, glancing about at his children. "Go. All of you. Find something else to do for a few minutes."

Amongst the protest rising from them all, Dulsey herded and shooed them along, casting her own last reproachful glance back at Thomas.

This was not going well.

"How long will it take?" Gruener said at last.

Thomas spread his hands. "No way of knowing, really. On horse-back—I can make the towns in a few days, but depending upon where they go, it might take me longer to find her. Then a few days back."

"What trust can you put in that Shawnee you knew?" Jenkins asked.

Thomas shrugged. "He was a friend once. But they're hurt and angry that I never returned—even though many of us came back unwillingly."

"How can you say that?" Mrs. Gruener said.

He regarded her calmly for a moment. How to make her understand? "Many were so young when taken, 'tis all they knew. Some had husbands, wives, children by the time they were returned. 'Twas complicated."

Her eyes welled again, and she turned, went to the fire, and poured a mug of coffee and brought it to him. Mouth tight, she examined him critically. "You're wounded?"

The coffee was hot and bracing. "A cut on my scalp, nothing more." He drank again, barely stifling a sigh of delight. "Very fine brew, ma'am."

Her gaze lost none of its severity. "Let me see," she said suddenly, and being too weary to argue, he tipped his head obligingly.

Fingertips probed, more gently than he expected. She huffed. "Let me get salve and something to clean it with."

"So," Gruener said, as his wife hustled away. "We've little choice but to provision you and let you go."

The hardness had returned to his jawline. Big hands rested on his knees. Beside him, Jenkins made no comment.

"Can you think of aught else we could do?"

Gruener swallowed, then slowly shook his head. He glanced up at Jenkins, who lifted a hand in a gesture of helplessness. "I think," the pack master said, "if anyone can get her back, it's Bledsoe." He looked from one to the other, then added, "And seeing as how you folk have more to talk over, which you don't need me for—"

He gave a small wave and strode away.

Mrs. Gruener returned and set to work cleaning the cut. "I washed in the creek during the night," Thomas said, "but I doubt I got all the blood out."

" 'Tisn't bad," she said gruffly.

While she dipped salve onto the cut, Gruener's jaw worked. He sat forward a little. "The question remains, what is your intention toward my daughter?"

That very question had haunted him all night. "To bring her safely home."

It earned him only another swift and bitter glare from Kate's pa. Her mama swung away and set the pot of salve next to her washbasin, then lifted the coffee pot to refill his cup.

Thomas gritted his teeth.

It wasn't that he didn't want to say the words. And the knowledge that he'd already done the very thing he swore to Truth that he wouldn't—to leave a woman behind to cry over him—the certainty of that, with Kate, took his breath away. *God, forgive me. . .for all of this.*

He drew a long breath and let it out slowly. Looked first at Kate's mama and then her pa. Both worn and haggard in their grief. "I love your daughter," he said at last. Something inside him broke open completely at the admission, and he had to swallow hard to keep going. "I—I'm not convinced I'm the man she needs, but if she'd have me, I'd be honored to have her as wife."

Mrs. Gruener's hands went to her mouth again, and Kate's pa—his shoulders heaved, the blue eyes sheened, and he nodded sharply. "She'll have you."

Thomas hesitated. "You know this?"

Gruener shook his head, slowly at first, then more vigorously, and he rubbed his eyes with a thumb and forefinger. "She's been enamored of you for some time now. If you hadn't noticed."

His skin prickled with more than the morning heat, and he fought the urge to squirm. "I—noticed." He sipped at his coffee, then frowned into the cup. "Regardless of what she decides, if it's in my power to do so, I'll bring her back."

CHAPTER 26

Three of the Indians were quarreling again. Kate crept behind a bush to tend her needs, and when she lingered too long, a tug came on the tether on her wrist. Her skin was already chafed bloody, but holding back a wince, she edged closer and stood as quietly as she could, head down, hands folded in her skirts. As their voices rose, harsher and louder, she shut her eyes.

If they slew each other, would she be able to find her way back to Thomas and her family? Would he be able to find her?

Abruptly, the arguing stopped. One sharp word from Crying Bird, who held her tether, then he and the other Shawnee hefted their packs and set off without the others, yanking her along.

"Where," she panted, "are we going?"

"Enough talk," he snarled.

Be brave.

She had to keep repeating the words to herself as the men set a blistering pace, dragging her up hills, across creeks, around canebrakes and mud flats. Sometimes she could hear Thomas's voice clearly saying it, see the pale blue of his eyes, feel his rough, warm palm against her cheek—and others it sounded more like her own voice whimpering, *Help, Lord.*

If Thomas finding her again was dependent upon her staying on her feet, she did not know how she'd accomplish it.

It was nearly noon before Thomas could get away again, mounted this time on Ladyslipper. He tried to calculate how long it might take him to reach the Ohio River and find a place to cross, but with all that had taken place the last few days, he could not. Perhaps not more than three days. Almost certainly less than a week, even if it rained, which meant he might get there before any decisions were made about Kate.

He had Ladyslipper packed with the few things the Grueners were able to spare, with plans to stop off in Harrodsburg and purchase anything else that came to mind. He knew the Shawnee tended to generosity in their own gift-giving, and he wanted to do the same. Especially since at this point, Kate meant more to him than any material goods he might own.

And what if they demanded Ladyslipper as well?

The thought made his breath—and heartbeat—hitch. But this was Kate. He'd do the same for any of his sisters, and—

She was most definitely not his sister. She'd somehow become so much more.

The words he'd spoken to Karl and Jemima Gruener under duress came back to him in a rush. A trembling struck his limbs. Fortunately neither of them had pressed him to explain his comment about not being sure he was the right man for Kate. They'd shown him nothing but kindness since that conversation, insisting he sleep for a few hours, making sure he was fed and provisioned enough for the ride north. Sadness still rimmed their faces, but there was hope in their eyes as well, though faint enough.

He wasn't at all sure he'd be able to find her, much less whether his plan would work or what would happen after. But he had to try. No one else had even the slightest idea where she might be.

"And thine ears shall hear a word behind thee, saying, This is the way, walk ye in it."

Now, where had that come from?

"Whither I go ye know, and the way ye know."

That made no more sense than the first. It was—it was the words of

Jesus, for heaven's sake, not some directive about Kate—

"But Thomas, you do know the way. I have made you for this moment."

And why did it matter? What were they, he and Kate, but two in the midst of countless others who had suffered hardship and loss. Why should God intervene for them?

"And ye shall seek me, and find me, when ye shall search for me with all your heart. . . . I am the Way, the Truth, and the Life. No man cometh unto the Father, but by me."

There was so much he knew or thought he knew after years of sitting in church beside his family. Enduring long sermons, overloud and out-of-tune singing, frowns and disapproving looks when he'd fidget. Staring out the window and wishing he was there, running the hills. In the midst of it all, losses and separations that he'd seen break grown men and women who he'd considered strong.

And the religion of the Shawnee had at times seemed more real, more tangible—but even that had been without a certain hope he'd remembered his childhood elders speaking of—

So many times, Lord God, I've asked where You were, all these years. If You were with me. If You could even see me or had turned away. And now, in this, You mean me to know that You let it all happen so I would seek You?

Because now, here he was. He'd gotten his boyhood wish to run the hills, had spent years doing so, crisscrossing the wilderness until he knew it better than his own mother's face. And to be in the wrong place at the wrong time, where both he and Kate were taken—but yet the right place at the right time, that he had a fair idea of where to start with looking for her.

Provided they hadn't just gotten mad and tomahawked her. The very thought choked him, made it hard to breathe—especially the closer he got, as he'd retraced their trail to where he'd left Kate with Crying Bird and the others.

The sun was lowering in the sky before he reached the spot. His heart hammered in his chest as he slid down from Ladyslipper.

No sign of Kate's body, or even of any struggle. Naught that would point toward her not still being alive somewhere. Just an abandoned campsite, barely visible even to one who knew what to look for, and a trail leading away.

And the memory of her cheek under his palm, and her mouth against his—

For the second time that day, Thomas dropped to his knees, overcome. Deep breaths like gasps or sobs—he could not tell which—tore at his gut.

God—oh God, I did not realize until this moment how desperately I want her to be alive. Need her to be alive. Not just to be able to deliver her safely back to her family, but—Lord, is it wrong to just want her in my arms?

When had he gotten so attached to Miss Katarina Gruener anyway? *Ah Lord. . .*

With a last, shuddering sigh, he got to his feet, cast a final glance about, then swung back into the saddle and set off again. It didn't seem they were trying too hard to hide their trail at least.

❧

Hours later as the sun was slipping below the horizon, he puzzled over it still.

He didn't want to stop for the night, but with no moon until later, he'd lose the faint trail Crying Bird had left. On the other hand, he was bound to lose it sooner or later, once they hit the Ohio River and crossed, because unless he found a ferry, he'd no way to get Ladyslipper across without swimming and thus wetting all his goods. So it might be best to ride through the night, angle toward Lexington and northeast to a ferry, then work his way up the river and inquire about Kate as he went.

Or just head straight for the Shawnee town that had been his home for a while. Because at this point, it was his best guess that Crying Bird would take her back there. Especially after he'd run across sign that the party had split, with three braves going back south, and three—one of those with a smaller print—headed on north.

Crying Bird making sure Thomas would follow and return to the Shawnee?

Kate's presence seemed confirmed by a single red-dyed quill and a couple of beads lying shiny in the dirt. Thomas stooped to pick them up, then closed his hand around them. The embellishment on her moccasins was wearing out already. Not that they weren't good workmanship, but he wasn't sure they'd ever been meant for a long run like this through the wilderness. He'd known that when he'd bought them, had only intended they serve until her feet were healed enough for shoes, impractical though those were, or until they reached the place they intended to settle, where someone might have the time and wherewithal to make a sturdier pair.

Maybe that someone would be him. He tucked the beads and quill into a pouch at his waist, down deep so they wouldn't fall out.

An entire day passed, then another night, and on the next day the country became markedly more flat, like a river bottom. The creeks were trickier to cross, and Crying Bird had to help her more than once. And then, with the growing sound of what she'd come to recognize as a river's flow, they emerged on the bank of a wide expanse—the widest she'd seen since, well, she couldn't remember a river this grand, and she'd thought the Shenandoah wide. It hadn't the Shenandoah's loveliness, surrounded by long, blue mountains, but in sheer majesty—

She could only stand and stare, her jaw slack. It was beautiful.

"Spelewathiipi," Crying Bird said, pointing at the river. Then indicated the bank. "Now wait here."

He and the other brave, Grey Hawk, disappeared into the brush, and after a great rustling, reappeared carrying a canoe and paddles between them.

They slid it into the water, and Crying Bird stepped in then beckoned to Kate, reaching out to steady her. Grey Hawk took his place at the front, and paddles in hand, they pushed off.

Seated between them, skimming across the river, Kate felt suspended in time as well.

"I will come for you."

Thomas's voice, warm as the river breeze. Did he somehow know where she was being taken? He must to make that sort of statement.

Regardless, God Himself knew where she was. He could see her out here in the middle of the wilderness on this wide, lonely river—indeed, was with her, cradled her in His hands as surely as the canoe did, carrying her in the flow of His will the way the river carried her. And how amazing would that be, if she were taken to a place Thomas knew?

Even her fears for her family seemed far away in this moment. Because if God held her here, surely He would care for them there.

Even so, Lord. . .hold us and keep us all safe! And Thomas, wherever he is. . .

As they neared the other bank, they paddled toward the mouth of a smaller river or creek. The canoe glided along, under a canopy of trees, surrounded by birdsong.

For the rest of the day, they paddled up the creek. Occasionally they'd pass other travelers, both on the water and on land, or settlements. Crying Bird and Grey Hawk would wave and call out a greeting. Only once did they stop to rest and eat.

They slept that night on the creek bank, then before light the next morning were out on the canoe again. Finally, about midday, with a spate of discussion that Kate wished she could understand, they angled toward the bank. Grey Hawk leaped out as the canoe scraped mud, then turned to catch the vessel and pull it up onto more solid ground. Crying Bird also hopped out, then reached back a hand to help steady Kate. She took it without hesitation.

Higher up the bank, she stopped and looked around while the two men stowed the canoe. On either side of the creek were hills, but nothing more to be seen other than forest.

Crying Bird and his companion had caught up to her, and without bothering to retrieve her tether, they beckoned and kept walking. So sure of her following, were they? She shook her head and trudged up the hill behind them.

The men conversed and laughed as they went, sometimes glancing back at her and so obviously snickering at her, she wanted to stick her tongue out at them as if they were only small boys. Then she'd remember with a jolt where she was, and where they were headed, and a spasm of something like fear would squirm through her.

As she walked, she wrapped the rawhide thong around her wrist and tucked the end in amongst the strands. At least this way it did not pull at bruised and tender flesh. She put her other hand through the slit in her petticoat and into her pocket. Amazingly, some of the items she'd had there the night she and Thomas were taken were still there—comb, sewing scissors, a small handkerchief. Her steps slowed then she stopped altogether. What if she slipped away into the nearest thicket, then ran back and got the canoe? Paddled away, back down the creek, across the river, and—

A wave of weariness swept over her, stealing her strength and resolve so thoroughly that her knees nearly buckled right there.

So—sleepy—

There was no possible way she had the strength to do all that on her own.

Dear Lord, forgive me for not even wanting to try right now. I know Mama and Papa must be frantic with worry. I just—oh Lord, help me!

As the day wore on, the Indians grew more lighthearted, if possible, while all she could do was trudge behind them. To the best of her reckoning, they were going slightly northwest now.

Would Thomas truly be able to find her? And what might happen to her in the meantime, even if he did? Somehow his assurances that she could hope to be treated well, if they'd not killed her on the spot, seemed to fade to naught. She'd heard tales of captives being made to run the gauntlet—would they make her endure that dread custom?

Almost certainly Thomas would not reach them before she had to find out.

CHAPTER 27

Mug in hand, Thomas stood on the porch outside the tavern in Maysville, on the edge of the bluff overlooking the Ohio River, and eyed the storm clouds rumbling in from the west. His only consolation was that Indians liked rain even less than he and would likely go to ground until it was past.

Lord, keep her safe. I know I've asked that a hundred times at least, but please. . .

Peace like a cool breeze trickled over him, easing the knots in his shoulders, untangling the threads of his thoughts.

You truly are here, aren't You, Lord? I can hardly believe it, but. . .somehow, I do.

Who was it in the Bible that had said words like those? *"Lord, I believe; help thou my unbelief."* It was another thing he'd puzzled over so many times—how one could say they believed but then confess the exact opposite.

In this moment, he understood.

"She must indeed be something, this girl," came a gruff voice, and Thomas turned to find himself joined by Abel Carter, a grizzled character who'd been running the traces of Kentucky and Ohio nearly as long as Dan'l Boone.

"She is, that," he admitted.

A peal of thunder punctuated the words, and the older man laughed. "You say you've asked after her at every station and settlement from here to Harrodsburg, aye?"

"I have." Just on the outside chance Crying Bird or his companion wearied of her and decided to sell her along the way, rather than drag her all the way to the upper Scioto.

"Any word?"

"None."

Carter sucked his pipe for a moment. "I wish you well in finding her. I never knowed you to let a skirt turn your head." He sucked for a moment on the stem, contemplating the storm alongside Thomas. "Life holds little enough comfort, 'specially out here on the frontier. Best take it where it's offered and not think too hard about it."

"This is the way."

He tried not to flinch at the way the inner exhortation echoed the spoken one.

"I plan to," he said quietly, "just as soon as that storm clears."

Kate woke, snug in her nest, amazingly dry after a long night's soaking rain under the tiny bark lodge the two Indian men had constructed as the rain began the afternoon before. For a moment, she could almost believe that she was safe in camp with her family—merely waking from an unsettling dream, with the warmth on either side of her coming from siblings and not these two strangers who seemed to know nothing of propriety, though neither had laid a hand on her in any untoward way.

Except, could she even think of them as strangers after so many days in such close quarters?

Crying Bird's gaze had taken on a little more of a gleam the last day or so when it landed on her. What thought lay behind that?

She opened her eyes and blinked in the gloom at the ceiling of their shelter. What if Thomas never came? What if—what if Crying Bird's intent was—something she'd rather not contemplate?

Be brave.

Her eyes snapped shut. How weary she was of hearing those words.

To her right, Grey Hawk stirred, and with a groan, rolled out of the shelter and to his feet. Crying Bird moved as well, but when his hand touched her hair, she twitched away and scrambled outside, blanket clutched to her chest.

The lean Indian followed, looking ridiculously unmussed—as far as she could tell from the past days of travel—his chin tucked, one dark brow quirked, his dark eyes holding curiosity, a silent challenge, and not a little admiration.

They do not generally ravish women, came Thomas's voice.

Kate fought to steady her breathing. "I am—not afraid of you," she whispered.

Crying Bird's mouth tipped in a smile she might have found handsome under other circumstances. "Are you his woman, or no?"

That question again. . .and a distant memory of that very thorough kiss. She felt her cheeks reddening, and could do naught about it.

The Indian laughed softly. "Since you will not answer me. . .if Eyes-of-Sky does not come for you by your next moon, you will be my woman."

Her heart plummeted.

The storm had erased any hint of a trail, and none had seen Kate and her captors—or leastwise admitted to it.

Thomas knelt beside a stream, filling his canteen. He'd exhausted all the main settlements south of the Ohio, and finally, early this morning, had taken the ferry across the river. From here on remained what truly felt like a leap of faith.

He stoppered the canteen and slung it over his shoulder, then with his rifle in one hand and Ladyslipper's reins in the other, he paused. Scanned the forest around him. Shut his eyes and drew a long, deep breath, savoring the early summer woodland sweetness.

Lord God, I've thrown an awful lot of prayers at You these past days. Been pretty sure I heard You speak in return. I ask now, if I have Your favor at all, give me direction. And protect Kate. Help her be brave.

Let her be alive. . .and waiting for me.

A single, hard breath heaved through him, and he lifted his face and opened his eyes.

Thank You, Lord God.

Resolute, he hung his rifle in its scabbard and swung into the saddle. To the town that was Crying Bird's home—and once, his. He'd find Kate or die trying.

There through the forest was a cluster of dome-shaped huts.

Crying Bird pointed. *"Hotewe,* town," he said, then pointed to the ground. "Sit."

Kate complied without question. She wasn't sure she could have stood.

For the last day, he'd been trying to teach her various words. She tried to repeat them after him, but weariness of mind had overcome her at last, and in disgust, he'd given up, until just now.

Grey Hawk stood, arms folded, while Crying Bird ran toward the town.

She closed her eyes and wrapped her arms about her legs, then laid her cheek against her knees.

Here was where she needed the most strength and where she felt she had none. Too many days of walking. Too many dark nights, tucked between these two men. *Merciful and gracious God, Giver of peace, Maker of the world and of peoples. Forgive my weakness. You promise to be with us to the end of the world, and I know You are here. Help me to face whatever may come next.*

She kept her eyes shut until the sound of Crying Bird's voice called to them. She started to unfold, but Grey Hawk's hand on her shoulder kept her where she was. The two men spoke back and forth for a moment as Crying Bird approached and came to stand in front of her. Behind him, folk were trickling out of the town and forming a double line, a few paces apart.

Her heart nearly failed her completely at the sight.

Crying Bird finally acknowledged her again, a strange excitement lighting his features. "Stand up." When she'd risen, brushing off her petticoat by habit only, he nodded at the gathering townspeople. "I will give you the word to run. You should run as fast as you can, all the way to the end, to the old man standing there. If you slow down, these boys coming will whip you. Do you understand?"

She wanted to heave up whatever was left of her breakfast, then curl into a ball and cry until she had no more tears left, but she nodded. *Lord in heaven, have mercy.*

A wave of dizziness swept over her, but her vision cleared. A pair of young boys, no older than Betsy, came trotting down the hill, switches in hand.

Crying Bird gave a hard nod as well, then moved her to stand in one place, while he positioned the boys a few paces behind. The line of people stood quiet and waiting, dark faces gone still and expectant, only the breeze stirring their glossy raven hair or the brightly colored shirts and the fringing on their leggings.

Kate clutched her petticoats in both hands. She tried not to look at the switches and clubs they held in their hands. Or the fact that the women and children looked as fierce as the men. Fiercer, perhaps, for all that they outnumbered the men.

For a moment, the entire forest seemed to hold its breath, then—

"Run."

She lifted her skirts and was in motion before she could give thought to it. Faster than she thought herself capable—although her feet slipped a little as she reached the edge of the column—and the sound of a switch cutting the air sent a bolt of fear jagging through her, speeding her along, just before a sharp burn touched her shoulder. A whoop rose just behind her, then another, and suddenly a chorus erupted as she dashed past, along with a couple more licks from the switches. She was nearly halfway along before she realized no one even attempted to actually strike her with the heavier weapons, only brandished them and gave those blood-curdling whoops.

Petticoats clutched higher, she ran faster.

And then she was there, at the end. The man standing at the end of the column broke into a smile, and held out his hand for her.

Crying Bird had called him *old*, but he stood straight and strong, his face quiet but set in lines that bespoke pride and the same sort of admiration she'd seen on Crying Bird's face. Silvering hair, cut just below the shoulder, fell from under a turban of blue silk.

It was the kindness in his dark eyes that made her decide to trust and reach for his outstretched hand. He spoke a greeting in a deep, soothing tone, and turning, tugged her along with him. Kate wrapped her free arm around her middle and, gasping for breath, followed.

Behind her, the column broke apart and streamed after.

He led her to a longhouse and inside, where several other older men sat, then pointed to an empty mat nearby. She sank down, dizzy again and still breathing a little hard.

While the rest of the town assembled—she could only surmise by the numbers that it was the entire town, and had they turned out just to look at her?—she glanced around. Many were so beautifully arrayed, she wished she could get a closer look at their ornaments and perhaps even touch them. And the faces—such high, round cheekbones and proud, beautiful looks. Except for those touched by age, every head of hair was glossy black, the women's divided into two braids that fell down their backs or over their shoulders. Most of the men wore theirs cut to the shoulder, loose, or in a scalp lock adorned by feathers, shells, or bits of fur.

The children were miniatures of the adults, although many of the boys wore only breechclouts and moccasins. She noted with an odd detachment that the embellishment on their moccasins was very similar to that on her own.

Crying Bird stood near the front and began to speak. He'd not gotten far before a woman who looked remarkably like him rose and began to argue. Crying Bird argued back, his voice still calm but rising just a bit in a tone Kate could recognize as nothing but defensive. The woman gestured angrily at Kate, spat a long string of words, then turned and stalked out of the longhouse. Brows drawn together, Crying Bird addressed a question to the entire assembly, and the older man who had led her here rose from his place nearby, and spoke, also gesturing at her. Once again, Kate felt her heart calming under his kindly tone.

One of the leaders said something, and the assembly began to trickle out. Several of the women lingered, peering at Kate with curiosity. She rose, still shaky but trying to appear composed.

After another exchange, Crying Bird turned to her. "You will stay with *Payakutha*—Flying Clouds—until it is decided what shall be done with you." His eyes bored into hers for a moment, and she could almost hear the unspoken, *or whether we see if Thomas really comes for you,* but he did not say it. "The women will find clothing for you and take you to bathe. They will show you kindness on behalf of Eyes-of-Sky."

The older man, who Kate took to be Flying Clouds, beckoned to her, and Crying Bird still followed, though the other women scattered. They went a short distance between various bark and skin huts, until they came to one that Flying Clouds ducked inside. Crying Bird waved for her to follow. "*Wegiwa*," he said, and Kate dutifully repeated the word.

Flying Clouds murmured to her encouragingly as she entered. The inside of the wegiwa was snug, and surprisingly neat and clean. He pointed to a low platform and spoke. "That is to be your bed," Crying Bird said in a curiously flat voice.

She blinked and looked around again. Other platforms, for sleeping as well? Her eyes came back to the older man, still smiling and regarding her with a suspicious amount of affection.

"What did you tell him?" she asked. "And does he speak English?"

"He does not speak the white man's tongue." Crying Bird's chin came up. "And I told him that you may or may not be Eyes-of-Sky's woman, that it remains to be seen."

"And—what is he to Eyes-of-Sky?"

"The one he called *Father* while among our people."

Her eyes burned. So her guess was correct. She drew a deep breath, turned to the older man, and gave him what she hoped was a respectful curtsy. "I am honored to meet you. Thomas—Eyes-of-Sky—is a fine man."

With the slightest hesitation, Crying Bird translated her words, and the smile became a grin, then an outright chuckle. The answer was surly, in Crying Bird's translation, but Kate heard only the warmth in the older man's tone. *"I am honored as well. You are very welcome here."*

And Kate would take being Thomas's woman—whatever that meant—for the small miracle that it seemed to provide her here.

The women came for her very shortly after, and while leading her off, they shooed Crying Bird away. If anyone spoke English, they weren't owning up to it. Their chatter and laughter so reminded her of Mama and Dulsey and the girls, however, that she nearly dissolved into tears right there and then.

But she also found it unexpectedly comforting. Despite the strangeness of language and dress. Despite the fearful stories and the difficulty she herself had suffered. And she wished above all that she could understand what the women were saying, that she could hear their stories.

It was a strange thing to be thinking, she was sure. Ought she not be completely terrified?

They led her down to the creek and made motions that she should go into the water. Did they want her to disrobe as well, or. . . A couple of them, laughing, began to remove their own clothing, without hesitation or apparent shame. Face burning, Kate looked around, but there were no men in sight, only the women and a few small children. The two who had undressed stepped down into the creek and beckoned to her.

Kate stood, frozen, but painfully aware of the itchiness of her scalp and her overall grimy condition. Beside her, an older woman plucked at her sleeve, and another unfurled a bundle to show her a calico shirt of a cheerful red, and a length of rough cloth Kate supposed was a skirt.

Disrobe then, yes, and after a bath, clean clothing. Kate caught her breath in a gulp, and fumbled for what pins were left of the front of her gown.

Shed of the half-muddied weight of her gown, she untied her petticoat and likewise let it drop, then stepped out of the heap and undid the string holding her pocket in place. The pocket she set carefully aside, glancing up to see all the women watching her. Several gave encouraging nods and smiles. Then her stays—which were still rumpled and twisted from the past several days, and she could not be sorry for the opportunity to unlace those and toss them on the heap of her soiled clothing.

But clad only in her shift, she stood again for a moment, shivering even in the early summer heat, then unwrapped the thong from her wrist and held up her hand, tugging at the loop still tied there. One woman produced a knife and helpfully cut it.

Another chorus of encouragement, and she bent to untie her moccasins, then scoop her clothing into her arms and turn toward the water—all needed a washing—

"*No, no,*" came the admonishment from one, who wrestled the bundle away from her, none too gently, then gave her a little push toward the water.

"What—" Kate started to protest, but the woman hustled away, and threw everything—gown, petticoat, stays—into the water.

And let the mass float away downstream.

Kate gave a cry of protest. A long explanation—or what apparently passed for one—followed, then the woman came back, took her hand, and led her down to the water's edge. When Kate would have stepped in, she tugged on Kate's shift and made motions for her to remove it.

Lord, what should I do?

But there seemed to be nothing for it, and at least it was only the women. She took another breath, pulled the garment up over her head, and at the woman's insistence, handed it over. It was likewise thrown into the river, along with her other clothes.

Kate could only stand there, arms folded over her naked bosom, hair tumbling down her back, hunching as if she could hide herself from sight. Did they truly just throw her clothing away?

And—was there significance in such a thing?

Forgive me, Father, if I sin in any of this. Perhaps it would be more noble to take the harder path and not accept whatever hospitality they seem to be offering, but—

One of the women in the water took her elbow and tugged her forward. Mud and rocks squished under her feet, and the water closed about her, cool and soothing, as she went deeper. Finally, she sank, letting the water cover her to her chin.

A third woman waded in, stripped to the waist, brandishing a bar of soap. She tipped Kate's head back to wet all her hair, then speaking in a singsong voice, began scrubbing the length of it.

She did not stop with the hair. At that point, Kate shut her thoughts to the humiliation of it all and submitted to being washed by another grown woman.

CHAPTER 28

At twilight, Thomas camped, unwilling to stop but knowing once again that he was no good to her if he arrived without sleep or strength.

Whenever that was. And wherever. He still had no guarantee that he'd find her in that old town, whether anyone who still knew him was there.

Bedding down that night, however, near the bank of a creek whose name he'd forgotten, he lay awake, thinking through a dozen or more possible ways this might happen. Whether those who had taken him in and considered him their own would forgive his not returning before—whether they might not just scalp him on the spot. Whether or not they'd shown Kate kindness, or even kept her alive. Whether Grey Hawk and Crying Bird might have sold her off elsewhere and he just couldn't track down where, yet.

Whether or not, if he found Kate alive and well, they'd even be willing to accept his gifts in exchange for her. He wasn't sure what he'd do if they seemed determined to keep her. Stay and become one of them again, likely.

He'd sure as anything not return to the Grueners without their daughter.

God. . .oh God.

He'd exhausted every angle of prayer. Nothing left but to go forward and simply. . .walk back into that town. See his Shawnee father again and try to explain why he'd never returned. At least speak with them about the state of affairs with General Wayne and his army, so he had something to offer Carrington.

But to think of doing all that and not also having found Kate—

Please, God. Have mercy on us both.

He slept at last, and woke to the sun already above the horizon. Panic seized him, but he forced himself to calm and prepared himself for the day.

Whether or not Kate was there, he reckoned that the Shawnee folk would be more amenable to his appearance if he made the effort to look less white. He rolled and tied the hunting shirt behind his saddle, along with his blanket—which he'd already done the last few days, with summer's rising heat—and after shaving and bathing, combed out the length of his hair and then tied a piece of it back with the feather he took from the brim of his hat. Then, after much thought, he took out the silver ornaments folded carefully together in the bottom of his haversack. One pair he worked through the slits cut some ten years before in the upper part of his earlobes, still amazingly open after all this time, and the bracelets he put on both arms, above the elbows. If he'd stayed with the Shawnee, there would have been more, and had been at one time, but these were the only ones he'd kept.

He'd washed his blue shirt the night before, and while plainer than many he'd seen, it would also have to do. The embroidered edge of his breechclout hung below the shirt hem, as was the native custom, and he hung tomahawk and knives back on his belt.

Then, one more moment to peer up through the sycamore leaves before remounting and riding on.

The morning's tasks had included fetching water from the creek, grinding meal, then shaping corn cakes to be baked in hot ashes. As the day before, several women took it upon themselves to guide her through the tasks, with varying degrees of patience. And just as the day before, Kate took a strange comfort in the familiarity of the domestic work.

Strange did not begin to describe how she felt, though, at odd moments.

Like she'd found herself in another's skin. The clothing she'd been given was on one hand wonderfully loose and comfortable, but she could not regard the simple shirt and wrapped skirt as anything but immodest. Never in her adult life had she appeared in the presence of men in less than proper stays and gown. But in this place, no one seemed to regard it as out of the ordinary.

When the women had led her back to camp three days ago, freshly scrubbed and dressed and her hair combed out and braided in two tails across her shoulders, Crying Bird had inspected her with a critical eye, asked the women a few short questions, then informed her she should now consider herself Shawnee. And that she should take it as an honor, since the arrangements for such a thing usually took many more days, but they had made an exception for her—many exceptions, in fact—on behalf of Eyes-of-Sky.

"And who was Eyes-of-Sky to you?" Kate had asked.

The Indian warrior glowered for a moment before replying. "He was my friend. And he should have been the husband of my sister."

Kate's heart sank. Well, that would explain the ire of the woman who had stormed out of the assembly. . .and her continued glares whenever Kate happened to be within sight. But if these people believed for the most part that she was something to Thomas—

What would happen to her if he actually did come? Or, if he never did? Crying Bird's brooding presence was a near-constant.

And the more days that passed. . .

Kate knew how fleet Ladyslipper was. Surely if Thomas were riding her, he'd have caught their trail by now. Unless. . .

Unless he had fallen ill, or worse.

She could not think of that. She could *not*.

Flying Clouds or Payakutha, as she'd learned to call him, remained very kind. Sometimes he made Crying Bird sit and translate for them, and he'd ask about her family, or Thomas's family, of which she knew painfully little, and it was nowhere near enough to satisfy him.

It also fed Crying Bird's suspicions. "You are his woman," he said, "and yet you know nothing of his white family?"

Kate would not let herself squirm, even as the heat climbed into her cheeks. *Oh.* Of course. She'd been quite the innocent, hadn't she? These people took the word *woman* to mean that she was his wife. But she lifted her chin and met his mocking gaze as steadily as she could. "And if you know him, you'd know how little he likes to speak of himself."

Crying Bird made a scoffing sound.

"Unless," Kate said, "unless he is changed that greatly."

"That may be," the younger warrior said. "But I believe less and less that you are his woman."

She did not blame him, but she'd certainly not say so.

There was only a single kiss, under the queerest of circumstances, to lead her to believe she was aught but a thorn in Thomas Bledsoe's flesh.

On that third day, she'd just laid the corn cakes to bake in the clean ashes of Payakutha's morning fire and was about to sweep the wegiwa when a great stir arose somewhere outside. Crying Bird came striding toward her, and with a hissed word to Payakutha, seized Kate by the arm and jerked her along.

"Unhand me!"

He growled and gave her arm an extra shake. "Be quiet, if you wish to live."

She bit back a yelp and tried to keep up. The older Indian trotted along beside her, a fierce look on his face.

Was that anger, or—excitement? It could be either.

And suddenly her own rising suspicion kindled and flared into a wild hope. Could it be—

Oh please, gracious Father in heaven, let it be Thomas!

They rounded the longhouse, and there, across the open field, leading a horse that gleamed chestnut in the sun despite being loaded down with provisions was a single figure whose stride she recognized.

All the breath went out of her lungs, and she thought her heart would burst. He came! *He came!* And all the oddity she'd ever noted about his appearance made sense now—the leggings, breechclout, and simple shirt—all of which he wore with as much pride and ease as any of the men here—and the length of his hair, which fluttered loose except for a portion along the top and sides.

He scanned the gathering as he walked, quietly alert in that way she knew and loved, and she saw the change in him the moment his eyes found her. His head came up and his gaze widened, an instant before his entire expression shifted to a smile.

A *smile*. For her.

Her knees buckled—or Crying Bird pushed her down, she could not tell which. Thomas's face and bearing went instantly rigid, and as he approached, he called out in that slow, musical tongue she'd been hearing continually the last several days.

Crying Bird answered, and then Flying Clouds, the former with scorn and the latter with a definite note of joy.

She was both here—and alive. *Oh thank You, God! Thank You, thank You.*

And then Crying Bird forced her to kneel, holding her there with a hand to her shoulder, his face full of thunder.

The man couldn't have claimed her already. That went contrary to all Thomas had known of their customs for such things.

"Greetings, my friend and brother! It is good to see you again."

Crying Bird's mouth curled. "What, after you left us so suddenly? I think you are no friend, much less a brother."

"He is both friend and brother," came a deep, strong voice from beside Crying Bird, a little rustier than Thomas remembered, but full of gladness. "You are welcome, my white son! Welcome indeed, *Shkipaki-Nishkiishako*."

The burn that had kindled in his gut both at seeing Kate and at Crying Bird's use of her swept upward to settle in his throat. How many years since a man had called him *son*? He swallowed heavily and forced the words out. "My father. Too long it has been. I am honored by you, and wish to speak further. But I must settle a matter with Crying Bird."

"If it is the matter of this woman, he has told me that she is yours."

Thomas's heart skipped, and just in time he kept from betraying himself with the flicker of his eyelids. They'd surmised this, on their own? He supposed it could have been gathered from how closely he and Kate had stood that night, in the forest outside camp. . .

"She is my woman, aye."

"You hesitate, brother," Crying Bird snarled. "And she also does not answer when asked if she is yours. I think she is not. And because our people have already accepted her, as you can see—"

"Either way, she shall be mine," Thomas said. He must not let his desperation show. "I have brought gifts to offer in exchange for her. And you will see already how she favors me."

He nodded toward her, still kneeling, but her joy undimmed.

Oh Kate. I am hardly worthy of that. . . . But oh, she was lovely dressed as a Shawnee woman. All she lacked were the silver brooches and other ornaments that most others sported.

"I have said she shall be my woman," Crying Bird said, head tilted.

"Release her, and see who she chooses," Thomas said. "Or would you take a woman unwilling?"

"You belong to Red Flower. Or did, once."

And as if summoned, a woman stepped out of the onlookers. Thomas's heart dropped again. Sure enough, it was her. And her appearance was enough to cause Kate to stiffen and look wary.

"Enough." An older warrior, one with hair gone to silver and his face bearing all the gravity of advanced years. "We will speak of this later. The elders will decide the matter."

Thomas considered the man, and what he remembered of his character. "Will the elders allow the girl to show her preference, at least, before we speak?"

The older man looked first at Kate, who swayed now with open longing on her face, then at Thomas. "We will."

With a nod at the elder, Thomas turned back to Kate. Without a word, he held out a hand to her.

A strangled sob broke from her, and throwing herself out of Crying Bird's grasp, she scrambled to her feet, then ran toward him.

So—beautiful—

Then she was in his arms, trembling, shuddering, both hands clutching the back of his shirt.

CHAPTER 29

Shh, shh, I'm here," he murmured into Kate's ear, where only she could catch the words. The silk of her skin, the soft, familiar weight of her against him—he fought to keep from being overcome himself.

A ripple of laughter and talk surrounded him from the townsfolk. They were doubtless enjoying this display.

"You came—truly," she mewled, face pressed to his shoulder.

"Aye. Though I was delayed—aye." Keeping his mouth near her ear, he cradled her closer. So soft, so sweet—"Do you trust me, Kate?"

She went still for a moment, then sagged against him again. "Yes."

"Then I promise I'll tell you everything you want to know. But later." She turned her head to peer up at him as if unsure what he meant, and those deep brown eyes, swimming in tears, nearly undid him. "Everything," he said. "Whatever you wish."

A fierce determination shone despite her weeping. "I know already," she murmured. "That you lived here. And that—you were engaged to another."

Was that what Crying Bird had told her? "Not quite engaged," he said. "But close enough."

Close enough that he should have felt a good measure of guilt standing here, holding her in Red Flower's presence. But somehow all he could do was tuck her in more tightly as she fell to weeping against his shoulder again, and lay his own cheek against her head.

After a few moments, she began to calm, and stirred from his embrace, looking abashed. He swept a thumb across her cheek. "I need to greet Flying Clouds. Will you hold Ladyslipper?"

She nodded mutely and took the reins. Thomas looked up. The townspeople had dispersed for the most part, but Flying Clouds still waited, with Crying Bird beside him, glaring. Thomas made his approach but had not far to go—the older warrior crossed half the ground between them. "My son, I have missed you. Why did you not return before now?"

Thomas could not speak for a moment. "I am—I am sorry. Partly it was because I did not think you would want me to return. And partly because the sorrow of my white sisters was so great when I was first taken. My white father and mother had both died under hard circumstances, and I did not wish to add to their grief again."

The older man's mouth firmed, but he nodded and pulled Thomas into a strong embrace. "You will always be my son. No matter the years or the distance. And I am glad you came back, even if it is only for a time."

"Thank you, my father."

Flying Clouds released him, then addressed Crying Bird, who looked only slightly less angry than before. "Let go of your anger, young one. This son of mine has come back from the dead but will not stay long. Your life is yet yours to live with joy, and to seek good, and mine has been lightened this day by knowing Eyes-of-Sky did not forget us."

Crying Bird made a noise of scorn and stalked away.

The aging warrior then peered at Kate, who stood watching. A smile crinkled his face. "She is both lovely and brave. Where did you find her?"

Thomas held his breath a moment. Here was where the favor of these people might prove most precarious. "I was hired to scout for her family's travel into Kentucky. She has proved far braver than I knew."

"Is she truly your woman?" Flying Clouds asked quietly, his gaze searching.

"It is my purpose that she be so very soon," Thomas said. He could not bring himself to do aught but be perfectly truthful with this man.

Flying Clouds's smile deepened then faded. "Red Flower wishes to cling to old hurt, but she has another man and children. Her husband is away north—but we will speak of this later, yes? Have you eaten? Your woman there had just laid corn cakes on the ashes when you came." He chuckled. "They may be burned by now."

Kate could not believe the corn cakes were still edible. Further still, she could not believe she was sitting here, watching Thomas and the older Indian converse as the father and son that Flying Clouds had avowed them to be.

Thomas had but briefly explained, while they walked to Flying Clouds's wegiwa, that the elders were calling for an assembly later to discuss what was to be done with Kate, whether they would allow her to leave with Thomas. He would not explain what Crying Bird had said. It was too little—always too little, and the old frustration rose to smother the initial gladness over his promise to tell her later.

He'd begged her patience once more as they'd reached the wegiwa, then given nearly his complete attention to Flying Clouds. But as she ground meal to set more cakes in the ashes—what she'd prepared before was only for her and Flying Clouds, after all, not enough to feed Thomas's appetite by far—and then resumed sweeping the floor while waiting for them to bake, Kate caught Thomas's lingering glances even as he remained in deep discussion with the older man. Flying Clouds gave her the occasional encouraging smile as well, but judging by the growing tension in both of them, what they talked about must be of great import.

She finished sweeping, checked the cakes, and found them done. Laying them carefully on the lovely blue-and-white china platter she'd been similarly astonished over, she brought them to the men. Thomas took his with the barest smile and word of thanks, but when she offered some to Flying Clouds, he placed a hand over hers and spoke a lengthy bit that had to be more than thanks. "He says," Thomas translated, without prompting, yet with a strange catch in his voice, "that you have done yourself proud as my woman, and he is glad to have welcomed you as a daughter."

Kate froze. Thomas's eyes were deep and shadowed, and held some emotion she could not in the moment name for the sudden fluttering of her heartbeat. She turned deliberately to Flying Clouds and smiled. "Thank you, sir. You honor me."

Another stream of words, as he beamed and patted her hand. Kate nodded then looked at Thomas, but to her shock, he opened his mouth as if to speak, but did not, his cheeks coloring.

What on earth?

Under Kate's stare, he shook his head, looking even more discomfited, and muttered, "Later."

If the situation were not so precarious, as they sat in the middle of a people she'd been led all her life to believe were the enemy, speaking a tongue she'd had no knowledge of, she'd insist he tell her more right then. But their very life might depend upon how much grace and courtesy they maintained in the moment.

Flying Clouds seemed as dissatisfied as she, however, and leaned forward, speaking with more urgency to Thomas. He spoke quickly back, but defensively, glancing at her and then away. Flying Clouds huffed and sat back.

"Do you wish to lose her to Crying Bird then?" Flying Clouds demanded, after Thomas's hasty explanation that Kate didn't yet know he intended her to be his wife.

The sly old man. Was he trying to make Thomas declare himself on the spot, with the comment Thomas had refused to translate—that she would be a fine woman for him?

"I think I am safe enough from that," he said, but his Shawnee father looked wholly unconvinced.

"She ran to you, yes, but do not leave this to chance. I see Crying Bird's anger and jealousy. If he finds a way to take her from you, any way at all. . . And I see from the way she looks at you that she knows there is more you are not saying. You should talk to her."

Thomas gave his attention to the still-hot corn cake Kate had handed him. His appetite was only slightly lessened by this being the second round, and these were baked to perfection, just as he'd remembered.

Somehow Kate had learned to do this in the few days she'd been here. Did the wonder of this girl never cease? He looked up and found her still watching him, dark eyes puzzled. "These are some of the tastiest corn cakes I've ever had," he mumbled around a mouthful.

A smile flickered, but her brow remained knitted.

He'd asked for her patience, and this was hard for all of them. With a frown of his own, he turned back to Flying Clouds. "You yourself said this matter should wait until the elders speak."

"That was when I thought she knew at least that you want her to be yours. If she does not know—" He shook his head. "You should settle this with her. We can talk of Wayne and the white soldiers later."

Thomas popped the rest of the cake in his mouth and chewing, leaned forward, elbows on his knees. "That is of importance as well."

Flying Clouds nodded gravely and rose. "But you will have time to decide your mind on that. Crying Bird may not wait on the other. And if your girl does not know for sure she is yours, she will be merely one more captive and not one of our people, after all."

The older man took the rest of his lunch and with another smile to Kate, left the wegiwa. Threading her fingers together, Kate watched him go, glanced back at Thomas, then turned and walked across the floor, where she sat down, back to him.

The last of the cake turned dry in Thomas's mouth. Of all the ways he'd imagined this might happen—

He uncorked his canteen for a long drink. Closing it again, he considered Kate's still, slender form, shadowed there on the other side of the wegiwa. *Lord, give me the words, please. She deserves better than this.*

He crossed the floor and circling, knelt where he could watch her face. She didn't look up, and he didn't dare—yet—touch her. "I meant to ask what they call you here."

The smooth line of her throat moved with a swallow. "You should ask them." Her glance skipped toward the doorway. "Likely something like *Chattering Squirrel.*"

A hard-won laugh bubbled upward from his chest, and her mouth twisted in a wry smile. "Not knowing the language presents something of a difficulty there, I imagine," he said.

Her chin tucked again. "Crying Bird translates. Sometimes." Her dark eyes came to his, briefly, before lowering. "Flying Clouds has asked me questions that I cannot answer, and—it makes Crying Bird suspicious."

"Of?"

Her cheeks flushed, and her fingers worried the edge of the serge skirt she wore. "He. . .kept asking me if I was your woman, and. . .I didn't know how to answer. So I didn't." Once more her gaze flashed to his and away. "He said I didn't know enough about your family—your white family, that is—to be your woman. But they were being so kind to me—on your behalf, they said—that I was afraid to say I wasn't."

Her face was a deep crimson now.

"And. . .and I realize now," she stuttered on, to his silence, "what they must have been implying by that question. Of course I should have told them the truth—"

He reached to lay his hand over hers, then eased close enough to trace the edge of her face where the golden strands of her hair framed it. Her breath caught and grew ragged, her eyes widening. Those lips he remembered as so soft, parting. "You can't possibly even like me," she plunged on. "But then—then—you kissed me, there in the forest, and it seemed easy enough to let Crying Bird believe what he wanted to."

Their faces were but a few inches apart. Her dark eyes luminous, not leaving his.

"Katarina Gruener," he murmured. "You've confounded me at every turn. Been—aye, you said it before—more than a bit of trouble now and again." He smiled, hoping she'd hear it as the tease that he meant. "But I'd not change a thing, except—I'd be less unkind."

Her eyelids fluttered. "You were justified. I was a pest. And you were seeing to my family's safety." The lashes lowered. "As I proved that night the Indians took us."

"Kate." He took her chin, made her look at him again. "I told your pa and mama already. Need to tell you now. I. . .I love you, and. . .and want you to be my wife."

She stilled completely, staring back at him with—was that hope?

Disbelief? Fear and love mingled?

This time, he took care to kiss her more gently, just a light touch at one corner of her mouth, then the other. Pulling back a fraction to gauge her response, before—

The door flap of the wegiwa flew open. "The elders are ready," Flying Clouds said.

CHAPTER 30

After pulling her to her feet, Thomas did not let go of her hand as they left the wegiwa and followed Flying Clouds to the longhouse. And it was a good thing, because she was still too stunned to have walked on her own.

Why on earth would Thomas have said those words? Was he trying only to protect her, or—but he'd said he'd already talked to Mama and Papa. Heat swept through her at the thought. And that—likely the entire disaster of her being taken captive made such a thing necessary. But she'd not make him feel obligated to marry her, not even under these circumstances. She'd make sure he knew that once all this was settled and—

But then he'd kissed her. Again. By all appearances looked as though he'd intended to keep doing so. And now with great determination led her through the town as if making sure everyone there saw that she was, indeed, his woman.

Her whole form trembled so badly, she wasn't sure she could go any farther than the longhouse.

Once there, they were ushered inside and shown where to sit—near the front, in nearly the same spot Kate had been put that first day. Thomas placed himself next to her, and a short argument ensued on that arrangement, but at last the other man gave up and let Thomas stay. He leaned toward her. "You didn't have time to answer me, but please, whatever else is said—please consider that you're mine." His eyes were a pale grey in the half-shadowed interior of the longhouse.

Somehow she could not look away, could hardly breathe, and could manage only a nod. With a smile, he brought their clasped hands up to his face and kissed the back of her wrist. "They might be speaking too quickly here in the assembly for me to translate everything they're saying," he said, "but I'll tell you as much as I can, later."

She could not stop the twist of her lips. "Always later."

His eyes gleamed suddenly. "Not always, Lord willing."

And that drove the last of the breath and composure from her, as one of the elders rose and began to speak.

Lord, grant me patience here, and presence of mind!

Because after that last exchange, all he wished was to haul Kate into his arms and kiss her as thoroughly as he had the first time. But their lives might depend upon him paying attention.

"Crying Bird, you told us that first day that you and Grey Hawk found Eyes-of-Sky with this woman, the one calling herself Katarina, and that you believed she was his woman. You have changed your belief of this?"

Crying Bird rose, with a bitter glance at Thomas. "It was my thought to see whether Eyes-of-Sky would come for her, because at the least he owed Flying Clouds the honor of a visit."

"We do not hold those taken away by the white soldiers responsible for what happened to them. Some returned, true, but those who do not? We choose to hold no bitterness over it. Why do you do so, Crying Bird?"

His face hardened. "My sister, Red Flower, cried many tears after he was taken. He had made promises to her. He should not have made similar promises to this white woman without first making it right with Red Flower."

"But many years have passed since then," the elder said. "Red Flower took a husband, has children, and has been pleased to live with them. Does she now wish to throw over her husband in favor of Eyes-of-Sky? Red Flower, what do you say to these things?"

It made Thomas's heart ache a little to see her rise from the middle of the assembly and throw him a look as dark as Crying Bird's. True, he'd been taken and never returned, but he'd loved her once and wished her no ill.

"As my brother says," her voice rose, "I have a husband now. A good man. I do not wish to give him up."

The elder turned back to Crying Bird. "So Eyes-of-Sky came for his woman. And he has spoken with Flying Clouds. What do you want now?"

"I wish to claim the right of the captor over this woman."

"To—keep her as slave then? The women have already sung the song of adoption over her, and taken her in as Eyes-of-Sky's woman. That would be breaking our own customs."

"It is not breaking our customs if she was never his to begin with. He escaped and left her alone with us. Why would he do that?"

The elder stared at him then nodded. "Eyes-of-Sky should speak now."

Thomas rose to his feet. Crying Bird remained standing, with arms folded over his chest.

Lord God, I ask that You help me. Give me continued favor with these people. And give me the words. I plan to be as honest as I know how, here. Please— please honor that. And if You choose that I lose my life over this, then—please do not let Kate suffer.

"I thank this assembly for hearing this matter out. I am Eyes-of-Sky, known among the white people as Thomas Bledsoe, and it is true that I've been too long away from my Shawnee family. I did not mean any hurt to them, and rejoice to see you all again, especially my father Flying Clouds.

"When I met Crying Bird some days ago in the white town of Danville, his companions were bitter men, intending harm to white families only looking for a place to settle and live, who do not wish for war with either the Shawnee or our Cherokee brothers. And when Katarina and I were taken, it is true that I escaped and left her behind, but only with the thought of preserving the lives of her white family. She felt that if it were a choice between her life or theirs, her family's lives were more important. And so I went to warn them that Crying Bird and the others meant to attack and thus stir up more trouble.

"It was a hard decision. I did not willingly leave her. We are so recently a pair—"

Thomas stopped and looked at her, face upturned, that same breathless hope and dozens of questions in her eyes as earlier. He smiled then reached down a hand. With the barest hesitation, she took it, and he tugged her to her feet.

As he surveyed the assembly again—so many familiar faces, but some that were not—he felt Kate lean slightly into his side. He squeezed her hand. Hopefully she took that as encouragement. Red Flower looked away from them both with a sulky expression on her face.

"Red Flower." He drew a deep breath, offered another prayer for the right words. "I am sorry and ask you to forgive me for any hurt I caused. If I could make it up to you, I would, but this is how things happened and maybe—maybe it's because the Great Spirit knows best what we need."

The bitterness did not completely leave her eyes as he spoke, but when he finished, she watched him for a moment, then gave a short nod.

"As far as this woman then—this Katarina, she is mine. I thank you all for giving her honor for my sake, and for caring for her as one of your own. If you give me leave, I'll take her and return to Kentucky, to her white family, but it'd please me to linger a few days."

He blew out a long breath, nodded to the assembly as a whole, and taking a firmer grip on Kate's hand, settled himself to wait. This was not over by any means. The rest was up to the elders—and the Lord.

Thank You for giving me the words.

Quiet settled over the assembly, and the oldest of the elders shifted on his seat. "I see nothing more here to talk about. Eyes-of-Sky and his woman should be free to stay or go, as they please. Crying Bird, you should lay aside your anger and jealousy and seek the sunlight. Red Flower, you also should walk forward from what is past and live with joy with your children and, when he returns, your husband."

A murmur of agreement followed, but Crying Bird surged to his feet. "No! He should not be allowed to simply come back and do whatever he wishes. He should decide which he wants to be, Shawnee or white. He cannot be both. When he was taken away and never returned, he turned his back on his promise to be Shawnee. Do his actions of leading the white settlers into our ancient hunting grounds not bear witness to that? Why, then, do we welcome him back as a long-lost son?"

A grumble rose at Crying Bird's words. The elder rubbed his chin thoughtfully. "What do you think should be done then?"

"I think—" Crying Bird turned the fury of his gaze upon Thomas. "That one should be burned. And then this one he claims is his woman should be given to me."

The elders shifted. Thomas could see their discomfort even through the calm expressions they wore. Kate leaned closer to his side, doubtlessly reading Crying Bird's intent, if nothing else.

"That is not our way," one elder said. "We do not burn those of our own people. And Eyes-of-Sky was, if nothing else, one of ours."

"And the woman was taken in under the word of Flying Clouds. Even if Eyes-of-Sky does not claim her, at this point she is Flying Clouds's daughter, and you should contend with him for marriage, if that is what you wish. But I think the woman herself would not choose you." A chuckle arose from the assembly. "It is a hard place to be in, Crying Bird. I would say as well that you should lay aside your black thoughts."

If anything, Crying Bird's look darkened. "You will be sorry someday when the white man has taken all our land. We gave up the hunting grounds south of the Spelewathiipi, and now they want everything to the north. Eyes-of-Sky is no different from those, helping this woman's family occupy our lands. Keep her as ours, yes, but the land should be cleansed of her family and others like them."

Another rumble, this time more obviously discontented. Many wagged their heads, including most of the elders, but one elder, and several in the assembly, looked troubled and thoughtful at the words.

The elder leading the meeting turned to Thomas. "You and your woman sit down. We will discuss this matter further."

"Perhaps it is best if they leave the assembly altogether," another said. "They may wait at Payakutha's lodge until we have come to a decision."

Thomas nodded, his heart sinking, and whispered for Kate to follow him. A path more or less cleared for them as they went and Flying Clouds followed behind.

They burst out into the waning light of afternoon, and Thomas dragged a long breath into his lungs. "What is it?" Kate asked, soft but insistent, but Flying Clouds stalked past them, beckoning.

Thomas shook his head and led her on, still holding on to her hand.

They ducked inside Flying Clouds's wegiwa, where Flying Clouds turned to face them. "I do not believe they wish to give in to Crying Bird's anger," he said without preamble, "but even if they judge in your favor, it will not dissuade Crying Bird or protect you from him. I am glad you have come, even if only for the sake of this woman here, but the winds have changed for our people and you no longer belong here. Unless you want to take up the tomahawk against your white brothers?"

Thomas released a hard sigh. "I do not."

Flying Clouds gave a decisive nod. "Then you should take your woman and go. Now, while they are yet in council. I will gladly keep the gifts you brought to show your good faith, but for the sake of your life and this one—" He sent Kate an affectionate glance. "Love her well, my son. Be happy and do good to all men wherever you can. This has always been the best of the Shawnee way."

Thomas found he could hardly breathe, and his eyes burned. "Oh my father. You have been my only father these past years."

Flying Clouds gripped the back of Thomas's neck and pulled him toward himself, forehead to forehead. "You are ever my son, Eyes-of-Sky. And if the years prove better for both of us, and you find it in your heart to come back—the door of my lodge remains open to you."

Watching the two men embrace brought tears to Kate's eyes. She'd felt the rising tension of the assembly, then thought whatever Thomas had said had won their case. But when Crying Bird had risen, she'd not been able to shake a sense of apprehension.

Thomas stepped back from Flying Clouds and swiped a sleeve across his eyes. "Gather your things," he said. "We must leave right away."

She glanced at the older man, who looked at them both with so much sorrow in his eyes. "Would it be—permissible—for me to give him a farewell embrace too?"

The barest smile lifted the corner of Thomas's mouth, and he nodded, speaking in the Indian's tongue. The older man chuckled then held his arms out. Kate stepped into his embrace, so strange and yet not. The rumble of his voice beneath her cheek was nearly as comforting as her own father's.

"He calls you *daughter*," Thomas said. "And"—he made a sound that was either a choke or a chuckle as well—"he wished you to know that he thinks you a fine wife for me."

Well, that was something else to add to the long list of things she and Thomas needed to talk about later. She pulled away and looked up into the old warrior's face. "Thank you for all your kindness. I will never forget." And, as Thomas translated, she dropped another curtsy.

Then she scrambled to pack—there was little enough, just what she'd brought in her pockets and the few items Flying Clouds and the women had supplied her with—and then the three of them slipped out of the wegiwa and hurried to where Ladyslipper was tethered with other horses. Thomas and Flying Clouds kept a steady but low conversation, and after he'd gotten Ladyslipper saddled, he turned and gripped the older man's forearm for a long, lingering moment. Flying Clouds took hers as well, patted it with his free hand, then skimmed a hand across her head.

Thomas mounted up then reached down to her. Flying Clouds offered her his clasped hands to step into, and between the two, she swung up behind Thomas, scrunching her skirt so she could straddle more easily. The deerskin leggings, which she'd barely begun getting used to, proved useful in that respect, covering her to midthigh.

"Hold on," Thomas said, and then they were away, faster than she could ever remember going on horseback, the forest blurring on either side of them.

Closing her eyes, Kate clutched his waist with both arms, pressed her cheek between his shoulder blades, and prayed.

CHAPTER 31

They didn't stop until dusk had overtaken them. Kate slid down, almost over Ladyslipper's rump, and stood, legs trembling from the exertion of the ride, while Thomas dismounted and tethered the mare. He'd chosen a spot tucked high on the side of a hill, which provided cover while giving them a decent view of where they'd just ridden from.

Kate brushed her clothing down then tiptoed away to find privacy. Thomas had said hardly a word since they'd left the Indian town, and she honestly did not know what to expect. Likely a return to his formerly taciturn self. Best she reconcile herself to that now.

When she returned, Ladyslipper was unsaddled, and Thomas sat on the ground, back against a massive rock, their scant baggage beside him. He handed her a portion of jerky. "We dare not light a fire. Any distance we put between ourselves and the town is, at best, simply buying a little time."

Kate settled herself on the other side of the baggage and took the jerky. "You expect Crying Bird to pursue?"

Thomas nodded shortly. Between bites he said, "Flying Clouds promised to deal with whatever difficulty came up with the elders, but Crying Bird—" He shook his head, tearing off another bite with his teeth.

Twilight in the forest suddenly seemed more lonely, more menacing. Suppressing a shiver, she glanced around.

"We should be safe enough for now," he added.

Working on her own bite, Kate watched him. He sat cross-legged, head down, one hand upturned and slack on his knee, cradling the chunk of jerky. Dark hair fell in strands over his shoulder, and those silver ornaments in his ears glinted even in the dusk. His voice remained low. "Flying Clouds thinks that Crying Bird might choose instead to give attention to the trouble brewing up at the new fort General Wayne has been busy building all winter." He bit, chewed, glanced up at her, and swallowed. "I have need to angle down through Maysville, maybe to Boonesborough. We might be a little delayed returning to your family, but maybe following the trace will haste our way."

Kate thought through what he was saying—or rather, what he had not said. "You know the wilderness well enough to not have to follow the trace?"

The corner of his mouth lifted briefly. "Aye, but it doesn't serve my needing to find a certain man and speak with him." He seemed to stare a moment at the jerky in his hand. "At least there we can find a tavern or ordinary and have a real meal. And not sleep in the open."

"This is just fine," she murmured.

After all that had taken place the last few days and the obvious sorrow of Thomas's parting with Flying Clouds, how was she to address this unexpected melancholy? Besides minding her own supper, such as it was—and she'd had many a supper of only jerky on the hard journey north with Crying Bird and Grey Hawk, so it was naught to complain about.

"My parents moved from Virginia to the Watauga Valley when I was about five." Thomas spoke suddenly into the growing dark. "I remember little except a long road, steep mountains, and deep forests. We lived under constant threat of the Cherokee and Creek. My father spoke often of avoiding the war between the colonies and England, except that the British stirred the Indians to trouble—and still do." He snorted. "My mama died of a fever just a few years later. Then when I was about twelve, word came from a British officer named Ferguson, threatening to lead the Carolina Tories over the mountains to slaughter us. Neither my pa nor the other men would stand for that, and they went to war against Ferguson."

He nibbled at the jerky, and Kate waited, spellbound. Of all the times she'd asked him to tell her more of his story, and he chose to do so now?

"They made a slaughter of Ferguson and his men, but—Pa didn't come back. In the meantime, my sister took in a Tory who'd run away after the battle and didn't know anymore where to put his loyalties. She thought only to show him charity, but—he helped save our family through a Cherokee attack, and the two of them got married shortly after." A genuine smile curved Thomas's mouth for a moment. "He's a good man, is Micah. And that's partly why I stood up to speak for your pa when I did. Might say I learned to not judge a man for whatever his loyalties had been before."

She offered a smile. "And for that, I thank you. Papa and I both were grateful."

He bobbed a nod. "Anyway, 'twas a couple of years after that when the Cherokee caught me out alone in the hills one day. They were on a raid just for taking captives—they do that sometimes, looking for folk they can adopt as their own to take the place of those who have been lost or died. Hard as that seems to understand, with the stories you hear—and some of those are true too. But I was a lucky one. A Shawnee brave saw me while we were staying in one of the Cherokee towns and bought me. Carried me north, eventually to the town we just left today."

"Flying Clouds?" Kate asked.

Thomas nodded, head still down. He now clutched the jerky in his fist. "I had to run the gauntlet, of course, but they made it easy on me— and I ran fast." He huffed a laugh then looked up at her. "Did you—"

"I had to run it too. But I also realized at one point that no one was really trying to hit me, though a few switches landed across my arms and shoulders."

He winced, but nodded. "When it's a captive they intend to burn or keep as a slave, the gauntlet is right terrible—but for those they've decided to keep, they don't do much, just scare them, mostly."

Kate sat a little straighter. "Did they—bathe you?"

Thomas laughed softly. "Aye, that was the other thing. Flying Clouds's wife must have spent half an hour scrubbing me down. Reckon I've never been so clean, before or since. Then gave me new clothing after." He sobered again. "They explain later it's to wash away all the white blood, make you completely Indian. I didn't know at first though. But they took such care of me, and with all the hurt of losing both my mama and pa—" He took a deep breath, released it. "I reckoned myself as good as dead to my sisters at that point. Gave myself up to being Shawnee."

"Right down to planning to marry a Shawnee girl?"

He nodded slowly. "I cried near as hard as she did, having to leave her. Cried again before having to face my sisters again. And after enduring all their tears on my return, I decided there and then I'd never leave another woman to cry over me." His gaze held Kate's in the gathering dusk. "If I could help it."

Her throat closed at the memory of their last parting. "You couldn't help it."

"I could have," he said softly. "And it may not have been enough to save your family."

"That's in the Lord's hands alone now." Despite the jagged fear that tore her all too often at the thought that they might not have survived.

He just looked at her for a moment. "True enough. And I suppose, so are we. In the Lord's hands, that is."

Kate felt her jaw loosening, and joy leaping up in her heart. Thomas, speaking such words of faith?

After another deep breath, he went back to examining his jerky as if it were something vitally interesting. "So because of all that—despite what Crying Bird said about me having to choose— you must understand I'm not sure I'll ever completely fit the white man's world. Nor completely with the Shawnee either, but there's still a good bit of that in me." His gaze flickered to her and away. "I came back to my sisters to find it wasn't home anymore, not really. No matter how glad they were to see me again. I've spent the last ten years wondering if I should just return to the Shawnee, but—" His voice broke. He cleared his throat and went on, quickly. "You saw how today went."

He'd promised to tell her. Told himself once they had a chance, he'd at least begin the telling of it all. But now, with her quietly watching him as she worked on her piece of jerky, it seemed too much. Too intimate.

And maybe it was just the shock of everything—he recalled it had been weeks before he felt anything approaching being used to life with the Shawnee. Kate's manner toward him now seemed cool and detached. *She'll have you,* her father said, but how could he be sure that her flinging herself into his arms wasn't simple relief at his arrival and not a sign of some deeper attachment?

He looked over at her, clad in the loose, simple shirt and wrapped skirt that all Shawnee women wore, her golden hair in two braids over her shoulders. She was prettier than anything he'd ever seen, dressed out as an Indian woman. And on her feet—she still had those moccasins he'd given her. "Were you treated well?" he asked.

She glanced up, her eyes wide and dark in the moonlit shadows under the trees, then nodded. "All things considered, yes. I did not expect that—their kindness. Even after what you'd said." She nibbled the jerky. "Even Crying Bird and Grey Hawk weren't as harsh as I thought they'd be, especially after we separated from the others." She frowned. "There's so much I wanted to tell you. Ask you about. And now. . ."

So he wasn't the only one. "We should sleep for a few hours at least," he said at last. "We'll make Maysville by nightfall tomorrow." They could talk more on the way.

For a moment she did not move. "So what did the council say? And what all did Flying Clouds say to you, at the last?"

That also seemed almost too fresh to speak aloud. He reached for his blanket, and she did the same, wrapping hers about herself. "Lie down, and I'll start back with when I left you." He waited until she settled, then stretched out beside her about an arm's length away, facing her.

This girl, who just hours ago he'd been talking about making his wife. Who had clung to him during the ride south. Who even now gazed at him with expectation. And now he was nearly afraid to touch her.

"I made it back to where we'd made camp just after sunrise," he began.

Those dark eyes widened. "You ran the whole way, all night?"

"Aye. And your papa was none too pleased to see me show up without you." He offered a rueful smile. "But when I made him see that I was their best chance of getting you back—"

Something in her expression shifted. "And so you came up with the idea of asking to marry me."

The idea of—?

Thomas levered himself up on an elbow. "It wasn't like that."

She shut her eyes. "You don't have to keep pretending now. I understand when we were back in the Indian town you thought to protect me, but—" With a huff, she rolled away from him and to her feet, nearly in the same motion.

He scrambled to follow her. She ran maybe a dozen steps away then stopped, half hidden in shadow, her back to him and head tucked, still swathed in her blanket. He came to a halt as well, close enough to touch but not doing so.

"Kate," he breathed. "Your father liked to have killed me until I explained what had happened—how hard it was to make that decision to leave you. And even then—dear Lord, dying would have been easier, if I knew it might have spared you. But I had a good idea where Crying Bird intended to take you. And I'm the only one of all of us who knew how to get there."

She swayed a little but did not turn. "So was Crying Bird's intent all along just to take revenge on you?"

"I think he did feel real concern for Flying Clouds, and if he thought that was the best way to make me come. . . ?"

A moment's hesitation, then she nodded, once. "And come you did."

"Aye. As I promised you." He so wanted to just pull her into his arms—

"And why. . .why did you kiss me, Thomas?"

"Because. . ." He edged closer. "I wanted to."

She threw him a startled glance over her shoulder, then swung around, stepping back—but not as far as she could have. "You. . .*wanted* to."

"Aye."

Those soft lips parted and trembled. "But why? When have I ever been anything but a pest to you?"

"When—"

He needed to dig deep for the words to explain. *She* needed the words. *Ah, Lord, help me. . . !*

Another huff. "See? You can't think of a time."

And she would have turned away again, but he caught her shoulder and gave in to that crazy urge to gather her against him. She struggled, then stopped, half sobbing against his chest as he pressed his face to her hair and inhaled the smell of her—of woods, of horse, of whatever soap they'd used on her. "That day I pulled you from the river," he said, "and I told you to stay with us. Do you remember that?"

Another sob caught in her throat. "I—no. Perhaps."

"I didn't know it then. . .but as the days passed and I carried you with me on Ladyslipper, held you. . .I was growing attached to you. Falling. . . aye, falling in love with you. But I fought it, wouldn't let myself think about it, because—well, I already told you why. And I had to watch Jacob Hughes follow you around like a puppy, like he had a chance at catching your eye—"

She stirred in his arms, tipped back her head to look at him, lifted one hand to touch the edge of his jaw. "Which he never did. There was always you—"

Her face dipped again.

"You kept coming to me," he whispered. "And I kept turning you away, although I wanted—deep down I wanted—" His own breath caught. "So when we decided that I'd try to escape, and I didn't even know whether I'd see you alive again—I wanted that kiss. I wanted you to know, at least a little, how I felt. To—give you a reason to hold on, to wait for me to come."

Her face lifted again, her dark eyes luminous in the light of the rising moon. "It did give me reason. Sometimes remembering it was all that kept me going. The hope that—that you would come, and then—"

She hesitated, and in that moment when words seemed to fail her, he reclaimed that sweet, soft mouth with his own.

She sank against him, arms sliding up around his neck, answering his kiss in that way he'd hoped he hadn't imagined the first time. Heart beating against his, clinging as she had earlier that day, embracing him—even after hearing of his past with the Shawnee.

He broke the kiss but kept her tightly in his arms. "Oh Kate. . .I was so afraid I'd lose you before you were even properly mine."

Trembling, she nodded. "I hardly dared believe you meant what I thought you did—"

Ladyslipper's whinny broke the evening stillness.

CHAPTER 32

Kate knew, without being told, that it was Crying Bird. Thomas released her and signaled for quiet, and she'd hardly time to gather the blanket back around her before he took her hand and crept farther under the trees and back to their camp.

Another horse's whinny answered Ladyslipper, down the hill and back up the trail where they'd ridden a bit ago. Thomas froze, head cocked, then pointed at the ground and a palm-down motion. Kate sank to her knees as he retrieved his rifle and slung powder horn and shot bag around his body. Crouching, he offered her a pistol. "You know how to use this, aye?" he whispered.

Her heart was racing now for reasons wholly unrelated to earlier, but she nodded. "Papa taught me."

"And this." He reached inside the top of his leggings and pulled out a small knife. "Do you think you could stick a man, if you had to?"

She caught her breath. That indeed did seem a harder thing, but considering all they'd already endured—

"Crying Bird isn't likely to spare either of us this time." Though his voice was a low murmur, it held all the weight of a boulder. "He might, you, but you saw how furious he was. If it's this or your life, don't hesitate. Do you hear me?"

"I—would do my best." She took the knife from him.

"My brave girl." He pressed a quick kiss to her forehead, then stepped back to tuck the matching pistol into his belt and stood listening again.

The sounds of approaching hooves had stopped.

He held out a hand to her and led her higher on the hill, just above Ladyslipper. Kate tried to be as quiet as he, but was sure she failed miserably. They reached the summit without mishap though, and he stopped yet again to listen. "Wait here," he breathed, pointing to another cluster of rocks.

Then he disappeared through the moonlit shadows.

Thomas ran lightly from rock to rock, taking advantage of the shadows. He had no strategy here, only blind instinct. Crying Bird would do everything he could to take them by surprise. His weapon of choice from boyhood was the tomahawk, but so many years had passed, that might have changed, and all the Indians involved in their capture had rifles. Regardless, Thomas would not knowingly expose himself even in moonlight.

He could count on Ladyslipper's greeting giving away at least an approximate location. The only question was from what direction Crying Bird would take an approach. By setting Kate to wait uphill from the horse, he hoped to keep her out of the conflict, but he couldn't expect that the Shawnee brave would simply walk into their camp either. Maybe if he couldn't intercept Crying Bird, he could come up from behind.

It was like old games of hide-and-seek, out here in the moonlit forest—but deadly. Crying Bird wouldn't take him prisoner this time. It was unlikely enough that he'd show mercy to Kate. Yet his very gut congealed at the thought of having to strike the first blow with one who had been as a brother.

Lord. . .oh Lord, is there any way around this? I know You can preserve us here, under the shadow of death—but will You? There are others who have cried out to You, but You didn't see fit to save them. Will You do this for us?

Once again a longing seared through him, not just to hold Kate in his arms and steal kisses under the wings of danger, but to be able to live out a long and even possibly unremarkable life, with her at his side.

Please, merciful God, let it be!

A rustle of leaves came from just below him, which might have been a breath of wind, except. . .no wind stirred the air tonight. Not at this elevation.

Kate crouched on one knee, pistol in hand but resting across her leg. From her perch, she could trace Thomas's descent, but barely, and she thought there might be movement over in the direction of the trail, but she couldn't be sure. There was no way to warn Thomas.

She closed her eyes against the agony of waiting. *Father in heaven, we have no hope but You. Save us—we are Yours!*

Whickering again, Ladyslipper swung on her tether, ears pricked toward something off to the left. Not where Thomas had gone. Kate swallowed against the pounding in her throat and took a better grip on the pistol. Only one shot, and she'd nothing for reloading.

She touched the knife, sheathed and tucked into her leggings as Thomas had carried it.

Would Crying Bird try to steal Ladyslipper, or would he try to ferret them out first?

For a few moments, there was only stillness. Ladyslipper tossed her head and snorted then peered into the brush again.

'Twas definitely not Thomas that the mare saw, or smelled. A lean figure eased its way under the trees toward the horse. Kate's fingers flexed on the pistol grip. Should she try to stop him, or would Thomas—

With a bloodcurdling screech, another figure launched from the side, colliding with the first, and the two men went rolling, scrabbling at each other. Kate sucked a breath to keep from releasing her own scream. Should she stay or—

The tug of her heart was stronger than her fear, and holding tightly to the pistol, she scrambled from her perch and down the hill, as a grunt, growls, and an angry cry punctuated the night air.

Crying Bird fought like a wildcat, as Thomas knew he would. But to his dim surprise, he found himself a match for the Shawnee brave and, after a frantic scuffle, had Crying Bird pinned to the ground.

At least for the moment. Both of them were breathing hard, but the fury in Crying Bird's gaze made it clear he'd not be down for long.

Thomas dragged in a deep breath. "Stop this madness. For the sake of the bond that was once between us. For love of our people."

"There is no longer any bond between us," Crying Bird snarled.

"You were as a brother to me!" he roared back.

"You are a traitor and no brother to me! I will cut out your heart and take your woman."

"And add to the bloodshed between our peoples? Do not do this—do *not* make me take your life!"

"I am not making you do anything—but die!"

Crying Bird bucked against his weight and got an arm free, landing a blow to the side of Thomas's head. The forest blurred around him, and Crying Bird scrambled out of his grasp, then came up in a crouch, blade flashing in one hand.

Pulling his own knife, Thomas dodged the blow he could feel coming even as Crying Bird lunged. But not fast enough. Fire lit across his arm and gut.

Crying Bird stepped back, teeth bared, eyes gleaming. "See? You are too weak to fight. You—"

There was a flash behind Crying Bird, a puff of smoke, and the crack of a pistol shot. The Shawnee brave staggered forward.

Thomas caught him, wrenching the knife from his grip and dropping his own. His eyes wide now, Crying Bird's mouth worked.

"I am sorry, oh my brother," Thomas whispered.

A dark froth appeared on Crying Bird's lips, and he collapsed. Thomas did his best to ease him to the ground, but—

Oh God—nay—I did not want it to be like this!

And suddenly Kate was there, kneeling beside them. "Is he—"

Thomas shook his head. "Dead. And you—that was you?"

He hauled her into his arms, and for a long time they could do naught but cling to each other.

"I've nothing to bury him with," Thomas murmured at last. "We'll have to cover him with rocks."

Kate stirred and looked up at him. He fairly sagged with exhaustion. "We could wait until morning. . ."

"Nay. Tonight or naught."

He trudged away to scout a place, and for lack of anything else to do, Kate retrieved the two hunting knives, still lying near the Shawnee warrior's body, and then the pistol, where she'd dropped it, several paces away. The piece was still warm from firing.

Had she really done that—to shoot so true that she took a man's life? She'd been a fair enough shot when Papa had taken her out to teach, but—

The enormity of it swept over her, and she dropped to her knees. *God. . .oh Lord.*

"Kate?"

Thomas knelt beside her, his hands gentle on her shoulders.

"I—" She could hardly breathe. "I shot a man—"

He pulled her into his arms again. "And you were very brave about it too."

"I could not bear that he hurt you." She pulled away a little and looked at the stains on his shirt. "Wait. You're hurt. How bad is it?"

Thomas winced a little. "Not as bad as it could be. As it should have been, to be honest." He kissed her softly. "Come. Let's finish here and be gone."

CHAPTER 33

They set themselves to the somber task of providing a decent burial for Crying Bird. Thomas found a rocky outcropping not far from their campsite, and after he'd found the Shawnee's horse, wrapped the body in the blanket tied on his mount. It took close to an hour, by Kate's reckoning, to find enough rocks to close the body in properly. Both she and Thomas were near to dropping from weariness by the time they finished.

Neither of them wanted to linger, however. And Kate did not relish riding either horse alone in the dark, so when Thomas suggested they tie all their baggage on Crying Bird's horse and both ride Ladyslipper, she readily agreed.

Thomas led both horses down the hill until they reached the trail, then helped Kate mount first before swinging up behind her. "This way," he murmured, "if you want to sleep, you can. I'll hold you up."

"'Tisn't like you haven't done so before," she whispered back, and she could see his smile even in the patchy moonlight.

But her heart felt too heavy, her thoughts too full for sleep. They rode for a good while in silence, then as the moon rose to its zenith, Thomas began to speak about his family and various events during the war and after.

Dawn was lightening the sky and the moon sank halfway to its resting place before Kate could close her eyes without seeing it again—Thomas and Crying Bird scuffling in the moonlight, and that terrible, wild slash of Crying Bird's knife, and then him falling forward when she fired the pistol.

Thomas was safe, she was safe, and that's all she need worry about now.

The next thing she knew, the rumble of Thomas's voice was pulling her from slumber. "Kate, wake up. We've reached the river and need to take the ferry across."

She sat upright, swiped her hand across her face, and smoothed her hair as best she could. Dawn had turned to grey with the threat of rain.

"Surprised to find them on the north bank this morning, already," Thomas said.

Normally, Kate knew, they'd have to ring the bell or halloo for the ferry to come across to get them. Thomas dismounted and, handing Kate the Shawnee horse's lead, went to speak with the ferry operator. When he beckoned to her, she nudged Ladyslipper down the bank to the loading point. Thomas caught her as she slid down from the saddle, then led both horses onto the flat-bottomed boat.

The crossing was uneventful. Thomas chatted with the two men who first poled the boat out into the current, then took up oars when the river became too deep. Besides the lapping of the water on the sides of the boat, the only other sounds were the calling of crows and the occasional snort of their horses.

Kate sat at the edge and watched the water but could feel the occasional glances from the ferrymen. "Your wife?" one asked, finally.

"Aye," Thomas answered, with no hesitation, from just behind her.

She could feel his presence even before he spoke, but after he said it, his fingers slid across her shoulder, and she reached up to cover his hand with her own.

'Twas the strangest thing, touching each other like this, and so openly... yet the most comfortable and natural. A shifting of the boat caused his leg to brush her side, and they stayed that way, leaning subtly against each other, until the ferry approached the other bank.

Scattered buildings stood along the riverbank, some more weathered than others, and once they docked, Thomas thanked the ferrymen and led Kate on foot up the slope of the bank. "There's a tavern that might let us a room for a few hours' sleep."

More stares followed him, partly, she decided, for the oddity of a white woman in Shawnee clothing and partly for the bloodstains still darkening Thomas's shirt body and sleeve. The first thing after finding a room would be getting water and tending his wounds, and she'd not let him say her nay this time.

The tavernkeep looked reluctant until Thomas laid down extra coin. While he went to see to their horses, Kate asked for water and cleaning cloths and took them up to the room the tavernkeep indicated, along with the baggage they'd brought in. The room was dingy and wanted a good sweeping, but it would do after she spread Thomas's blanket across the bed.

She smoothed her fingers over the crown of her hair and down both braids. 'Twas best to wait to comb it out until after they'd slept, but she hated feeling mussed.

Thomas came in and shut and barred the door, then set the rest of their baggage on the floor and his rifle against the wall. His eyes came to hers, and despite the weariness so obviously pulling at him, a shy smile touched his face.

She had to catch her own breath at the thought of the two of them, so perfectly alone. "Come, sit here by the window. Let me wash those cuts now."

He pulled off his hat and tossed it aside, then removed all the gear slung across his body, one or two at a time, and set them in a pile as well. With only the barest hesitation, he unbelted his shirt and stiffly drew it over his head.

Kate's breath stopped completely. She'd never seen him without a shirt, and now she knew why. Encircling his upper body was what looked like a fringed band of dark strands, but she realized were marks on the skin. Tattoos, likely from his time with the Shawnee.

And a thin, reddish line traced down one arm and across his lean belly, still seeping blood.

He watched her, his gaze guarded suddenly. "See? Always at least a little Shawnee."

Kate seized his hand and pulled him toward the window. "Sit." Once he'd settled onto the rickety stool she'd placed there, she wrung out a cloth in the water and set to work, cleaning the cuts. Her eyes kept going back to that decorative band across his upper chest and arms, but she forced her attention to the wounds. "There's none deep here, thankfully. A place or two that might bear stitching, and I should wrap them at least."

His face remained impassive. "Do what you must."

She took the longest of the cloths given her and, with his help, wrapped that around his belly, then bound another around his arm. After tying that one off, she lingered, hesitating, then skimmed her fingertips across the markings just above it, spanning his upper arm. She could hear the catch in his breath, felt the tremor run through him at her touch, but when he didn't object, she let herself trace the length of it, across his chest, around the other arm, and to the other side, across his back, under his hair.

Another hesitation, and she lifted the length of it, a glossy dark brown, to see how the tattoo traced across his shoulder blades and a short distance down either side of his spine.

"That's—beautiful."

Thomas's gaze glimmered, but still he said nothing. Rain pattered suddenly at the window, and on the roof.

She let both hands linger on his shoulder. "And you think this makes you somehow—less whole? Less worthy?"

Another long moment of silence.

"I think—it rather makes you more." She touched his hair again, smooth and silky under her fingertips. "And if you were not in jest in asking me—"

She stopped, bit her lip. Could she say the words, and risk that he was?

"In asking you what, Kate?" he asked softly. "To marry me?"

She gave the tiniest nod.

"Nay, I was not." His hands, resting on his knees, twitched. As if—as if he wanted to reach for her as well. Because all his heart was in his eyes, or seemed to be. "Despite wondering how I could ask any woman to be my wife if I've no idea who I am or where I belong."

Kate swallowed. How many times had she thought similar things with all their travels—where she'd wind up, how many miles before she found a place to settle with a family of her own, not just with Papa and Mama, however much she loved them?

"I—I've heard it said in scripture," she said, "that we're all strangers and pilgrims, journeying through this life. Is any place fully ours, before we reach heaven? And if—if that woman loves you enough, she'd be willing to follow you wherever you feel led to go. Like my mama has, with my papa. He was—well, he considered himself nothing, because of how he came to this country, and how they met, and Mama is descended from an old family that first came over on the *Mayflower*. But God brought them together and now—"

She faltered. She, who loved words, floundering, barely able to breathe—

Thomas's gaze remained steady, luminous, and almost silver. "If you're willing to be that woman for me—aye, Kate. I'm asking you to marry me. Even knowing what I am. That I've no earthly idea where I'm to go next."

"I'd be honored to be your wife."

He did reach for her then, gently tugging her around until she stood between his knees, then gathering her into his arms, his face pressed into the curve of her neck. Murmuring words that sounded suspiciously like—

"Are you speaking in Shawnee?" she asked, at the edge of a giggle.

His breath tickled as it fanned her skin. "Aye." She felt his slow smile. "I said, 'my beautiful woman.'"

"But I'm only a silly, chattering female." She tried to laugh again, but it broke into a sob.

He stilled. "My darling Kate," he breathed against her ear, as she wept into his chest. "You're anything but silly, and I'm sorry I ever said it."

She couldn't seem to stop crying. "I. . .I can't believe. . .you'd really want me—"

"Hie there." He nudged her chin upward until she had to look at him. His eyes glimmered pale silver in the near-dark. "Even Flying Clouds was taken with you. Both brave and beautiful, he said you are. And he's right."

Her breath caught. "Now you're only flattering me."

"Nay." All hint of humor fled his face. "He would not lie, and—neither do I."

The moment hung suspended. She was abruptly aware of their closeness, the shared warmth through the thinness of her shirt, and his, and the wild beating of her heart like the call of a distant whip-poor-will.

"Kate," he whispered, and his thumb swept her cheekbone then touched the tip of her chin. "If I'd realized that first time I saw you how much I'd love you. . ."

She was melting, right here in his arms, but she thought about that moment, across the room at the tavern at Bean's Station. "Nor I. You were so stern, so fearsome—" Her fingers traced the edges of his jaw. "Eyes-of-Sky. May I call you that, sometimes? I love the sound of it. And. . .you."

Thomas's head tipped. "They should have called you Joy-of-the-Heart," he said, and then his lips were on hers.

"You should sleep," Kate said at last, breathless.

"We should find a preacher."

Her entire body flamed at that. "The sooner, the better."

"Aye," he breathed, his nose brushing hers.

"Would this town even have one?"

Kissing her again—and oh, the warmth of his mouth was so pleasantly intoxicating, she could think of little else—he shook his head. "That I don't know. But we'll ask."

"Before or after you sleep," she teased.

"Kate," he said warningly, and the look in his eyes made her want to simply fall into his arms. But he drew a deep breath and stood, shoving the stool back with one foot, and led her toward the bed. "Sleep only, for now," he pronounced, and stretching out, patted the space next to him.

"I—I can lie down on the floor," she stammered.

He smiled a little. "You slept next to me in the woods, with five Indian braves surrounding us. You'll not share this blanket with me now when we might marry in a few hours?"

She couldn't move, couldn't breathe. Surely what every fiber of her wanted in this moment could hardly be lawful under any circumstances, but finally, gingerly, she lay down beside him. Let him tuck her into the crook of his arm, with her head pillowed on his shoulder. Stretched her free arm across his chest. And gradually, with his warmth soaking into her, she let herself sink toward slumber.

"In the eyes of the Shawnee," he murmured, a soothing rumble under her ear, "we're married already."

That brought her back to wakefulness. "Are we?"

He chuckled shortly. "Aye. And had we stayed—and the council ruled in my favor—they'd likely have insisted on giving us a wedding feast."

"That would have been—very kind of them."

Thomas tucked her a little closer.

"So then—last night might have been our wedding night?"

He stilled. "Would you have wanted it to be?"

No hesitation tied her tongue this time. "Yes."

"Well then." He let out a long breath. "A preacher, sooner rather than late, please God."

CHAPTER 34

Thomas woke suddenly, aware of aches he'd been ignoring for hours—and the sweetest of weights stretched along his side.

Please, gracious Lord, let us be husband and wife before the day is out. Or by the time we reach her family again at least.

The sun was shining again, but he couldn't see its angle from their tiny window. Even so, it was likely past noon, he didn't relish facing the trace again just yet. Nor did he wish to disturb Kate, but—

She whimpered in protest as he eased his shoulder and arm out from under her, but settled quickly enough when he shushed her and tucked the edges of the blanket over her. "Sleep, sweet Kate. I'll be back."

He pressed a kiss to her cheek, warm with slumber, and left reluctantly to find a fresh shirt and finish dressing.

Downstairs, he found that it was only just past noon. His inquiries yielded the news that Nat Carrington hadn't been seen in a while, but there was a preacher lately come to offer folk encouragement. Thomas thanked the tavernkeep, who'd offered that information, and armed with directions, set out to find the preacher.

His pulse hammered at the mere memory of Kate's dark eyes, soft and liquid, and the way she melted against him. He seemed to remember something from some preacher, years ago, thundering that it was *better to marry than burn*, but this was about so much more than the sweetness of her in his arms. Although he'd not deny that was something he looked forward to enjoying more of. . . .

A spare, greying man and woman in worn clothing of a very eastern cut worked in the garden next to a cabin, and both looked up at his approach. "Are you the preacher?" Thomas called out.

The man swept off his hat and mopped his face with his sleeve. The day was indeed more warm and sticky after the brief rain. "I am Reverend Foster, yes."

"I'm Thomas Bledsoe, and I've need of you for a wedding."

Foster's brow creased even as he offered an uncertain smile. "Yours, I presume?"

"Aye."

"Have you a license?"

Of course that would be necessary. "Not yet. I'm guessing with this being a county seat, I can purchase one?"

The preacher's head bobbed. "You'll need a special license, unless you're willing to wait. . . ?"

"Nay. We'd like it done today." He smiled thinly. "She's been through a lot, my Kate." Oh, but that felt just so good and right to say. "I want this done properly, and spare her any more difficulty at us needing to travel alone together."

Foster blinked, straightened, and nodded his head. "My wife and I, we'd want to speak to the girl as well, first."

"Of course," Thomas said, and offered what he hoped was a more disarming smile this time.

Foster told him where to find the clerk's office, and thanking the man and his wife, Thomas strode away to accomplish what needed to be done.

Getting the license was a simple enough matter, and the clerk hardly blinked at Thomas's request for them to marry the same day. That accomplished, he fairly ran back to the tavern.

He found Kate still sleeping, and for several minutes, just stood watching her, lashes fanned across her cheekbones, lips parted, breathing softly. Tonight—tonight she'd sleep in his arms as his own lawful wife, with none to separate them, or judge as wrong—

Most merciful God, how do I merit this? I don't, I know. It's naught but grace. . .Your own grace.

Kate woke to feather-light kisses along the side of her face and the warm rumble of Thomas's voice urging her to wake.

She sighed, half in regret but half in delight of the novelty of being kissed awake. Cracking an eyelid, she peered at him. "Mm, I could sleep for a week straight."

He chuckled, still leaning over her, perched on the bed beside her. "Myself as well. And maybe we should do just that—*after* we go make use of this."

He rattled a paper, and she squinted, trying to catch the words through the bleariness of having just awoken.

"It's a marriage license," he said, grinning.

"Oh!"

Another chuckle. "Aye. But for some reason, the preacher and his wife want to make sure I have a willing bride. So I'll need you to come along and reassure them of that fact."

She sat up and touched her hair.

"You're more than lovely enough. Let's go."

"I need at least to comb it out and braid it again."

He didn't look displeased by the prospect. "Fair enough. Mine too then."

They accomplished the task, respectively, with as much haste as they could, and Kate ignoring the itching of her fingers to run through Thomas's hair when he had it loose, while trying to give her own proper attention despite the warmth shining in Thomas's eyes as she worked out the tangles. But at last they were ready and, after stopping by to give the tavernkeep payment for the additional night, hurried out into the sunlight.

Kate clung to Thomas's hand, dodging mud puddles and other folk walking and on horseback, once again ignoring the stares they drew. What if the preacher disapproved for some reason and decided against marrying them? The humid air, and her worry, drew an itch down the center of her back, but she and Thomas had already discussed it at some length, and there was no way to know until they arrived—

Thomas was angling toward a log house with a neat, fenced garden beside it. He rang the small bell hanging at the gate, and called out to the half-open door.

An older woman appeared, dressed in one of the high-waisted, light muslin dresses Kate had seen so much of before they'd headed west. She gave both of them a quick, nervous smile, and held the door for them to come in.

At their entrance, her husband rose from a chair beside the hearth. "Reverend and Mrs. Foster," Thomas said, "this is my intended, Miss Katarina Gruener."

Both extended their hands to Kate, and she curtsied and thanked them for their kindness. But she could see the surprise and dismay in their eyes, and her heart was pounding.

Still—she'd faced worse. And just in the past day or two. Straightening, she tucked her hands together before her and tried to keep her expression pleasant.

"Will you sit and take tea?" Mrs. Foster said.

"That would be lovely," Kate said, and the woman nodded before turning toward the hearth, where a kettle already waited.

Reverend Foster blinked a few times, then firmed his mouth. "What brings you to Maysville then?"

Both Kate and Thomas took a breath and exchanged a glance. He lifted a hand to indicate she should speak—or could, she wasn't sure which. "My father engaged Thomas as a scout for our recent journey into Kentucky. We traveled with a small party from Bean's Station up through Cumberland Gap and over Logan's Trace, nearly to Springfield, when he and I were taken captive. He—escaped to warn my family, it being impossible for me to get away, but then came after, to bring me back. And so we are just lately come from the Shawnee town where I was taken."

More dismay and not a little astonishment filled the Fosters' faces. "Poor dear!" Mrs. Foster exclaimed. "How you must have suffered."

"They. . .treated me very well, I own," Kate said. "It was. . .well. . ."

She stammered and looked up at Thomas. How much could she reveal?

"It's all right to tell now," he said softly.

With a nod, she turned back to the preacher and his wife. "Thomas was a captive for a while, adopted by the Shawnee, before being returned to his white family in Tennessee. The one who took us was as a friend to him during that time, but—though he meant us ill in carrying me back to his town, God worked it for our good, and Thomas's Indian father showed me kindness on his behalf. They already thought us married, but—"

She felt the blush overtaking her cheeks, and peeked at Thomas again. How to explain precisely how this had happened?

"Ahh." Reverend Foster rubbed his chin, while his wife laid out her china tea service on the table. He too looked at Thomas. "So. Your wish, based on what you said earlier, is to protect this young woman from untoward speculation. Or—is there more?"

Thomas stood, back straight, hands clasped behind his back. "There's much more," he said evenly. "My Shawnee brother took her to begin with because he saw something of the attachment between us. Even though I hadn't yet spoken." He smiled a little. "I've had permission already from her father to marry her. A command, possibly—" He laughed shortly. "Regardless, if it's Kate's wish to wait until she hears that from his own lips, I'm willing to delay, but. . .she and I both think it advisable to go ahead and marry."

"And what is your wish, young lady?" Reverend Foster said.

"I've no stronger wish than to marry now," she said firmly, her gaze locked with Thomas's.

The preacher chuckled. "Well then. Shall we have tea and discuss particulars?"

How strange it was to sit at a table and take tea as if they were in the finest house in Virginia. Even Thomas's manners were very good as he tucked in beside her and took both cream and sugar and drank. Reverend Foster continued the conversation by asking more about her family, where they planned to settle, and what her father hoped to do there, then chatted with Thomas about the troubles with the Indians and the whiskey tax.

At last they finished their tea, and Reverend Foster cleared his throat. "Very well. Let's get on with this."

Thomas slid the blank marriage license across the table to him, and while the preacher skimmed it, Mrs. Foster sat straighter and looked at Kate. "Husband, if Miss Gruener and I could have a few minutes, and. . . if she would not be offended. . ."

"What's that?" her husband said.

"Well, I'd like—that is, a young woman should have a proper dress to be married in." The older woman's eyes skimmed Kate's form. "Not that you aren't already lovely, or don't wear the Indian costume well."

Kate exchanged another glance with Thomas, and he shrugged.

"Come with me," Mrs. Foster said, rising. "And at least—see."

Half an hour later, Kate stood staring at herself in the half-length glass Mrs. Foster said they'd brought all the way from Boston. This was not the girl she'd been used to seeing, but a young woman whose slightly hollowed cheeks made her eyes look huge, especially with her hair caught in a knot at the nape of her neck. And the dress—

She smoothed a hand down the skirt of the gown, the deep gold silk rustling under her fingers. Lace ruffles fell from her elbows, and a delicate ruching edged the neckline. The bodice was pinned over a stomacher embroidered with small flowers.

Mrs. Foster stood back, tears shining in her eyes. "I am sorry again for the outdated fashion. But it gladdens my heart to see you put it to use, and it would make my daughter glad as well, were she able to see it. You are a vision, dear girl."

"My deepest thanks," Kate murmured. "It's very kind of you, and I care little for being fashionable or not."

The older woman had explained that they'd brought the gown with them before the style had changed, and the daughter in question had died of fever just a few years ago. Kate felt touched, and honored, that the woman wished her to have the gown.

"Now—if you wish—these are simply to borrow—"

With a rueful smile, Mrs. Foster lifted out a gorgeous necklace of pearls and tied it about Kate's neck. Several strands of pearls framed a small cameo. She touched the piece, while Mrs. Foster fastened matching earrings in place.

"There. Now you are ready for Mr. Bledsoe."

Mr. Bledsoe. Once merely their scout, now her Thomas.

Heart in her throat, body held stiff by the stays she wore under the gown, Kate let herself be led out to the main room by Mrs. Foster.

There, near the table, stood Thomas. Wearing an obviously borrowed coat, but wearing it well. And—had he taken shears to his hair? For it looked different, somehow, neatly tailed back at his nape with black ribbon. The pale eyes widened, amazement spreading across his face.

"Here is your bride, Mr. Bledsoe," Mrs. Foster sang out, amid her husband's effusive praise. Kate spared the older man the barest glance and saw his eyes shining with emotion as well.

Thomas smiled then, an expression of wonder, and came forward to offer his hand. She put hers in it without thought. "I thought you could not be more beautiful," he breathed. "I was wrong."

She laughed nervously. "Did you—your hair—"

He turned his head so she could see. Indeed, it was freshly shorn just below the shoulders. "Reverend Foster thought I should dress up a bit as well." He grinned. "Now I'm glad I did."

"Do you two wish to marry today, or would you rather simply admire each other?" came the older man's voice.

Sharing a laugh, both of them blushing a little, Kate took Thomas's hand more firmly and stepped forward to face the preacher.

CHAPTER 35

Not a morning had been made that was sweeter, nor could the forest be more perfectly beautiful along the northern stretch of Boone's trace, and Thomas had ridden it enough times to know. But this time he rode it with his wife at his back, more dear to him than he could ever have imagined. 'Twas their first morning as a fully wedded couple, though they'd left the sanctuary of their little room in the tavern attic reluctantly enough.

Kate sighed and leaned into him, one arm snugging tight around his middle, both of them swaying to Ladyslipper's stride. Her form was soft against his back, made more so by her choice of the Shawnee clothing while they traveled. More practical than the gown Mrs. Foster had given her, and more convenient than any other with proper stays, which she'd confessed she couldn't yet face, still being chafed from wearing her old ones for days on end.

Thomas found her so darling in the Shawnee outfit, he didn't mind.

"Must we rush back as quickly as we can?" she asked. "Not that I'm not concerned for my family, but—"

He thought of the difficulty sure to be had of stealing away alone once they reached the others, and of the almost complete lack of privacy in the camp itself. "Nay. We can take our time. My only urgency at the moment is finding Carrington and relaying what I've learned about plans for attack on General Wayne's new fort."

"Ahh, so that's what you and Flying Clouds were discussing."

"Aye." He clasped his arm across hers. "Among other things." He sighed.

She tightened her hold on him briefly. "So what was it he said to you at the last?"

Thomas thought through the bits that he'd shared with her already, and so much more that he still ought to. "That he still considered me his son, and we're welcome back any time."

Kate was quiet for a long moment. " 'Tis extremely generous of him."

"Aye. I almost wish—"

She stirred. "What?"

"I wish we could bring him to live down here, with us. He seems weary of the constant war."

"Maybe. . .someday. . .we could."

"The Shawnee nation plans to go to battle before the month is out. Not sure if Flying Clouds will go along, but if he survives, maybe we could send him word. Once we know where we plan to settle."

"I'd like that," Kate said.

He lifted her hand from his waist and brought it to his mouth. How was it this girl could seem such a complete match for him, after such a short time? And that he felt such a deep connection with her already? As if. . .his heart had found its home, at last.

They caught up to Carrington at a tavern in Lexington. Thomas determined to ask at every establishment on their way, and Kate bravely trailed along without complaint, even when it meant traversing every tawdry street in the sprawling settlement that already boasted itself a city.

The older woodsman rose to shake Thomas's hand. "Well, here you are! We've heard quite the tale about you." His gaze slid past Thomas to Kate, with a speculative gleam.

"None of it true, I wager," Thomas said, then reached back a hand for her. She slid hers into it and stepped forward. "My wife, Kate. Lately Katarina Gruener."

Carrington's jaw dropped for an instant. "It *is* true then. The girl from Bean's Station, whose family you led up over the gap and to Springfield."

"We didn't make it quite to Springfield," Thomas said then smiled. "But aye. She was taken by the Shawnee, and I got her back. We were married just two days ago."

The older man's eyebrows climbed even higher, then with a half bow, Carrington shook Kate's hand as well. "I wish you both very happy, Mrs. Bledsoe."

She flushed prettily and smiled. "Thank you, Mr. Carrington. 'Tis good to meet you."

They sat, ordered food and drink, and Thomas launched into telling what he'd learned.

"The Shawnee are planning to move against the fort by month's end. Most of the town will pick up and set up a war camp elsewhere. They think it'll be an easy win because of St. Clair's defeat, but—" Thomas shook his head.

Carrington nodded slowly. "This is really no more than what we've guessed already. And I think General Wayne is more prepared than they know. But—thank you for sharing it."

"I tried—" Thomas hesitated. "I tried to dissuade them. Many are so weary of war, but most I think are even more weary of being pushed back, over and over. The younger warriors especially are spoiling for a fight."

"Well, it's a fight they'll get," Carrington said.

The bitterness rising in his throat at the memory of Crying Bird's fury, Thomas idly rubbed a gouge in the table. Beside him, Kate looked just as somber. Likely thinking of the same thing.

The tavern maid brought a platter with mugs of ale, bowls of stew, and several slabs of rough bread. They all set to without comment.

"What plans have you now?" Carrington asked.

Thomas exchanged a glance with Kate. "Return to her family. See them settled on their land over past Baird's Town." He scooped stew with a chunk of bread. "Beyond that, not sure."

Carrington took a pull of his ale. "Could use another man in Indian Affairs. If you're interested."

Thomas eyed him. "Does that mean protecting the United States government's interests or that of the Indians?"

The other man stilled, met his gaze with a hardness Thomas did not like but expected. "I reckon that would be up to you."

"I'll think about it," Thomas said.

"Fair enough."

They finished the meal with talk about other things, then Carrington excused himself and left the tavern.

"I do not care for that man at all," Kate whispered.

He squeezed her hand, where he held it beneath the table. "Me neither."

"Are you seriously considering his offer?"

Thomas shook his head slightly. "Don't know. Might. . .later."

She leaned toward him. "I'll be praying about it."

"And so," he said slowly, "will I."

June was growing old, and the full moon had come and gone by the time they meandered down Boone's Trace and up the western branch of the Wilderness Road toward Danville. They'd dawdled enough and needed to return to Kate's family and the rest of the traveling party.

But when they reached the station where the party had camped when Kate and Thomas were taken captive, they found another group in temporary residence there. Kate's family and the others had moved on. "Decided to press on to the land they'd all purchased," the station owner told Thomas. "Jenkins and his team are capable enough, I reckon, even with Injuns."

So he and Kate wasted no more time but pressed down the road to Springfield and beyond that very afternoon. Having provisioned well enough at Danville, they waited until sunset to camp and tucked up in a thicket with no fire, both Ladyslipper and the Shawnee horse tethered nearby. Curled up together, loosely entwined with both blankets around them as protection from mosquitos, they lay listening to the whip-poor-wills and the sound of each other's breathing.

"What if," Kate whispered, "what if Papa's angry that we already married."

Thomas huffed. "He'd be more angry, I wager, if we weren't." He shifted in order to give her a long kiss that left them both breathless. "Because with all these nights alone, I'm not sure I could have held out—"

With a laugh, she was the one to swoop in for the kiss this time, and for a while all questions were lost in a delight they still could hardly believe they found in each other.

But with daylight, Kate's questions came sweeping back. They were near enough to where Papa had purchased the land, by Thomas's reckoning, to be there by nightfall, or to catch up with them wherever they'd camped—and so far everyone they inquired of affirmed that yes, the Grueners and their party had moved on up the trace.

"He warned me so many times, to leave you alone. . .let you do what he'd hired you to," she fretted.

Thomas chuckled, long and low. "Did he now?"

"Thomas. . ."

She felt him sober a little.

"Likely, he saw, or felt, something between us already as well. . . enough to know, maybe, how it could be between us." He hesitated. "And from what he said to me, things were hard enough between him and your mama's father. . ."

That was something she'd have to ask Mama and Papa later, for certain. And then, with the sudden understanding of what it meant to be fully married—

"Oh Thomas."

"What, sweetheart?"

"We—" She collapsed against him, wrapping both arms around him as tightly as she could.

"What's that for?" he said, laughing again.

"I'm truly yours, am I not? And you—are mine."

" 'I am my beloved's, and my beloved is mine,' " he murmured.

" 'Let him kiss me with the kisses of his mouth: for thy love is better than wine,' " Kate returned.

Thomas hummed deep in his chest, and she could only chuckle in response.

"That would be why he warned you away," Thomas said.

Evening shadows were grown long by the time they found the path that, by all Thomas and Kate both knew, led to the tract of land Karl Gruener had purchased. It had lately been widened enough to accommodate a wagon, if need be, and as they continued, the sounds of children shrieking and laughing came to their ears.

Thomas pulled Ladyslipper to a halt, and the Shawnee horse beside them, and glanced back at Kate. Her eyes wide, lips parted, her breath came in small gasps.

"Your family loves you, sweet Kate," he murmured. "They'll be over-joyed to see you, regardless."

She seemed to collect herself, shut her mouth, and looked at him, eyes swimming in tears. "They love you as well."

Trembling, she clung to his shoulders, but as soon as they rounded a bend that brought a rough clearing into sight, with several folk moving about a pair of tents and the beginnings of a cabin, Kate didn't even wait for him to stop the horses. She slid down and ran, squealing, toward the midst of her family.

And he couldn't stop his own laughter welling up, nor the blurring of his eyes, though he swept a sleeve across his face and pretended it was just the sultry summer evening. Kate was caught in a knot of young'uns—Stefan, Betsy, and Jemmy—and then Jemima and Dulsey came running, and Karl himself. All of them, laughing, weeping, shouting with joy, sway-ing this way and that—

Only his own sisters and their young'uns would match the like of it.

He dismounted, hanging back to let them have their reunion, but then Kate burst out of the midst of them and came running back to him. And they all followed.

She got there first, her cheeks wet but grinning radiantly, and seized his hand. "Mama, Papa! Everyone. Thomas and I are married!"

And another round of jubilation broke out as they all surrounded him, hugging and pummeling and in general making him one of theirs.

Over the heads of the others, Karl Gruener stood back, the rough former Hessian weeping without shame, grinning fiercely, and nodding his most enthusiastic approval at both Thomas and Kate.

EPILOGUE

"*One last thing I need do before we settle,*" Thomas had said.

Her heart pounded in her throat. Again. Had she not enough of adventure this summer to fill an entire book of stories? And it was both Papa and Thomas who'd insisted she sit down every spare moment and record all that had happened—including Thomas's own tale, which she herself had become part of.

She rode beside him, this time on Trillium, with the pony they'd simply taken to calling Shawnee carrying baggage, as they headed back down the road that had brought them here.

Only for a while, Thomas warned. He wanted to return to her family, help get the big dogtrot cabin finished and weathertight before winter.

But first—first he wanted her to meet his sisters.

One lived up on the Clinch River, with her husband and a pair of little ones. Thankful, she was called. The next oldest, Thomas had warned, called Patience, they might not be able to meet, but he'd sent word ahead for both of them to come. The youngest, Mercy, they'd almost certainly get to meet, and the family matriarch, called Truth, would be waiting, and gladly.

Thomas watched her now, smiling, those pale eyes all too knowing as she gave attention to simply breathing in and out. "I'll tell you the same thing you said to me," he said at last. "They'll love you. They can't help but love you."

She could only look at him helplessly.

"Remember Flying Clouds," he said softly.

Across a creek then, and up over a rise—and there was the prettiest farmstead, against the backdrop of steep mountainside, bluish green in the summer heat.

Thomas rose on his toes in the saddle. "Halloo the house!"

A lean, gowned form appeared on the porch. Three or four children swarmed from the woods behind, and a bearded man stepped from the barn. Thomas nudged Ladyslipper to a trot, but Kate held Trillium back. A wave of dizziness swept over her.

Ah, this was not a good time for that!

Swallowing hard, she drew a deep breath. Thomas fairly flung himself off of Ladyslipper and swooped the woman into a hug that had them twirling around the yard.

"Thomas! What in the world—"

Kate could not help but grin at the mingled exasperation and joy in the woman's voice. And as her attention fastened on Kate, the eyes widening, Kate could see the resemblance between her and Thomas.

Oh yes, this was her husband's sister.

She pulled Trillium to a stop, and Thomas was there with a steadying hand as she swung down. She felt his trembling joy as he drew her to his side.

"Truth," he said, "this is my wife, Kate."

Author's Note

All authors, I suppose, look back at a story and think of all they could, or should, have written. I once heard that novelists can expect to only use about 1 percent of all the research they've done for a book, and I can attest to the truth of that. When I started digging into this particular slice of history, tucked in between the American Revolution and the Lewis and Clark Expedition, I didn't expect to be so immediately drawn in to the precarious world of westward expansion, although it's the next logical step after the colonial era and the Revolutionary War. I'd studied the history of the American War for Independence intensively for more than a decade at this point and found my knowledge of that time not only useful, but also crucial for understanding the events unfolding over the next decade or two.

During my study of the American Revolution, sparked by my interest in a particular facet of British camp and family life during that era, my husband often teased me about being a Tory sympathizer. It's true that history is so much more complex and nuanced than we think. So much wrong is committed on both sides of a conflict, most times, and no nation is without its share of bloodguilt in some form or another. But historical events are told through the filter of individuals and their unique perspectives and prejudices, so when I write a story, I do my best to capture that individual mind-set as it might have been without imposing modern sensibilities. That includes attitudes toward native peoples, slavery, or at what age and under what terms marriage might be acceptable. So if you run into something while reading this story that makes you cringe in one of these areas, please keep in mind that we are all very much products of our own time.

That said, let me highlight a few areas of study I found interesting but was unable to further expand on within the story itself.

When these characters first presented themselves to me, I found them not only easily rooted within the overall family history of Daughters of the Mayflower, but also deeply rooted in their own family histories. I first heard Kate's voice reciting her father's experience with the British army early in the Revolution—an event I found my interest and imagination captured by from the account, told by Colonel Rawdon himself, in the pages of a volume that in turn tells the story of the American Revolution from the British viewpoint (*Redcoats and Rebels*, see bibliography). Other accounts give provenance for the possibility of a young Hessian soldier falling in love with the daughter of his host family and later deserting his military duty. Countless family histories trace the migration of peoples from the Eastern Seaboard, down the Great Road along the Shenandoah Valley, into the Carolina backcountry and what is now eastern Tennessee.

I was also delighted to get to return to the Bledsoe family, which I'd first discovered during my research for the novella "*Defending Truth*" (*A Pioneer Christmas Collection*, Barbour Publishing). This particular branch of the real-life Bledsoe family provided historical backdrop for the heroine of that story, and then again for this one. My interest was initially sparked by the coincidence of name between Anthony Bledsoe, who served as captain of the home guard during the foray by the Overmountain Men in answer to Ferguson's threats in the fall of 1780, and the last name of one of my daughter's fellow ballet students. Come to find out, after spending some time tracing the Bledsoes' migration from Virginia, through Tennessee, then into and across Missouri, they're probably related.

The issue of slavery was so interwoven with the fabric of society that most gave it no thought. So many people didn't even own slaves, and I debated long before deciding that Dulsey, the African American woman who serves as nanny and second mother to the Gruener children, was a freedwoman and not enslaved. Some might find fault with that, some would doubtlessly find fault no matter how I portray this issue—whether I have more characters of various ethnicities or fewer—but all I can say is that I can fit only so many things into the scope of one story. I did touch on the fact that the native tribes also took and used slaves, and by several accounts they liked in particular to take captives of African Americans because of the status it gave them within their own people. Again, I must portray folk as they would have been in their own time.

Another theme I found I had to treat with a light hand was that of the church. Lest anyone take my comment about the Baptists as an insult, let me assure you, I grew up in a Baptist church and owe that upbringing with much of my knowledge of scripture and church history. I've found it both interesting and amusing, however, that early Baptists emerge in colonial history as quite the upstart group whose emotionalism and zeal were looked askance upon by other, more settled, denominations. . .rather how modern Baptists have tended to view the Pentecostals and charismatics of our day. That same zeal helped carry the Word of God into the heart of the wilderness. I'd hoped to make some reference to the Travelling Church but could find no way to do so without sacrificing story flow, and the faith of scattered individuals was just as important as larger moves such as the Travelling Church.

The native conflict and the dilemma of a wandering people from one sort of nation trying to find a place peaceably with those already established are never-ending sources of interest—and distress. Reading the accounts of treaties made and either forgotten by the next generation or broken by the very ones who made them was exhausting. William Penn, when writing of his dealings with the native peoples of the New World, actually believed the Shawnee and others to be descended from the ten lost tribes of Israel, because of physical type and customs so similar to Old Testament laws, and that conviction led him and his followers to extend the utmost respect to native tribes. Others who followed Penn did not share that conviction or had forgotten the excellent relations that European peoples enjoyed with Native Americans during Penn's lifetime. While digging into the history of the Shawnee people, I've ended many a research session in tears, begging God's mercy on those of us who did not know, who cannot change history, but who must find a way to go forward and seek peace "as much as lieth in you," with those around us. I've always been fascinated with learning "the other side" of a particular conflict—much of my study of the Revolutionary War era was of the loy-alist viewpoint—and I've come away from my study of the Shawnee and other tribes with a new appreciation and love for these people.

Yet all people share the bloodguilt. The horror stories of captivity and slaughter were a very real force during this time. As I wrote in my story, the apparent contradiction between the brutality of Native Americans and their very tangible generosity and love to those they chose to adopt as their own is difficult to understand with our modern minds, but it is no less a reality among our own people, in our own time.

Historical Note

The Cumberland Gap, originally part of the Warrior's Path (the route traveled by native peoples seeking war and trade), was first discovered and traveled by Dr. Thomas Walker in 1750, then later explored by men such as Daniel Boone, who blazed the trail from southwestern Virginia into Kentucky and guided settlers along that path. The gap itself is considered a Gateway to the West (one of several within the United States), as the largest natural opening from the Eastern Seaboard across the Appalachian Mountains, and it became a key meeting point for settlers, fur traders, and military forces.

By the 1790s, as the Eastern Seaboard became more crowded, settlers poured from eastern Tennessee and western Virginia into the lower Ohio Valley, beckoned by the promise of affordable lands and a better situation for their families. They did this despite the threat of the native tribes—some of whom tried to work with the settlers while others stood fast against westward expansion. The native tribes who opposed westward expansion by settlers were still encouraged in their resistance by the British, who continued to maintain forts along the American frontier in order to undermine the newly founded colonial government. Peace did not come easily or immediately during the infancy of the United States.

The Kentucky of this time was still a wild and terrifying place for those born in the East, but it was not nearly as wild as it had once been. Early explorers wrote of herds of buffalo as well as abundant deer, turkey, and other game. Travel was a matter of following waterways—trekking alongside rivers or weaving back and forth across creeks—braving mud, sand pits, and canebrakes. Still, plenty of stations had sprung up along the traces, and one man reported that by this time, there were enough ordinaries (the period term for an inn) along the way to stay at one every night. Many of the settlements were by this time thriving centers of white civilization. The backwoodsman was not always the ignorant, uneducated clod that some have painted him. I tried to show this with Thomas by his knowledge of scripture even in the face of doubt, but it wasn't uncommon for folk to be reading novels (such as *Gulliver's Travels*) or classic works of Greece or Rome. The post ran briefly between Danville, Kentucky and Bean's Station, Tennessee, 1792–94 and then again later. One of the first post riders, Thomas Ross, was indeed a casualty of Indian attack.

The spring and summer of 1794 marked a couple of notable battles between the Shawnee and other tribes and the United States forces led by General Anthony Wayne. An offensive launched against Fort Recovery, which Wayne built on the site of a previous win by Native Americans, should have been an easy victory but proved a disappointment. The Northwest Indian War, as it was called, culminated in the Battle of Fallen Timbers in August 1794, and the Treaty of Greenville in August 1795. Those two events decided the fate of the Shawnee, who mostly picked up and moved west afterward. Most native peoples had adopted the dress described in this story and the use of European household articles such as the china platter on which Kate serves corn cakes.

I drew much of my description of Kate's running the gauntlet from the memoirs of Jonathan Alder, who was taken captive at age nine and lived as a Native American for nearly twenty-five years. His account of native society encouraged me to paint the social life of the Shawnee with a much warmer hand than I otherwise might have.

And lastly, the history of the Wilderness Road itself is so rich I couldn't possibly fit everything I wanted into this particular story. I defer to authors such as Laura Frantz and Lori Benton for their excellent portrayal of the era, fifteen to twenty-five years before the setting of mine, but the groundwork was laid as far back as 1750 when Dr. Thomas Walker mounted that expedition into what was then western Virginia (which extended all the way to the Mississippi). Daniel Boone and James Harrod followed after, initially traveling companions but later separating after a difference of opinion. Both blazed new trails, Boone from Cumberland Gap northward, and Harrod branching off to the west. Many others followed, and of those, some were driven back by the threat and heartbreak of native attack and other perils, but others stayed. Many men kept journals of their travels, and surely many women did the same. Most, if not all, of the difficulties I wrote about within these pages happened to someone, whether it's a horse sliding off the trail into a creek; travelers developing what was known as *foot scald*, a painful and dangerous condition caused by walking in chronically wet shoes; or coming across entire traveling parties slain by Indians. Many frontiersman had discovered the comfort and convenience of adopting native dress, and they also learned how much better suited moccasins were for the trail than European styles of footgear.

I found it difficult to pinpoint exactly when the Wilderness Road was opened for wagon traffic. Kentucky legislature commissioned a road in 1795, according to Pusey (1921). Wikipedia (which I do not recommend as a sole resource but can be very helpful for initial research) says 1792, with the road opened in 1796. (The Battle of Fallen Timbers put an end to Shawnee resistance in 1794.) There's evidence that the road was actually cleared for wagons as early as 1780, but was officially improved in the 1790s. Another article says that improvements started when Kentucky became a state in 1792 and then opened in 1795–96, and that's what I went with for the purposes of my story. Again, there was so much detail I could not include, but I'm indebted to Pusey for descriptions and images of the road from the 1920s, before much of modern development occurred.

The internet is a marvelous thing. I'm indebted to Bing Maps and Google Earth for letting me go where I otherwise would have been unable. I had to rely on memory—from many trips over the years—for the atmosphere I tried to capture of the beauty that is Tennessee, Kentucky, and Ohio, but satellite maps helped me trace the route in certain places, figure out about how long it might have taken them to get from point A to point B, and envision what the countryside might have looked like along the way. Various websites and Facebook pages (thank you, Cumberland Gap and Pine Mountain Facebook pages for providing photos of your area during spring!) also helped tremendously in pinpointing what might have bloomed when—but I'm sure I didn't get it all perfectly correct.

For further resources, I point you to my bibliography.

Acknowledgments

No book is written without the help of many people and resources, and this journey has been so long, time would fail me to mention everyone, but here are notables for this particular story:

Michelle Griep, dear friend, critique partner extraordinaire, fellow history geek, who decided I should be dragged along on this adventure. So glad you did!

Kimberli Buffaloe, dear friend, sometime critique partner, and now Boone cousin! Who shares my love of the Carolinas and history and, being from Kentucky herself, pointed me to various resources to kick-start my research. . .and whose anticipation for this story truly humbles me. I hope it doesn't disappoint!

Lee S. King, dear friend, critique partner, and so much more! Whose patience in converting ancient WordPerfect files enabled me to resurrect the story of my heart and apply myself to writing again with the hope of publication. (Do you realize that was more than fifteen years ago??) Thank you so much for reading every word I've tossed your way and always saying, "More!" (As well as cheering me on.)

Jennifer Uhlarik, dear friend, critique partner, sister in faith. . .whose prayers and encouragement helped me hold on through some of the darkest seasons.

Breanna and Corrie McNear, beautiful daughters, first readers, amazing encouragers. . .your enthusiasm (and reassurances that it wasn't stupid!) often kept me going.

Elizabeth Goddard, a.k.a. Beth, dear, *dear* friend, critique partner, and nudge from behind. . .the one whose encouragement led to that very first novella contract. Thank you for being the one to whom I could tell anything!

Ronie Kendig, dear friend, encourager. . .so glad the Lord has had us on this journey together! You always believed this door would open, didn't you?

Joan Hochstetler, Laura Frantz, and Lori Benton, fellow authors of the time period and region, whose work I respect so much. . .to Joan for her kindness in answering questions and sharing research sources, Laura in welcoming me to Kentucky (figuratively speaking!), and Lori just for being the amazing storyteller she is. Your stories all provided inspiration and a very high bar for excellence!

Becky Germany, country girl and editor, so willing to give many "nobody" writers a chance in this industry as she did me. Thank you—and the entire team at Barbour—for your dedication to producing beautiful stories! And I still remember a particular conversation around the table at an ACFW gala with fondness.

Tamela Hancock Murray, agent, encourager, beautiful and gentle soul. Thank you for caring, for listening, and for believing in me. I'm still astonished to be in possession of a contract with my name next to Steve Laube's.

Susan Brower, my first agent, who directed me to Tamela to begin with. Thank you so much for encouraging me to hold out for traditional publishing, and for being such a comfort that hard last year of my mother's life.

Troy, Cameron, and Meeghan, who along with Breanna and Corrie have continued to love a story-crazed and cranky wife and mama through her very first legit book deadline. I'm well aware of what y'all suffered for the sake of this one. . .and I love you more than I can possibly say! Same goes for all your older siblings—Alistair, Ian, Erin, and Ross—and the darling spouses—Aaron, Leah, and Jenn—for your amazing love and support over the years. Once again, I would not be who I am without you!!

New Hope Free Lutheran Church, especially Mary, Barb, Teri, and Cheryl—Wednesday night fellowship supper ladies who let me bounce story and research questions off them, were patient with my slackness during deadline, and were so wonderful to pray and ask how things were going. Pastor Steve for understanding when I needed to step back. And last but not least, New Hope Youth for all their enthusiasm and support.

Sarah Wilson, steadfast farmer's wife, bearer of her own beautiful ministry, sister in spirit. Thank you so much for your hands and your heart, and a listening ear just when I needed it!

Terri and Dan Thompson, visionaries in ministry, whose viewpoint often challenged me to think deeper, wider, more tenderly. Thank you both for fellowship, hospitality, and encouragement to step up and let God make me more visible.

Jenelle Hovde, beta reader and fellow ACFW Dakotas member, for your incredible enthusiasm and insightful comments on native culture and society.

My HAH sisters—Homeschooling A Houseful, online community extraordinaire, for years of love and support and just plain real life.

Kimberley, Kathleen, and MaryLu—what an honor to get to work beside you on this series!

A certain exchange student from Germany who made my senior year of high school ever so much more interesting and whose name I've borrowed without permission. I hope you are doing well all these years later.

All the brave men and women who traveled the Wilderness Road to start with, especially those who left behind a written record for us to follow.

God our Father, King of the Universe, Maker of heaven and earth. . . who lovingly reminded me that since He had opened this door, it was a very small thing for Him—as the One who spoke the entire creation into existence—to help me with a little word count.

BIBLIOGRAPHY

Ancestry.com.

Calloway, Colin G. *The Shawnees and the War for America*. London: Penguin, 2007.

Charles River Editors. *Native American Tribes: The History and Culture of the Shawnee*. CreateSpace Ind. Pub. Platform, Sept. 22, 2013.

Harvey, Henry. *History of the Shawnee Indians: From the Year 1681 to 1854, Inclusive*. Cincinnati: Ephraim Morgan & Sons, 1855.

Hibbert, Christopher. *Redcoats and Rebels: The American Revolution through British Eyes*. New York: Norton, 1990.

Kincaid, Robert L. *The Wilderness Road*. Indianapolis: Bobbs-Merrill, 1947.

LaCrosse, Richard B., Jr. *Frontier Rifleman*. Union City, TN: Pioneer Press, 1997.

Native-languages.org.

Nelson, Larry L., ed. *A History of Jonathan Alder, His Captivity and Life with the Indians*. Akron, OH: Univ. of Akron Press, 2002.

Pusey, William Allen. *The Wilderness Road to Kentucky: Its Location and Features*. New York: George H. Duran Co., 1921.

Ross, Jane Barks. *The Magic Moccasins: Life among Ohio's Six Tribes*. 2 vols. Columbus, OH: Avonelle Assoc., Ltd., 1979–80.

Wikipedia.com. For overall framework and initial research only.

Transplanted to North Dakota after more than two decades in Charleston, South Carolina, **Shannon McNear** loves losing herself in local history. She's a military wife, mom of eight, mother-in-law of three, grammie of two, and a member of ACFW and RWA. Her first novella, *Defending Truth* in *A Pioneer Christmas Collection*, was a 2014 RITA® finalist. When she's not sewing, researching, or leaking story from her fingertips, she enjoys being outdoors, basking in the beauty of the northern prairies. Connect with her at www.shannonmcnear.com, or on Facebook and Goodreads.

Continue Following the Family Tree through History with. . .

The Liberty Bride (December 2018)
by MaryLu Tyndall
War Forces a Choice Between Love and Country

A trip home from England to Maryland in 1812 finds Emeline Baratt a captive on a British warship and forced to declare her allegiance between the British and Americans. Remaining somewhat politically neutral on a ship where her nursing skills are desperately needed is fairly easy—until she starts to have feelings for the first lieutenant who becomes her protector. However, when the captain sends her and Lieutenant Owen Masters on land to spy, she must choose between her love for him or her love for her country.

Paperback / 978-1-68322-617-8 / $12.99

The Alamo Bride (February 2019)
by Kathleen Y'Barbo
Will Ellis Lose All at the Alamo?

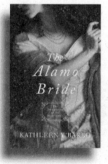

Ellis Dumont finds a man in New Orleans Grey unconscious on Dumont property in 1836. As his fevers rage, the man mutters strange things about treasures and war. Either Claiborne Gentry has lost his mind, or he's a spy for the American president—or worse, for the Mexican enemy that threatens their very lives. With the men of her family away, Ellis must stand courageously and decide who she can trust. Will she put her selfish wants ahead of the future of the republic or travel with Clay to Mission San Jose to help end the war?

Paperback / 978-1-68322-820-2 / $12.99